ADMIT TO MAYHEM

By

D. J. ADAMSON

HORATIO PRESS

MYSTERY-SUSPENSE-SCIENCE FICTION

ISBN: 9798988659327

Other Books by D. J. Adamson

Mystery
Suppose, Lillian Dove Book Two
Let Her Go, Lillian Dove Book Three

Suspense/Thriller
At the Edge of No Return

Crime Thriller/Science Fiction
Approaching Storm
Into the Storm

To
my mother Dortha, who believed in me when I didn't,
and
to my husband Tom and son Shayn who have put up with all my
stories.

In the Midwest, if we can't
count on anything else, at least we can count on the weather.
-Unknown, but, I bet, a Midwesterner

I admit I am powerless over
what life gives, but powerful in my choices.
-Lillian Dove

CHAPTER ONE
POWERLESS OVER STORMS

My name is Lillian Dove. I am a recovering alcoholic, five years sober.

Five long years, yet the clink of ice in a glass still sets me on edge.

There is no graduation from alcoholism. Or life, for that matter. I am also addicted to Pepsi, chocolate, men, being afraid, being afraid of not being afraid, men—again--and my independence, co-dependence, and unsettling ability to fail no matter my attempt. There are other compulsions and bad habits, but I can't think of them right now. Memory loss, see? And I obsess about how much I forget if I remember. Giving up alcohol turned out to be easier than changing some of my other behaviors.

Especially my bad judgment when it comes to men. The type of man I'm most attracted to is like a tall Tom Collins on a sweltering summer day: gin, a little lemon--but not too sour—with sweet syrup and bubbly soda. It's hard to resist, even if I know it's not good for me.

I've pledged a Tom-Collins-abstinence.

Yet, Chief Charles Kaefring began offering me his attention. I thought my sobriety realigned my sexual magnetism. I was attracting a different type.

He started coming to my desk to tell me he was leaving and instructed me to send all his calls to his assistant. At first, I couldn't figure out why he thought I needed this instruction. I already transferred his calls as a manner of routine. Then a week after making sure I was aware of his whereabouts, I bumped into him lakeside at Louise's Italian Kitchen.

Louise's is my Friday night routine. I celebrate making it through another week—one spaghetti dinner at a time.

After that Friday night, I saw him at Louise's every week. If he got there before me, I'd see him glancing toward the entry as if waiting for me to arrive. If I got there first, I'd pretend I never expected him to show up--which was the truth. Each and every time he arrived, I was flabbergasted.

I wasn't sure what was happening between the two of us or who started it. I mean, how could a man like him seriously be interested in me?

And even after weeks came and went, I still didn't trust him. He'd ask if I'd like wine with my meal at each dinner. "Of course," I'd say, letting my glass set without drinking it. If he worried the wine wasn't good, I'd bring the glass to my lips without sipping. If he knew I had a drinking problem, I figured he'd beat the hell out of there. Eventually, though, he stopped asking if I wanted wine and only ordered one glass instead of two.

Still, he kept showing up.

I knew I was slipping into a situation that could toss my sobriety into the toilet, but meeting for dinner didn't seem like backsliding into emotional drunkenness. Although, it never feels like slipping until you find yourself in a ragged heap of discontent. Our routine altered when he telephoned, giving me a weather report on a Sunday afternoon. He said the day was hot and getting hotter. He said he was putting a steak on the barbecue. He just happened to have two. *Are you hungry?*

I'd just consumed a Dairy Queen double-double with fries. "Famished."

The steak was delicious. The company was savory. Being with him—scrumptious.

I knew I should have left at the first warning a storm was shifting and heading my way. Storms are dangerous. They don't discriminate. Rich or poor. Religious or atheist. Functional or Dysfunctional, or like me, slipping between the two. Storms stir up trouble and ruin things or people, whether they were made to withstand fierce winds or fall in the slightest breeze.

They are also easy to deny. How bad could a little thunderstorm be?

I ended up staying for dessert.

Need I mention he had a healthy appetite, too?

When I gained consciousness, I found the clock showing six in the morning.

I clawed my way out of Charles' big, comfy bed and tip-toed out of the bedroom. Cooper, his Australian Shepherd, came off his rug when he heard me come down the stairs. I grabbed a piece of leftover steak and bribed him quiet.

Luckily my Mustang convertible started first try.

But I didn't get more than two miles before I caught a whiff of burning wood and saw smoke. I followed the scent like a bloodhound, steering between tall, green cornfields and driving a gravel road of puddles and hard, dry ruts. At its end, I found a house engulfed in flames.

I grabbed my phone and punched in 911. Helen Curtis, the third-shift dispatcher, answered. "Frytown Police. What is your emergency?"

"Helen, it's me, Lillian."

"Lillian? What's wrong?"

"There's a house fire. I'm on Rohert Road, just this side of the crossroad and Black Hawk. It's a house that sets off a way."

"East or west of Rohert?"

"West. No, hold it, east. From Kaefring's place."

Once reported, there'd be no stopping the fact I was coming from the chief's farm at the now logged-in time of 6:36 a.m. It would be breaking news on the tittle-tattle circuit.

"Sounds like the old Dillard place." Her comment went to whoever picked up at the fire department.

She came back on the line. "Did the Carters get out?"

"I don't see anyone. Hurry."

"Trucks are on their way. Stay in your car 'til they get there."

I clicked off. I got out of the car.

The acrid fumes multiplied twenty times stronger outside. I glanced at the waking morning. The sky is clear of clouds.

Where was a good rain when you needed one?

An explosion sounded. Glass cracked. Yellow-red flames flared. I saw someone in one of the upstairs windows where the fire hadn't reached. The Carters? From the sound of the sirens, the trucks were still a couple of miles away. But why hadn't the Carters called the fire department?

I took off in search of a ladder. Two sheds stood not far from the house. The larger was an old, falling-down garage, aged-ready for a spark. It was empty of cars but full of stacked boxes, used bikes, a rusty lawnmower, a faded-red gas can, paint cans, and what some might call antique furniture. But, of course, no ladder.

Bikes? Children?

The possibility of trapped children spurred me to run the short distance to the other shed. When I reached it, another blast came from the house. I opened the door, finding this smaller shed full of shovels, rakes, a dirty tarp, and, surprise—a ladder. Hefting it, I dragged the ladder over the dry, splotchy lawn to the side of the house. I arranged it beneath the window. And climbed.

My hands slipped on the rungs. My pulse pounded in my ears. Seeping wetness pooled beneath my arms, dribbling a small stream past my breasts.

I yelled, "I have a ladder!"

I locked my knocking knees against the ladder's rails, stretched, grabbed the window frame's bottom, and lifted. It was either painted shut or locked or just plain old.

"Can you hear me? I need help with the window."

The house shuddered.

I twisted around, hoping to see fire trucks coming down the road. There were blue and red halos, but the trucks were nowhere close. They looked stalled.

The halos were right about at Sam Roe's place. His cows were always getting out on the road.

Good grief.

Stupid trucks. Stupid-ass cows. Damn Sam.

Another explosion. This time launching wood and flame. A flare lit from the roof. Time was running out. I twisted back to the window. "I can't stay much longer. Help me get the window up!"

Three rungs remained before the very top of the ladder. It was too dangerous to stand on the last rung, but the next to last might hold me.

Good god. I was going to kill myself and the person inside.

Somehow, I unlocked my knees and coaxed my gravity-dependent feet higher. I steadied myself, then took hold of the rail. I gritted my teeth and stepped onto the next two rungs. The ladder tipped and slid. I took hold of the window.

Steady. You're okay. If you can't open it, you'll think of something else.

I cupped my hands against the glass. So hot. Whoever was in the room had to be in trouble if still alive.

Boom!

The ladder shook.

There, I saw someone crouched over by the door.

I pulled off my blouse, knotted it around my hand, and banged it against the window. The glass cracked and burst, releasing a mighty hot wind to my face. The force and surprise of the impact shook me off balance, and my uneven weight tilted the ladder. I lurched forward, pushing my weight against the rungs, forcing the ladder to remain standing.

Miracles happen.

"Please, hurry," I yelled.

I laid my blouse over the sill and wrestled halfway through the opening, teeter-tottering. Then, dizzy with the effort and realizing where I was and what I'd done, I panicked. I kicked to regain my footing on the ladder, this time sending it clattering to the ground.

"Help me!"

This was my voice.

I fell into the room, hitting my head. My vision warped. My fingers came back bloody.

A hand touched my naked shoulder. "Are you okay?"

With my head reeling, I opened my eyes to find an indistinct face. Alien. Something out of a science-fiction movie.

Sirens screamed.

The face disappeared.

Another gust of heat moved over me. I lowered my head, my hands worrying my hair. I glanced to each side, checking the room as best I could.

There was only me.

Outside, voices called to one another, and other voices answered. Then, a gushing waterfall hit the house, squelching, sizzling, smothering insistent destruction. Inside, fumes and heat and a hammering pulse in my head muffled any thought of salvation.

I'd failed. Yet, for the first time in my miscarried life, my ineptitude didn't flood me with the same sordid worthlessness I'd shouldered so many times before. This time was the last.

I was going to die.

I saw Ben Weaver. Not a specter, but a paramedic for the Frytown Fire Department.

An oxygen mask cupped my nose and mouth. The air tasted good if lungs could taste it. I moved to take the mask off, and that's when I found my hands bandaged—my left hand attached to a saline bag.

Hold on there." Ben pushed my hands away. "You're in no shape to be getting up."

He was right. My movement caused coughing. Smokey phlegm filled my mouth. Nasty. My body ached, my head was killing me, and my hands burned.

"You've got some superficial wounds," Ben was saying. "You'll need stitches in your forehead. But overall, you're okay."

A pinprick stung my left hand. He must have checked the intravenous tubing to see whether I'd disturbed its flow.

"It's Tim Johnson who you owe thanks to. Hey, weren't you told to stay in the car? What were you doing in the house?" Ben didn't wait for an answer before placing his hand on my breathing mask, ensuring I was getting oxygen. "Tim got you over his shoulder and down before the roof caved in. He saved your life."

I tried to speak, but my throat closed on each syllable, causing the words to come out as, "In...ous."

"Someone else is in the house?"

I accepted the translation.

"Hey, Chief," Ben shouted.

Chief Simms of the Frytown Fire Department, in an orange-yellow jacket and a black helmet, came up to the gurney. He asked, "How is she?" His face was sweaty and streaked with soot.

"She's going to be okay. She says someone else is in there."

Chief Simms cupped his hand and shouted, "Tim!" He gave a wave. "Over here."

Tim Johnson appeared, lifting off his mask and helmet. He wiped his blackened forehead with his dirty jacket sleeve. "She okay?"

Chief Simms asked him, "Could there still be someone in the house?"

Tim shook his head. "I got a good look around before the roof caved in. No sign of anyone."

Chief Simms gave a nod. "Kaefring told me he found and contacted the Carters. They're over at Carrollton Lake camping. I can't think who else she would've seen." Abruptly, as if he caught sight of someone, he yelled, "Kaefring! She's alert."

Charles's voice, "Pete, set up another blockade halfway up the drive. We need to keep those goosenecks out of here." He came to stand by Chief Simms. "You okay, Lil?"

I nodded and mumbled, "Tars...'one...ous."

No one paid attention.

"We're letting the house go," Chief Simms said to Charles. "Our goal now is to ensure the fire doesn't jump to one of these sheds, or hell, catch this grass on fire." He sounded angry, as if the fire was set to ruin his day. "This grass is dry as straw and itching to burn."

"I got barricades at all the entrances," Charles told him. "Two on the drive and two on the highway. The other place is evacuated. Davis took them over to the Reverend Keiff's." He returned his attention to me. "Good thing you were here, Lil. Like Simms says, there's no saving the house, but it could have been a hell of a lot worse."

"Barricades won't keep 'em out." Chief Simms spat. "People will track through the damn cornfield, as hot as it is, to take in someone else's bad luck. And this place has never had any luck." He shook his head. "Stupid bastards." He turned. "Damn, it's goin' to be hotter than hell today."

With Chief Simms gone, I received Charles's full attention. "What in the Sam Hill got into you? You're lucky you weren't seriously hurt."

I reached to pull my mask off, wanting, this time, to do so before Ben could stop me. As distinctly as I could, I said, "There... was... someone..."

A flash of heat moved through me, and behind it came a heaviness in my stomach and chest. I struggled to get beyond the discomfort, my words now choppy. "Up...stairs... window."

Then everything blended into a fuzzy image. My head reeled like after a three-night binge. My stomach heaved. I leaned over the gurney and retched.

Ben and Charles stopped me from falling. Charles held my head.

Ben's voice, "She knocked herself good on something. She might have a concussion."

They helped me lie back down, and Ben replaced the mask.

"Take it easy, Lil. You're safe." Charles put his hand on my shoulder.

"Hate to see this happen to the Carters." Ben was somewhere behind me.

Everything, including me, drifted.

"I'm taking her on in," Ben said.

CHAPTER TWO
OVER CHARLES

"Think Burt had insurance on the house?"

I knew without opening my eyes that the voice belonged to April McDonald, a nurse at Frytown General Hospital.

"Doubt it." This voice belonged to Laura Dell, the emergency room nurse. She met the ambulance when it arrived and got me set up in a room. Had she given me something more to make me sleep? How long had I been out? Laura said, "You can't afford insurance if you've lost your job. This economy's gone to hell.

"They were in a world of hurt with him laid off at the city," April said. "Carol doesn't make much as a teacher."

"You heard, didn't you?" Laura asked. "They may be cutting staff here at the hospital, too."

"How can they?" April squealed. "This is the main hospital for Johnson County unless you go into Iowa City to Mercy."

"You know, you're right," Laura agreed with her. "We're over-loaded and underpaid. You should go right on up there to the office and quit."

It got quiet.

April changed the subject. "We could take a donation or something."

"That's a good idea. Their boys are going to need clothes. School's going to start in a couple of weeks. We can have a huge community garage sale."

"Burt and Carol aren't the types to take charity."

"Maybe not," Laura said, "but there comes a time when you have to swallow your pride. I'll put up some fliers and get the Frytown Women's Club to do a phone chain. It won't take much to get a sale going."

I opened my eyes. My hands hurt. I lifted them and saw what looked like two red lobster claws.

"Don't worry, hon," April said. "Your hands aren't as bad as they look. They'll be stiff and hurt for a couple of days, but they should heal fast. Not more than a bad sunburn. Are you hungry? Tonight's fried chicken. I think you'll be able to handle a fork."

I shook my head, dizzy, and reached to find a lump on my forehead.

"Yep, you got one nasty bump." April came over to the bed and gave my head a good look. "Your head is worse than your hands. It took seventeen stitches. What did you fall on?"

"I don't know." I shut my eyes, thinking back. Did I see what I fell on? I shook my head, dizziness again.

She maneuvered around the bed. "The doctor gave you a tetanus shot just in case. If you start getting a headache, buzz me." She lifted a remote from the bed rail and showed me where to find the buzzer. "I can give you some Tylenol."

When an attendant brought in the dinner tray, I found I was hungrier than I'd thought. My hands were painful, but the back of my hands hurt the worst. April was right; I could maneuver the fork well enough to scoop mash potatoes and gravy.

Dinner wasn't long past when Charles appeared in the doorway. "How're you feeling, Lillian?" He was wearing a clean uniform, never less than a military press in the trousers, and held his cap in his hands.

"I'll live."

He pulled up a chair and smiled, nodding to the plastic container of Jell-O left on my bed tray. "Is that all they're feeding you?"

I'd licked the plate clean, and only a chicken leg bone remained with a smear of potatoes and gravy. "They're wrong. There isn't always room for Jell-O."

He laughed. "Well, I'd take it. Jell-O beats the hell out of the stale tuna I found in the refrigerator at the station." He looked at my hands. "They look sore. What did the doctor say?"

"I haven't seen the doctor. I'm told he'll come by in the morning, but it's my guess he's going to tell me to stay out of the sun for a while."

A funny yet sour expression came over his face. I didn't think it had to do with my joke. "Charles, are you all right?"

"Just tired." His squared shoulders slumped. He smiled. "I didn't get much sleep last night."

I avoided the subject. "You realize that tuna had been in the refrigerator for a while?"

His expression turned worried. "Why the hell didn't someone throw it away?"

"Didn't it stink?" I never eat anything out of the fridge without a good sniff test.

"I didn't stop to smell the damn thing." A burp escaped his lips.

"You should ask a doctor to give you something before leaving the hospital," I said. "Just in case."

"I don't have time to be laid up." He wiped his face with his hand. The skin took its time to spring back like a rubber band pulled too many times in too many ways.

Charles wasn't much older than me, seven years maybe. Forty-five was my guess. But he looked ready for retirement. "We've got double the crowd at the lake with this damn hot weather," he said. "It was over a hundred again today, and they're saying we're in for the same tomorrow." He wiped his forehead. Beads of perspiration pimpled his brow. "The city keeps busting my butt for cutbacks. Hell, I've cut shifts as far as I dare. With the crowd down at the lake, and now this fire, I won't have any other choice but to put my men on time and a half."

He took a pad from his shirt pocket, along with a pen. "Why don't you start from the beginning and tell me what happened."

When I got to the part where I broke the window and fell into the room, I noticed his blue eyes fading to gray. He sat with his mouth clenched. His stomach rumbled.

He noticed I noticed. I looked away to save him embarrassment.

He said, "You've got a nasty bump." He added, "I bet it won't leave much of a scar."

"How often do you win your bets?"

"Often enough." He put his hand tenderly to my face.

I wanted to tell him how good it felt to have someone worry about me. Could this be the start of something good? Could sobriety lead me into a good relationship?

When I'd arrived at his place on Sunday afternoon, he'd set the table with water goblets, not wine. After dinner, we went out to the rockers on the back porch to take in the night. Chit-chat wasn't necessary. We sat and listened to the approaching storm, heard the soft roll of thunder, then a flash of light.

"We should go in," he said.

"I should be going home," I said.

As the wind pulled above its whisper, we remained sitting, rocking, and listening, tension mounting. I knew I should leave.

An enormous blast of thunder crashed overhead. Charles stood and moved beside my rocker. Rain began falling. He bent low, his lips lightly touching mine.

"You should stay," he whispered. "It's dangerous."

I looked out to the storm, wondering about its strength. Would there be damage? Could I survive its ravage?

Charles grasped my hand and tenderly kissed its palm. A spark flashed between us. His eyes sought mine.

It won't work. He doesn't know me.

I slipped my arms around his neck.

He pulled me out of the rocker and crushed me to him, thunder, lightning, the wind howling, *can't go home*, his hands asking, my body answering, *yes, yes.* He lifted me into his arms and carried me into the house.

The wind roared. Tree limbs scratched and banged against the house. Thunder boomed. Lightning cracked. Yet, I wasn't afraid.

We laughed when he threw me down on the bed and leaped in after me. His blue eyes, full of boyish fun, took me in as completely as his arms. His hungry lips found mine again and again. He kissed my neck. Unbuttoned my blouse before pulling it open to give way for his fingers to caress my breasts. I clasped his head in my hands, thinking no, wanting yes. I lifted my breast to meet his lips and trembled at the lick of his tongue, the playful nibble at my nipple.

While he removed my clothes, I kissed him and took him in my hand, finding his desire as great as mine. When he lowered himself onto me, my heart raced.

I wanted it to be true—him, me, the storm inside taking us in, here—tomorrow?

Sitting now in my hospital bed, I needed him to put his hand back to my face, look into my eyes and tell me I wasn't wrong. I wished for him to say he desired me with all my faults.

A disquieting silence developed. We were no longer swinging on the porch. I was a patient in the hospital, and he came by to follow up on a house fire. The storm had passed. The *me* he knew was the Lillian Dove who'd moved to Frytown. Not the one left behind.

    I wasn't sure where to take the conversation.

He glanced at his writing pad, where he'd made a couple of notes. "Just a couple more questions, and I'll let you get some rest. First, can you describe the person you saw?"

"I didn't see him good. I think he was wearing a mask."

"A mask? Like a ski mask?"

I shook my head. I tried to bring the image to mind but couldn't.

"You keep saying 'he.' Are you saying it was a man?"

Again, I had to shake my head. "I can't say. Not for sure."

He made another note and then put his notebook back in his shirt pocket. "I didn't expect you to come up with much, but getting a witness statement right away is important. Details are fresh. But in your case, the details may take some time coming back with hitting your head." He stood. "I doubt you'll need to make an official statement. My bet's on faulty wiring or a lightning strike. I'll have Simms's report tomorrow."

After he had left, I got out of bed and went into the bathroom. It wasn't the first time I saw the black-and-blue bump with the Frankenstein stitches, but I hadn't noticed I was missing an eyebrow over my left eye.

By the time I got to my condo the next afternoon, my hands were stinging. I never considered how much hands do until I hurt mine. The lotion they gave me at the hospital was helping, but each time I buttoned a button on the shirt, the skin on the top of my hands crinkled and burned.

It wasn't enlightening to find out how many things I owned that pricked, rubbed, and stabbed.

I emptied the contents of my purse on the corridor floor to search for the door key. Once I had it, I used both hands like shovels and pushed everything back inside. I shouldered my purse and moved on to tackle the lock.

Angry yowling came from inside the condo. I opened the door. Bacardi was sitting in the middle of the living room, tail twitching. I placed my foot between the door and the jamb to prevent him from escaping. After wrangling the key out of the lock, I squeezed in, holding the door to my body and scraping my hand, causing me to yowl.

Bacardi's my cat, named for his brown and yellow coloring, and my first drinking preference for rum and Coke. At the age of twelve, if you add enough cola, you forget all about the sweet tang of rum. Plus, Bacardi's hair frizzed out of his body as if he'd stuck his claw in a light socket. I'd woken up many a morning with that same look when my hair was shorter.

I dropped my purse on the floor. Toed off my shoes.

When the taxi had dropped me off, I spotted my car parked in front of the complex. A note left at the hospital desk stated I'd find the keys in my maildrop. But thinking about maneuvering the tiny mailbox key kept me from wondering if I'd got mail, and besides, I wasn't planning to go anywhere.

Another yowl. Bacardi moved to sit in front of the kitchen entry-way. I went in and found his kibble bowl and water dish full. Funny. Generally, they would be close to empty by the end of the day. It was now well over thirty-six hours since I'd left home.

Using my thumbs, I gingerly pulled the cupboard open. I took out a can of cat food, using both palms, and placed it on the counter. I got the can opener out of the drawer in much the same way and then stood to stare at it. Not as easy to manage. As I was giving the possible techniques some thought, I noticed a fork in the sink. Odd. Plus, the fork appeared rinsed, which I call washing dishes. I opened the cupboard again. I was pretty sure there had been three cans of Feline Delight before leaving on Sunday, but one remained after taking this can out. Someone had fed Bacardi. Someone had been in the condo.

"Did you have a visitor while I was away?" Bacardi meowed and rubbed against my legs. "Did Earl come over and feed my hungry boy?"

Earl was my next-door neighbor. He had a key to the condo in case of emergencies. He must have heard what had happened and made sure Bacardi had food.

After maneuvering the can opener without as much pain as I'd imagined, I went into the bathroom. I took a long shower, enjoying the relief of cool water on my hands. I lathered the prescription lotion per directions. It was late afternoon, but I put on PJs.

After finished eating, Bacardi sat cleaning his face. I checked the fridge for something for me. My choices were yogurt, mayonnaise, mustard, and a half head of lettuce. I found the last of a carton of Rocky Road ice cream in the freezer.

I was a connoisseur of Rocky Road. So much so that I kept a box of plastic spoons, disliking the taste of ice cream against metal. Okay, I know, it was chocolate.

I picked up the remote and flicked on the television. Local news meteorologists, whose voices lull during average temperatures, tittered this afternoon like girls getting ready for their senior prom. I switched from one channel to the next. Each weather announcer offered explanations on how low systems collided with high systems and forecasted another hottest day. Finally, I stopped at the local news channel, KETV, where a video showed a blackened house at the end of a cornfield.

KETV's reporter, Bobby Bowen, was speaking. "Chief Simms of the Frytown Fire Department said an investigation is undergoing and his department's not willing to eliminate the possibility of arson." He pushed his microphone up to Burt Carter, standing next to him. "Do you have any idea who might have done something like this to you, Mr. Carter? Known enemies? Are you or a member of your family under investigation?"

Burt blinked. "What do you mean? Why would we be under investigation? This was our home." Burt wore a T-shirt depicting a man fishing and the words MY WIFE THINKS I'M WORKING. Local camping apparel. His wife, Carol, and two sons, Darrell and David, stood beside him. Carol wore jeans and a midriff top. Darrell, the older son, wore a gray T-shirt with IOWA FOOTBALL imprinted in yellow. David's yellow T-shirt said WHATEVER.

Bobby stayed resolute. "I understand this is the second time someone has attempted to burn down this house. You're aware the Dillard family experienced this exact same tragedy?"

Burt's reply was a blinking frenzy. Bobby stuck the microphone closer to Burt's face as if forcing a response. Burt stammered, "Before…before my time."

"But you do know the story?"

Bobby Bowen continued. "Over sixty years ago, the Dillard family was murdered by an arsonist," He remarked to Burt, "If you hadn't gone camping yesterday, your family might have suffered."

Carol Carter nodded as if to say, "Yes, we have that, if nothing else." Then, the younger son offered a peace sign.

"How do you feel about what has happened to your family?" Bobby asked Darrell.

"I'm happy my family wasn't hurt. I heard lightning also hit a house over in Oxford."

"That's right. The Oxford fire department confirmed lightning struck the house. But is that what happened here?" Bobby's next question went back to Burt. "According to Chief Simms of the Frytown Fire Department, Lillian Dove, a civilian phone facilitator for the police department, reported the fire. Have you spoken to Ms. Dove?"

I was dumb-struck that my name was being offered so freely.

"Are you aware she said she saw someone in the upper floor window of your house?"

"I don't know…"

"Have *you* spoken to her, Mrs. Carter?"

"No. We just came back. We have seen no one except for Chief Simms."

"If they link arson with this fire, Mr. Carter, and the fire department finds lightning wasn't the cause, then Ms. Dove may be the only eyewitness to this crime."

My mouth went slack. He was making me sound far more important than I was.

Burt looked like someone had hit him in between the eyes. "Crime? This…this wasn't any crime. Lightning hit the house. It stormed last night. Who'd want to burn down our house?"

I picked up the carton of Rocky Road and licked off the leftover chocolate on my fingers and the plastic spoon. Yet I still felt unsatisfied. The memory of the cool, gummy texture of lime Jell-O returned.

Cool, light Jell-O. Jell-O shots. One package of Jell-O, one cup of hot water, stir, add one-half cup of vodka or gin, or tequila if you're on the wild side, then a one-half cup of cold water. Hell, if you're really the wild and crazy type, make it a half cup of hot water and a cup and a half of booze. Chill.

I fell into a stupor as soon as my head hit the pillow.

The air held an aroma of algae, dust, and small animals' leavings. All horizons offered only cold, gray water. I stood in a dense thicket of oaks and brambles. My mother, Dahlia, was standing before me with a skeleton key. "No, sir," she goaded. "Not as long as I got the key."

If I could just get that key, then everything would be different. "Give it to me."

"Come an' get it." She laughed and dangled the key like a feather strung on a pole.

I jumped. My fingers clipped the metal as she jerked the key out of my reach. She cackled, thoroughly entertained by my failure. "Got to jump higher in life, Lilly, if you want to make something out of yourself."

I hated her. More than I could ever remember hating her. "Like you? I don't want to be you, Dahlia."

"Worse things in life. You could stay being you." She hooted and jiggled the key.

I jumped and missed. She'd ruined my life. I jumped again, missed. *I wish you were dead.* Jumped. Jumped. Jumped.

Then, from somewhere in the bushes, I heard Cressie's voice. "Lilly, stop. You're the key, not her."

I stopped jumping. I stared into the undergrowth, trying to find her. "Cressie?"

I needed the answers still plaguing me. "Why did you kill yourself?" She'd promised me the pain would go away. But, it hadn't for her. "Cressie? Come back." Branches whipped me as I ran. Tree roots tripped me. Thorns ripped my arms, hands, and face. The tip of my tongue licked the blood off my bottom lip.

I woke up.

I shook off the despair from the thought that, like Cressie, I would only struggle to fail.

Help me, Cressie.

I thought it was morning, but it was dark outside.

Thirsty, I went out to the kitchen and turned on the light. The ceiling fixture flickered and popped. Bacardi dashed between my legs, almost knocking me off my feet. The fridge offered cold, neutral light as I reached in and pulled out the yogurt. I peeled off the foil label. Sniffed. A faint peachy scent.

The telephone rang, and the answering machine picked up. The voice on the machine said, "Hope you weren't in bed, Lillian. I hated to call and bother you so late."

The voice was Nelly Crow's, head RN down at Oaks Manor. "I heard about the fire. I hope you weren't hurt."

I picked up the phone. We discussed my injuries and treatment. Drug addiction is a secret in the medical world. Nurses may not be taking a lot of drugs, but they can't quit talking about them. No different from dieters sharing cookie recipes.

"I'm going to work tomorrow," I informed her. Then I asked, "Is something wrong with Dahlia?"

"Well..." I could visualize Nelly biting her bottom lip. "I could be calling about a stolen horse before checking the barn, but I can't find her."

I gave that some welcomed thought. Life without Dahlia?

My mother Dahlia was the reason I lived in Frytown. Frank, my eldest brother, moved her from our hometown of New Liberty to Frytown after her first stroke, thinking a senior condo would care for all her needs. After her second stroke, he called me.

Frank and I weren't close. I hadn't spoken to him since I'd left home at eighteen, abandoning him and my other younger brother to an alcoholic father and our mother who denied a problem existed.

Fifteen years later, I picked up the telephone and didn't recognize his voice. Needless to say, our conversation was short, not sweet. And it soon came down to pointing fingers. "You owe her, Lillian."

"I owe her nothing but the bill from my therapist." This was an exaggeration on my part. Therapy might have sped up my sobriety if I'd admitted I had a problem and gone to therapy.

"Some of us had to stay and bear the burden."

My chest tightened. I wanted to tell him that I would've gone back and done it all differently if I could have. Even at eighteen, the voice in my head said that running away wouldn't fix what I was feeling. But like my feelings, the next drink quickly drowned the voice.

"Who do you think took care of all of them after you ran off?" he snapped. "Did you think of that? I took care of Patrick. I took care of the old man until we buried him. When Mom got her first stroke, I put her in a place where she could be safe. This time, I moved her into a convalescent home." His voice raised, and my stomach clenched. "I've got a life, too, Lillian. I've done my part. It's your turn."

He was right, yet I retaliated. "We aren't talking about who will wash the dishes, Frank. We're talking about the woman who dragged me out of bed late at night to help her carry our father into the house after he'd passed out on the front lawn. Summer, winter, it didn't matter. He could never make it into the house."

"He's dead."

"I was eight, Frank. Eight. By twelve, I had to manage the house. I was given charge of my two brothers and dragging in the old man."

"As I said, Lillian, he's dead. She doesn't have long to live. You can stay at the condo. There's not much money left, but there's enough to get her through the next few years."

"No, Frank. I won't do it."

"You don't need to bother calling if she dies. I'm done." He hung up

When she died, I would call Frank and give him the good news. I would have called if he'd left me his phone number.

Nelly's voice disrupted my thoughts. "Lillian?"

"Nelly, how far could she get with a bad heart in a wheelchair?"

"Hold it. There she is."

"You see her?"

"She's coming from the TV room." She added, as if puzzled, "I just checked there."

"Is *Gunsmoke* on tonight?"

"I'd swear she wasn't watching television." She said in a rush, "I've got to go. She's heading for the front door."

I went back to the kitchen. I ate the peach-like yogurt over the sink and threw the carton in the trash.

Here comes more trouble, I thought. Lately, Dahlia had gotten it into her head that she would leave Oaks Manor. A week ago, the Oaks staff searched for her and found her in her nightgown several blocks away, wheeling her chair in the bike lane, trying to thumb a ride. When I confronted her about the trouble she was causing everyone, she'd said, "One day, you're going to show up and find me dead."

When I talked to Marilyn Yoder, the manager of Oaks Manor, she explained Dahlia's behavior as delusional paranoia brought on by her strokes. Marilyn suggested that small undetectable strokes may continue to occur.

The end was near.

I opened the freezer. I wasn't looking for more ice cream. Ice cream couldn't deaden the nightmare still looming in my mind. How was I going to grab that key before Dahlia kicked the bucket? I knew ice cream couldn't silence Cressie's voice or my secret dread that I'd find myself in the scrub in one of those dreams because I'd be standing right beside her.

Cressie was the one who'd preached sobriety to me. The coroner's report stated the cause of death was a barbiturate and alcohol overdose. Cressie's dying stopped me from drinking.

I have yet to determine if I will make it beyond her sobered-eight years before falling and slipping off the cliff.

Please help me, Cressie.

I took out a fifth of Absolut from the freezer. Drinks with lower alcohol levels, like beer, burst, but vodka is unequaled in its ability to resist freezing.

The seal was still intact. I'd purchased this bottle the day I moved into Dahlia's condo, which had triggered an episode, and I came close to the edge of a cliff in nowhere-land. After some deep breathing, reciting the steps, and reminding myself of the promise I'd made to a sober me, I'd put the bottle in the freezer. I took it out now and again when things got bad to remind myself just how close the line between sanity and insanity walked beside me. It glided, wrapped in a mantle, whispering, *remember Cressie.*

Like other times, I put the bottle back into the cold. I pushed Dahlia away in my mind. No worry. She'd pop back—no stopping Dahlia. I turned on the news.

A weather reporter pointed to a screen, updating viewers on the storm, which was now moving south and terrorizing other towns and cities. "Stay inside, folks, and drink lots of fluids."

Wednesday morning. Back to normal. I showered and dressed in my professionally casual black slacks and a white cotton blouse, the regulation uniform for civilian workers. Sipping my first cup of coffee of the day, I jotted down a list for a stop at the Hy-Vee grocery. Feline Delight was at the top, and under it, I added the other necessities of life, like toilet paper, bread, cereal, milk, something to go with the bread, and lettuce.

The Frytown Police Department comprises fifteen officers: Chief Kaefring, Lieutenant Manville, Major Investigations Detective Jacque Leveque, two sergeants, and ten patrol officers. In addition, there are three dispatch operators and the three of us who handle the office. I work the five-hour morning shift, eight to one.

Only a handful of patrol cars were parked in the lot. I entered the station by the back door. I grabbed my second cup of coffee and a donut. I chewed and sipped and started my day as usual by checking in with Donna Stockman in dispatch. Most days, I enjoy another cup of coffee and go in to hear "the latest" from her until eight-thirty.

Donna Stockman was a better source than Wikipedia.

She was unmarried, other than for her job. She'd answered the phones in the lobby, a full-time job before dispatch was funded. That was twenty years ago. Today, she worked the first dispatch eight-hour shift.

As with most mornings, she was sitting in her custom-ordered ergonomic chair positioned facing the doorway. "Lillian, how are you feelin'? Oh, dear, look at that nasty bump. You poor thing."

My hands didn't hurt as badly. The bump was a little better, too. Its swelling had lessened, and the color had changed from purplish-blue to a purple-pink Easter egg. I'd penciled in an eyebrow as best as I could. Things were looking up.

"I'm fine." Then, as casually as possible, I asked, "Is Chief Kaefring in?"

Of course, I'd seen his own black Ford Explorer in the lot and the chief's cruiser with CHIEF OF POLICE on the sides. But this conversation with Donna was mandatory, so I figured I might as well get it over and done.

Donna's eyebrows moved to uneven positions, one lowering below the frames of her retro, rhinestone-studded glasses and her other eyebrow arching high in a question. "He's in. The car's in the lot." She was letting me know she knew I knew he'd arrived. "He went straight to his office and closed the door." A sly grin moved across her lips. "He seemed to have something on his mind. I barely got a "Good Morning" out of him." She sipped some coffee. Timing was one of Donna's talents. "Sweetie, what happened before you got to the fire?"

I sipped my coffee, figuring out how to maneuver around her questioning. Donna was a skilled interrogator. It wouldn't help by trying to sideline her or circle around what would eventually need to be said. I aimed toward the truth. "So, this is what happened, Donna. The chief called and said he had two steaks and was putting one on the grill."

"Uh-huh. And?" She raised her cup and peeked over the brim.

"It's not like I have a social calendar. I went." I shrugged at the casual, innocent decision I'd made. "And if you remember, it started storming."

"Uh-huh. I hear you." She sipped and savored.

"There were tornado warnings."

She closed an eye, giving me the "Donna-Eye." Donna's social life depended on good, juicy chit-chat, and her "Donna-Eye" was popping out of its socket.

I wasn't about to confess. "We got to talking, and it got late. Charles was worried about me getting home."

"Chief only lives six miles out of town."

I went over to her private Mr. Coffee, wanting to distance myself between her questioning and my answering. I groaned when refilling my cup, faking the effort and hoping the redness of my hands would grab her sympathy and attention. When she said nothing about the horrible, yet pretended, pain I was in, I helped myself to a piece of watermelon from the small bowl on her desk. "Is this diet working?"

"I've lost two pounds," she replied.

Donna considered even a pound a notable amount. But this morning, the success of her diet wasn't going to distract her from getting enough out of me to supply her rumor mill. She wiggled her naughty finger. "Don't think you'll get out of what happened, Lillian." She settled herself more comfortably in her chair. "Now, fill me in on the juicy parts." She popped a piece of melon into her mouth and smacked her lips.

"Will you quit? Nothing happened." I waved off the thought and her speculations. "We ate dinner. It started storming. I stayed for a while. That's all."

"More than a little while, hon." Both her eyebrows arched so sharply that her glasses slipped to the middle of her nose.

I warned her, "Don't get any ideas or start stories where there are none. As soon as the weather let up, I told you, I headed out."

"So, you say. Let's see, I don't recall hearing it thunder after midnight." She devilishly chuckled, covering her mouth as if she could say a whole lot more, but not now, not here, or to me.

"It's my story," I said. "I'm sticking to it. And I would appreciate you setting straight anyone else who's asking."

The console buzzed. She put the call on speaker. Garth Davis, a rookie parole officer, rescued me from Donna's interrogation by calling to ask for a ten-zero. Donna said, "You asked for one not more than fifteen minutes ago, Garth. What's up?"

He groaned. "Ah, Mary Beth cooked meatloaf last night."

Donna's voice now sounded like a naughty finger. "I should call Mary Beth's mother and tell her to teach that girl how to cook, or we will have to hire a new rookie."

His voice became more than anxious. "Don't, Donna. I'm begging you. Give me five."

"Ten-four." Donna swiveled around laughing. "Now, what did Mary Beth put in that meatloaf to give him the shits this early in the mornin'?"

Was it her meatloaf, I wondered, or had Garth been slumming the staff refrigerator like the chief? "I think I'll hold off from accepting a dinner invitation anytime soon."

Whoops.

"Dinner?" Donna's face lit, remembering our conversation before Garth's call. "Which brings me back to…"

The general line rang. She held up her index finger, ordering me to stay where I was while she picked it up.

I retreated to seek refuge at my desk.

I didn't get far. Charles stood in the hallway. He said, "I thought that was you. Could you come to my office for a minute?" He turned and preceded me in.

Peggy Hudgins sat at her desk in the outer office of the chief. Assistant to the chief of police and higher in seniority than me, she got away with being habitually late. This morning, I could only imagine what brought her in "on time."

Charles took his chair behind his desk and shuffled paperwork. A vast feeling of unease stretched between us. Finally, I said, "Garth called in sick. He said Mary Beth's trying to kill him with her cooking."

He began sorting the papers. "Mitch Miner called in sick, too. I think there's a bug going around. I'm a bit under the weather myself." He pulled a business envelope attached to some paperwork from under a stack of files. Then he placed a manila file in front of him, opened it, and read what was inside. His brows furrowed. His attention returned to me. "How are you feeling? You should take more time off." His voice sounded conflicted.

"I'm fine."

He took a sheet of paper and raised it. "Chief Simms gave me his report this morning. He's notified the state fire marshal's office. It's his opinion arson started the fire." He slid his fingers up and down the sheet, smoothing any wrinkles.

I was just about to tell him I'd caught all this on the television news when he began reading the report. "An eyewitness to the fire stated they saw someone in an upstairs window. Adding an unidentified person on the premises to the fact that the remaining structure indicates the possibility of liquid used to stimulate flame, I notified the state fire marshal, requesting a forensics unit to complete a more thorough investigation."

He replaced the sheet in the file and closed the folder. His expression was without emotion, professional. "I will need you to give an official statement of exactly what happened and what you saw. The fire marshal will also want to interview you." He paused. "I need to warn you there is a discrepancy. Tim states there wasn't any evidence the room had been inhabited that morning. The bed was made. The closet doors closed. He says the bedroom door was wide open when he entered. The stairway and first floor were completely engulfed, allowing no escape. The report also states no human remains were discovered."

I tried to take in what he was implying. "Are you saying I'm a suspect?"

He scratched his cheek. Not yet nine a.m., and already a ghost of a shadow. "No. But I want you to understand the consequences of what you might say. If you insist you saw someone, you may be an eyewitness to first-degree arson. A felony."

He waited for me to speak. I said, "I'm pretty sure I saw someone."

"You need to be absolutely sure."

I wasn't been absolutely sure about anything in my life, but I said, "There was someone. I'm sure of it. I can't remember what they looked like, and I'm not even sure I saw them. But there was someone in that window. And when I got to the room, there was someone inside."

"Okay, then. I want you to be careful until this is resolved. If someone thinks you could identify them, you're a threat."

"I'm sure I'll be fine." I thought we were finished, and I got up to leave.

"Wait." When I didn't sit back down, he said, "I need to talk to you about something else. Sit down, Lillian."

I continued to stand. What more could I say about the fire? I wasn't ready to talk about what happened between us.

He must have figured I wasn't going to sit down because he said next, "I have to lay you off."

I sat back down, hard. "Why?"

"They've been on me to cut back." He busied himself again as if to avoid what must have been an unmasked, veritable guise of desperation on my face.

"Are you firing me?"

"Lay-off. If we rehire for your position, you'll be hired back."

My mind raced like a greyhound's let out of the gate, searching for any damn unlucky rabbit it could find. "If this is because of …well, you know. I have told no one. Donna asked me when I got in this morning, and I told her you had an extra steak and couldn't find anyone home to ask over for a barbecue but me. So when it started storming, I stayed for a while until it was over, on the couch."

He grinned. "Think she bought that story?"

"No…but…"

"Look. My hands are tied." He held them out towards me as if to show the ropes binding him. "I have the choice of laying off either lobby receptionists or Garth, and I can't afford to pull off officers. I also laid off the second phone shift if it makes you feel better. After that, dispatch shifts, and Peggy will handle the general lines." He pulled out an envelope from under the manila file.

I gave him a silent stare. *Please?*

He looked away, rubbing the back of his neck. "I hate doing this. The timing couldn't be worse."

I bet. The timing was perfect. He'd tricked me into his bed, and now he was kicking me out of the office.

I couldn't trust you.

Humiliation and anger bubbled simultaneously. I stood as calmly as possible. And with the best Scarlett O'Hara imitation I could muster, I said, "Don't worry, Charles. That night meant nothing to me. I'll save you the trouble. I quit."

His professionalism dissolved. His expression became the look of a puppy scolded for being a bad boy. "Now, Lillian. Don't be putting words in my mouth. Laying you off has nothing to do with us. And by laying you off, you can collect unemployment until I can hire you back."

"Either way, I have to look for another job."

Peggy, who was busy on a telephone call connected to an unlit console, glanced at me as I walked by her desk.

Charles followed me into the outer office. "I'll fix this. Give me a day or two."

Tears welled in my eyes. How did this happen? Why did I let myself get into this situation? I liked my job. I needed this job. "Fix what, Charles? It's just a job."

He held out the business envelope as if holding out an olive branch. "Your check."

I survived by check to check but said, "Put it in the mail."

Still trying to keep my panic from overcoming my composure, I kept a normal pace walking from his offices to the back exit door. When I passed Lieutenant Manville's office, he got up and came out. "Hello, Lillian. This won't take long." He must have thought I was coming to give him my "official" statement.

I kept moving forward, trying not to change my pace, trying not to run as fast as I could, out of the office, away from everyone before more humiliation struck.

Tears blurred my vision. I passed the dispatch office, and Donna called out to me. I bet she knew. Lieutenant Manville knew, too. Officers Richards and Officer Stiller standing by the coffee in the break room, both looked away, embarrassed. Everyone knew!

Cheeks burning, unable to see anything clearly, the back door swung hard, banging into the outside handrail.

Stupid, stupid, stupid.

I brushed the tears off my face and ordered myself to stop crying. That's when I saw Detective Jacque Leveque drive into the lot. He was Frytown's only detective. Which made sense since the biggest ongoing crime in Frytown was meth use and dealing—and most dealers barely scraped out a living with rehab having become so popular. What celebrity hadn't done rehab?

The last time there was any major crime needing investigating was when I was a new hire. Louis Feller found his wife in bed in the afternoon with the UPS delivery man. Donna told me Detective Leveque put the evidence together and arrested Louis the same day. She also said it wasn't a complex investigation since everyone in town was waiting for Louis to start asking why so many packages were being delivered to his place. Louis Feller shot buckshot into the UPS guy's butt and got twelve months on second-degree assault, with time served.

Someone told me his wife took up house remodeling and an interest in handymen.

Donna and I were friends, or so I'd thought. Lieutenant Manville rarely noticed me when I was in the office. Not seeing me around would be a typical day for him. I got along with officers Richards and Stiller, and the rest of the officers, fine. We'd joke away a dull day.

If any person would be thrilled when hearing about my lack of employment, it'd be Detective Leveque. He couldn't get up in the morning without planning how to ruin my day. It'd been that way between us since I reminded him it was against office policy for employees to fraternize. Leveque's a Tom-Collins-type. Drink enough of those, and you're sicker than a dog.

My car was parked across the street. I blinked hard, telling myself I wouldn't let Leveque see me cry. I stepped off the curb into the crosswalk. The sun glinted off a windshield. I froze.

"Move!"

My feet left the pavement as I was pulled out of the path of an upcoming car. So close, I could smell its exhaust.

"Are you nuts?"

I jerked out of his grasp. "Don't touch me."

I looked for the culprit of my narrow escape and saw a dusty, green car with a trunk pleading a finger-streaked message: Wash Me. The car accelerated and then turned a hard right at the corner.

Glory, this was turning out to be one messed-up day.

When I tried to start the ignition in my car, the engine coughed and died. I pumped the gas pedal, turned the key again, and this time, the car started. As soon as I'd gotten in the car, the tears trailed down my cheeks, dripping off my chin. I couldn't get away fast enough.

I drove around the same corner as the car that almost ended any more anguish. It was long gone. I put my car into park and blubbered like a baby until there were no more tears left.

I checked my watch and found it wasn't even nine o'clock. There was still a whole day ahead. So what else was going to happen?

Instead of the expected freeze, hot air blew out of the car's air conditioning vents. Not a surprise for a '96 Ford Mustang convertible decorated with dents, three bullet holes, and a duct-taped back window. It'd been a bargain at a police auction. I flipped off the A/C switch, reached for my purse, and checked my wallet to find thirty-nine dollars. I immediately regretted leaving without my check.

I pulled down the visor's mirror to survey the damage. My eyes appeared normal, which was more worrying since normal for me hadn't been bloodshot since I'd quit drinking. However, my left eyebrow was still missing, and the penciled brow was wiped away by the tears. And the bump appeared purple-pink on a face, red and blotchy.

Still, I'd seen worse. I remember one time I got so drunk that I went home by bus, although my apartment was a simple walk from the bar I frequented. Guess I didn't want to get arrested for a DWW, Drunk While Walking. I ended up passing out and falling onto the floor. The bus driver didn't realize I was still back there, hidden away and snoozing it off until he checked the bus at the end of the shift. I ended up then with two black eyes and a cut lip.

I went to Hy-Vee as if it was like any other Wednesday. I strolled my grocery cart steadfastly, ignoring all four wheels going in opposite directions. Up one aisle and down the next, I took my time. I picked what I needed carefully. Considered pricing, volume, and expiration dates. I picked up a giant size jar of peanut butter. Protein—it'd go the distance. I hate peanut butter by itself, so I threw in a jar of strawberry preserves. Yes, preserves, none of that jelly stuff.

I discovered the gelatin aisle—grape, orange, pineapple, and strawberry-kiwi, which sounded very exotic. Then I spied six-packs. Ready-made Jell-O. Who would have thought? I picked up several six-packs and tossed them in. The ready-made was triple the cost but more suitable considering my culinary skills.

This spontaneous action of being frivolous created a spurt of giddiness. I'd planned to buy five cans of Feline Delight when I left the house this morning, but I counted eight into the cart. Why the hell not? Eat today, starve tomorrow.

I trolley'd my treasures to check out. Sylvia Collins, the veteran checker at the Hy-Vee, stood at one cash register, and at the other, a teenage boy handling a month's load of groceries. I got into Sylvia's line. She and the customer she was checking spoke quietly between one another while items crossed the scanner with beeps and burps. Several times, the two glanced at me. I tried not to notice.

When it was my turn, Sylvia gave me a look of sympathy. "How are you doing, Lillian?" I thought she meant my red eyes, missing eyebrow, and badly sunburned hands, but she said, "I couldn't believe it when I heard you got laid off."

Okay, I'd sat in the car crying for what-- five, ten minutes? It took me another ten to drive to the Hy-Vee. The news of a world disaster wouldn't move as fast as bad personal news in Frytown. I said, shrugging, "It's no big deal. Actually, I wasn't laid off. I quit."

She stopped scanning. This angle of the story hadn't gotten passed around.

"I decided I needed to get a career. Working part-time isn't taking me anywhere. So I've been thinking about going back to school."

She nodded and repeated, "School." She pulled the six-packs out from the cart.

Ah, the good old days.

I could hear the next conversation between Sylvia and her customer in my head. "You heard, didn't you? They fired Lillian Dove, and the poor thing's saying she'd quit. And do you know what she had in her cart? I'm afraid she's going to drown herself in Jell-O."

I glanced away from her only to set eyes on a shelf of brightly colored bottles: Mango Margarita, Strawberry Daiquiri, White Russian, Piña Colada. Someone shelved handily mixed drink bottles available in all sizes for those who didn't want to take the time or trouble to learn the concoctions.

Sylvia said, "They say this economic slump isn't just a recession but a depression, like the Great Depression."

I swallowed the increased saliva from the images of accessible temptation. Finally, I said, "It's hot enough outside for a Dust Bowl."

She sacked the Jell-O six-packs, saying, "You eat these?"

A rhetorical question since she was well aware I wasn't married and didn't have any children.

She continued. "My kids like them. They taste pretty good on a hot day when you're hungry, and it's too hot to eat."

With nothing more to bag, she gave me her full attention. Her tone became more serious. "I heard you were hurt out at the Carter house." She glanced over her shoulder at the next register. It was now vacant. "I didn't want to say anything with Darrell able to over-hear us. Poor kid. He's beside himself with worry."

I looked around for the kid who'd been operating that register. Darrell Carter? I found him. He'd gone across the store and was stacking packages of toilet paper.

Sylvia called out, "When you're done there, Darrell, remember to get the recycling ready."

Without turning to see who'd given him the order, he said, "Al-ready done, Syl."

She lowered her voice again. "You know, Darrell started a week ago. He came in saying he needed to get a job to support himself. He said his mom and dad were planning to move, and he didn't want to go with them." She sighed. "He's such a good kid. He doesn't sit around playing computer games or wait to be told what to do. You know, he doesn't just work here? He works for the humane society and helps at the Senior Center. I don't know how he finds the time to be captain of the football team, a junior firefighter, and keeps on the honor roll list. You know this is his senior year?"

I didn't. I knew very little about Darrell and almost as much about his mom and brother. Burt Carter and I exchanged street closure information over the telephone to answer questions by the general public.

I did, however, remember being young. I was sixteen when I ran away from home for the first time. Dahlia found me and dragged me back. At eighteen, I ran far enough away that she couldn't find me. I went off with Bill Cunningham to Davenport, Iowa. Two weeks later, he dumped me, and I had to learn to survive independently.

Still, it was better than at home.

Sylvia broke my thoughts about Dahlia and my memorable childhood. "Darrell is determined to go to UI. I swear that boy's crazy about going to college. Why he's been wearing UI colors since he was a little-bit. Carol told me she couldn't get him to wear anything else."

I now noticed he was wearing the yellow and black Hawkeye colors of the University of Iowa under his Hy-Vee apron.

I hefted a filled sack and went to take the other, but Sylvia picked it up instead and carried it to the end of the counter. With her free hand, she pulled the grocery cart behind her through the checkout, set her sack in it, then took mine from me. She leaned toward me. "I heard you saw someone." She glanced both ways, then said, "I hope you got a good look. I always say, what goes around comes around."

I didn't have the chance to ask what she meant by the remark because someone came into her register aisle.

Extra, extra. Hear all about it.

Each condo at Lake View Residential Complex had one or two bedrooms with a bath, a small kitchen, and a living area. Each condo shared a common wall, and each had a small patio. Earl Langley lived next door to me. He came out of his condo dressed in a suit and tie.

"You're looking pretty fine for so early in the morning, Earl. So where are you going?"

"Funeral." He brushed a scattering of white flakes off his shoulders.

Earl Langley was friendly with the married ladies in the complex. Mainly because he popped little blue pills like he was taking vitamins. Whenever the women were caught coming or going from his place, they offered excuses for having baked a plate of fresh cookies or pie, and they were bringing him a piece. Their voices would tremble with excitement and embarrassment as if they'd just been caught with their hand in the cookie jar. So to speak.

Not much taller than me, Earl was of average build. His white hair, what was left, was neatly combed. Pants pressed. Shoes shined. Usually, he'd give me one of his sly, naughty boy grins, but this morning his face held a complexity of emotions I rarely saw.

He said, "They're dropping like flies around here, Lillian. One of these days, I'll be attending my funeral."

The friend he played checkers with passed a month earlier, and he'd taken his friend's passing pretty hard. In fact, he'd refused to play checkers for a couple of weeks.

"Ah, Earl. I'm so sorry. Who is it this time?"

"Susan Porter." When I didn't respond, he added, "Lemon cake."

The mention of her pastry brought an image of a fairly tall, slender woman with white hair and milky eyes, who carried her Tupperware'd lemon cake forthrightly in her hands as if daring anyone to admonish her for where she was going and what she was about to do.

I couldn't say I knew her, but I admired her ability to shrug off the judgment.

Earl had once shared a piece of her lemon cake with me and confided the woman's husband was no longer ambulatory or sexually functional. "I do what I can to comfort her."

That's Earl, the emotional caregiver.

I continued to give him my condolences. "Her lemon cake was great. I'm sorry for your loss. What did she die of?"

"Old age." He waved off the sympathy. "Let's see, she must have been what, eighty-two?" He grinned, "Although I never ask to see a driver's license."

There was no secret all his ladies were married. "Will her husband continue living here?"

"Nah. I spoke with her daughter. Susan introduced me to her a couple of years ago and gave her my number in case anything should happen."

Daughter *and* mother cooperating? How novel.

"Susan's daughter said she'd have to put her dad in a home closer to where she lived in the Fort Dodge area." He glanced down at his watch. He startled. "Hey, what are you doing home this time of day?" He studied my face. "Your bump looks worse than it did yesterday. You all right?"

"I got laid off," I told him. Then I remembered I'd quit.

"Sorry to hear that, Lillian. If you need any help…"

"No, I'll be fine. I still have my job at Discount."

My other part-time job was afternoon clerking at the AAA Discount Liquor store, most everyone called Discount.

"Layoffs are happening to everyone nowadays," he offered to explain my dilemma.

Older people dying and people losing their employment were how Earl was seeing the world that morning.

"Sign of the times," I summed up. "I'll find another job." I smiled. "Or maybe I'll learn how to make a lemon cake."

He couldn't keep back an even more enormous grin than before. "If you do, bring me over some."

"Careful, Earl. I might show up one lonely night."

He became thoughtful. "You should find someone special to chase away the lonelys, Lillian."

"Heck. I'm not lonely. I've got you, haven't I?" I kissed him on his grizzled cheek. "Besides, I don't want a boyfriend. They get in the way. They tell you what to do and what not to do. I like being in control of my own life."

"We're two of a kind, there."

He said he'd be home later in the day and continued to his funeral.

I opened the door. Bacardi was immediately underfoot and out. "Bacardi, come back here."

Earl grabbed him before he got too far. "Got him."

Bacardi yowled and hissed in Earl's arms.

"Just a second." I went in and set the groceries down on the couch. I yelled out the door, "He's going nuts in this heat."

Earl came back and handed over the cat. "He was thumping around in your kitchen the other night. He was making a racket."

"Sorry. What night?"

He thought a minute. "Let's see. It must have been Monday night. Yes, that's right. The night you were in the hospital. I guess it's what set him off. You hadn't come home. It was pretty late when I heard him."

I thought back to the kibble and the fork in the sink. "Then it wasn't you who came in and fed Bacardi?"

Earl shook his head. "Guess I should have thought to do it. If you hadn't come home the next morning, I probably would have."

If it wasn't Earl who'd come into my place, then who? And how? I told him, "If you hear any more thumping, let me know, okay?"

"Ah, don't be hard on the fella." He reached out, giving Bacardi's head a scratch.

Bacardi hissed. Usually, Earl was one of his favorite people, but I guess Earl's preventing him from taking a hallway stroll put Bacardi in a mood.

After I closed the door, I stood a moment. But, of course, the only two people who had a key to the condo beside Dahlia were Earl and Albert, the super for the complex. Unless that is, my brother Frank had kept a key. But it wouldn't have been Frank. He'd never have taken the time or trouble to feed my cat. But then, it wasn't like Albert to enter the condo without notifying me, either.

It couldn't have been Dahlia. She was confined to a wheelchair.

I was back to the only logical possibility, Albert. I called him. His answering machine message said, "Your dime, my time. Tell me what's wrong, and I'll come to fix it.'

"Albert, this is Lillian Dove in number three-two-four. Did you come in and feed my cat while I was in the hospital? If you did, I want to thank you."

I hung up. It had to have been Albert.

I went back to the kitchen. Bacardi jumped on the counter, spooking me. I laughed.

"Get down. You don't get any more food until I get back home. You were a naughty boy hissing at Earl."

I lifted him off the counter. He sat on the floor, giving me his back and twitching his tail in retribution. The rejection did the trick. I opened a can of Feline Delight.

Men might come and g, but Bacardi would never leave me.

AAA Discount Liquor, or Discount, offered the lowest-priced booze this side of Walmart.

Yeah, an alkie working at a liquor store doesn't sound like someone working her program. But you wouldn't believe how many bartenders *are* or *were* drunks.

Clarence Salzman, the owner, was clerking for a customer when I jingled the bell coming in the front door. "Hot enough for you?" he said to Mrs. Atkins, a bi-weekly regular. She routinely purchased a small bottle of apricot brandy and a dry sherry for Mr. Atkins. She once told me a little drink while watching the nightly news helped their digestion.

She never purchased more or less the amounts, or more often, at least she didn't on my watch. The Atkins were a prime example of people who could manage their drinking habits. Unless you count their daily routine as a compulsion. If Mrs. Atkins didn't show up every Wednesday, I'd worry about them.

Mrs. Atkins was now saying to Clarence, "Was it cold in the ground when you woke up this morning?"

Clarence seemed to understand. "You're right. It's not that hot. It could be worse." He bagged her bottles. "Although it'll be a lot hotter where I'm heading."

"Now, Clarence," she said, "you're as good a man as my Paul, and they reserved a penthouse suite for him at the Pearly Gates Hotel." They both gave that some time for a good chuckle. "But my," she admitted, fanning herself with her hand, "it is hot today. When I drove by Western Heritage, the digital sign showed it'd already reached a hundred. And this morning's news said we'll go as high as one-five, one-ten." Then, she said in a more confidential tone, "It's the humidity that's hard for Paul. It hinders his breathing."

Paul Atkins suffered from chronic obstructive pulmonary disease, COPD, caused by forty years of smoking two packs a day. Mrs. Atkins told me she got rid of all his cigarettes, matches, and the ashtrays in their house before he came home from the hospital. I guess she was still on the winning side.

She gave Clarence her money, and she turned around and saw me standing in front of the fan. Of course, Discount was air-conditioned like any other store, but Mother Nature beats technology every time.

"Are you all right, Lillian? I heard you were hurt in the fire."

"I'm doing just fine, thank you."

Mrs. Atkins was wearing pink today, a color favoring her creamy white, always-wear-a-bonnet complexion. She turned around to Clarence and pursed her returned change. "Clarence, would you mind if I put a notice in the store window about Saturday's garage sale the lady's club is arranging for the Carters? You know they lost everything." She repeated. "*Everything.* Just imagine."

Clarence nodded toward the front door. "Didn't you notice that sheet of paper taped on the door when you came in?"

"Why no."

All of us looked. Clarence read, "Don't miss the huge garage sale to benefit the Carter family. Two p.m. to six p.m.' "Laura Dell came bright and early this morning to put it up."

"Oh, good. That Laura is a do-er. You don't have to ask her twice." Although she was still addressing Clarence, she included me in the next bit of conversation. "You saw, then, that the sale's being held down at the lakeside? We're hoping to empty some tourist pockets, too. There should be plenty of them down there if this weather keeps the way it has." She gathered her sack of bottles, tucking them under her good arm, and said to me, "I heard about you trying to help someone at the fire. It was a brave thing to do."

Her statement wasn't a prompt to get me talking. What I liked most about Mrs. Atkins was that she not only said people should mind their own business, but she minded hers.

I made light of her compliment. "You would have done the same if you'd spotted someone trapped."

She took a moment to think. "Possibly. When I was younger, maybe. Or I'd like to tell myself I would. Only I've never been called to know if I would or wouldn't. You were. It was a brave act. Don't let people tell you any different."

After she had left, Clarence worried I might not be up to a hot day in the store. I told him my hands were much better, and I had no more headaches. Apparently, the rumor about my layoff hadn't gotten around yet, so I filled him in on my need for employment. He proposed giving me more hours. In a recession, you can count on people continuing to drink.

"I agree with Maude," he said. "You were foolish, but it was bold what you did. You're lucky you weren't killed."

I agreed. "If it hadn't been for Tim Johnson, I would have died in the fire. So next time, I'll stay in the car like I was told."

"Let's hope there isn't a next time." He walked into his small office and came back out carrying his cane. "Damn it to hell," he said, opening the door. "It's hotter than a three-balled tomcat in a pepper patch out here."

"Hurry and close that door," I yelled. "You'll let the warm out."

He chuckled and started to close the door. Then he poked his head back inside. "I almost forgot to tell you. Oaks Manor called."

"They called last night, too. Dahlia's giving them trouble. Did they leave a message?"

He thought for a moment, then shook his head. "Didn't leave no message, exactly. It was Marilyn Yoder who called. She said your mother's not acting herself."

He closed the door and left.

I grabbed a banana popsicle out of the freezer and stayed by the fan, letting each bite of flavored ice lay on my tongue until it melted. Places like Hy-Vee sold mostly beer, mixers, and wine. The drinkers who came into Discount came for the harder, more expensive liquor. When I asked Clarence how he could sell so cheap, he said that he didn't need to make a profit from other people's troubles. Instead, he made his profit from cigarettes and snacks.

I would be dipping into his Popsicle profit big time if it was slow today.

And it was relatively quiet. Then, hours later, Stu Boil came in for his half a pint of Jack. He stopped to shoot the bull, saying he'd driven by the lake. "Everyone within ten miles is in the lake up to their pits. Nobody's shopping." Stu owned the fishing tackle store. "The fish don't bite when it gets this hot."

After Stu had left, it was an hour before another car drove up. I watched Percy Hastings struggle out of his small Dodge pickup and stagger up the cracked sidewalk. There's nothing sadder than watching a big man weakened by booze. It gives you the feeling that no matter how strong you are, there are some things you just can't beat.

He grinned a big one when he pushed open the door. "Ooo, wee. Cooler in here. Hey Lillian, hot enough for you?"

"Makes you thirsty, don't it?"

He licked his swollen lips as he came over and slumped down onto his elbows on the counter. He sighed big and loud from the exertion it took him to get from his car, through the door, to the counter. A hamburger with onions was what he had for lunch. Plus a couple of beers and a shot of whiskey to wash it all down.

I stepped slightly back to give myself some air. "What can I get for you?"

He gave the shelves behind me a good-looking over. His right hand fiddled around in his pocket and clutched a couple of bills and some change. It took him a few moments of concentration to separate the paper from the coin. Then, not finding a whole lot, he pulled out his billfold, found it empty, and after pausing in disappointment, he moved over to the refrigerated section and pulled out a six-pack of beer.

I rang up the beer and slid back some coins. Then I reached and snagged a couple of small bags of potato chips. "My treat."

"You'd make a good businesswoman." He ripped open a bag and pulled out a fistful of rust-colored chips.

Percy was stuck in middle life. Not old enough to retire, but still young enough not to go around appearing like he wasn't working. Mostly he did odd jobs around town or helped at the Gas for Less gas station on Highway 218.

After he took off, I helped myself to a bag of chips and took a cold Pepsi out of the cooler. I found a paper pad and made a list of all I was consuming, although Clarence never took any of what I snacked off my check. He said it was an employee's cost. Still, I liked to keep it honest between Clarence and me.

I emptied both the bag and the bottle before another car pulled in. When I saw whose it was, I pulled a bottle of Grey Goose vodka off the shelf and sacked it before Melvin Roth got in the door. He was a dirty martini type of guy. "Off early, Mel?"

Melvin owned Roth's Lumber and Hardware. He slid a twenty and a ten across the counter. "Not much business this afternoon, so Annie's handling things." Annie was his daughter, about Darrell Carter's age. "I heard you got hurt in the Carter fire. Good thing you were up and about so early in the morning."

I didn't bite on what he wanted to feed me. "I couldn't sleep. There was too much thunder and lightning. It stormed pretty bad."

"That's what I'm hearing." He winked.

Donna and his wife were friends. If he was fishing, his wife had already snagged the bait. "Have a nice day, Mel."

He winked again. "Will do. You do the same."

A couple more customers came in after Melvin left, but hardly enough to make my time worth Clarence's while. I had everything cleaned up by six o'clock and was ready to close.

The phone rang as I was about to head out the door. I knew it wasn't Marilyn Yoder. I stopped by Oaks Manor every night before going home. If she still wanted to talk to me, she'd wait for me there.

"Hello, is this Lillian Dove? This is Randi Quince from KETV. I am the assistant producer for *Iowa's History and Its People*.

"Bobby Bowen is hosting a program Friday night on the Frytown fire. He'd like to have you on the show. It's the first live show we've done. Usually, we tape interviews or just pull the film, but Mr. Bowen is anxious to put history in the making into his program. So he'd like to put you on."

"Thank you, but I'm not interested."

She gasped. "Maybe you didn't understand. He doesn't want to film an interview with you. He wants to put you on the program. Live TV. This is Bobby Bowen. Bobby Bowen of KETV News?"

"I understood. Tell Mr. Bowen thank you, but I have nothing to add to his program."

"Oh, he knows that." Her voice flattened on the word *that*. "You will not be the only guest. Chief Simms and Fireman Tim Johnson will also be here. Mr. Johnson is the person who rescued you, correct?"

It didn't surprise me that Chief Simms would be on the program to herald the heroic endeavors of one of his men. But why did they want me to come onto the program?

Randi said, "Mr. Bowen thought you'd want to thank Mr. Johnson publicly." She paused. I was about to decline again and hang up when she said, "A sponsor wants to give you a gift certificate for four at a restaurant of your choice or two hundred dollars in appreciation for your heroism."

I asked for the time and place.

CHAPTER THREE
OVER DAHLIA

The odors of sterilizing alcohol, urine, unwashed bodies, and the leftover aromas from over-boiled, soft food assaulted even my uncultured sense of good taste as I walked through the doors of Oaks Manor. The fragrances never varied no matter what hour of the day I visited.

I checked the obvious place first, finding a smattering of oldies but goodies sitting in the television room, wheelchairs braked around the flat screen, offering another rerun of *Everybody Loves Raymond*. Unfortunately, I didn't see Dahlia. So I headed for the reception desk.

"Aren't you off shift yet?" I asked Nelly, surprising her. She had her head down, concentrating on patient files.

"Oh, hi, Lillian." She stopped updating the file in front of her. "My, you don't look so good. What happened to your eyebrow?"

I kept my hand from fingering the penciled-in mark. "It got a little singed."

"And your hands." She stretched out her own, and I imitated her so she could get a better view of mine. "Do they hurt?"

"Only when I'm asked."

She giggled. Nelly was dressed in her nurse's smock and blue skirt, always looking clean no matter what she'd handled during her shift: bedpans, showers, vomit, spit, diarrhea. Her blonde hair braided in loops was partially tucked beneath a white net cap. Nelly's a Mennonite. "You were awfully brave to go into a burning house," she said.

"You're brave, taking care of these people." I added, "Especially Dahlia. How is the old girl? Still giving you trouble?"

"Your mother's sleeping." She bit her lip and glanced down the hallway towards Dahlia's room. "Did Marilyn get ahold of you?"

I shook my head. "She called Discount, but I wasn't there yet."

She seemed to search for words. "Well...Dahlia's been acting a little....well..."

I gave her some words to choose from-- "Pigheaded? Mulish? Insolent?"

"Let's say she's one of God's more challenging women. I'm sure He brought her to me so I could practice patience."

Funny, I was still wondering why *I* got Dahlia. "Do you know what Marilyn wanted?"

Nelly closed the file and placed it on top of the others. "Dahlia continues to hide on us. Marilyn opened the storage room this morning and found her. Asleep. We aren't sure that she didn't spend the entire night locked up in there." She gathered her personal items from behind her. She turned. "Hello, Mary."

Mary Niles came around the counter, taking off her sunglasses. "Sorry I'm late, Nelly." She pinned on her name badge. "Hello, Lillian." She was wearing a pink smock with teddy bears and matching pink pants. "You don't look too bad from being in a fire."

"Check her hands," Nelly said. "They sure look like they hurt. And she's lucky the bump on her head didn't give her a concussion."

Mary stared at me. "What happened to your eyebrow?"

"I'm thinking about shaving the other one and going without eyebrows for a while."

Mary gave that some thought. "Interesting."

Nelly brought her up to date. "Mr. Fielding has been having some tummy trouble." She patted her own. "I gave Mrs. Dove a slightly stronger sedative to help her sleep and stay in bed tonight."

Did Mary sigh with relief?

"I was just telling Lillian her mother seems terribly worried about something." Then, she turned to me, "Ever since she heard about you in the fire."

"It was before that," Mary said.

"You might want to check on Mrs. Goyen, too," Nelly told her. "I think some patients may be coming down with the stomach flu." She pushed the pile of files towards Mary, who took them in hand.

"A bug's going around," I said. "A couple of officers called in sick at the station."

Mary said, "I heard you were laid off."

Nelly said, "They're cutting back everywhere."

"I quit. I want to find something more permanent."

Mary said, "They're going to hold a sale for the Carters."

I was happy about the change in subjects. "Laura Dell's putting it together."

"They're in my prayers," Nelly said. She came around the counter. "Do you want to go to Dahlia's room before you leave? I'm going to give a peek in."

We found Dahlia sitting up in bed in the dark. If I'd told them once, I'd told them a dozen times, she could hold a pill under her tongue no matter how much water she drank. I looked around. No sign of the wheelchair. They'd taken away her wheels.

"Where've you been?" Dahlia snapped upon seeing me next to Nelly when Nelly switched on the light.

"Why are you awake?" Nelly asked.

"My eyes are open."

Nelly said, "I'll go tell Mary to give her something stronger."

Dahlia had twenty/twenty hearing when you didn't want her to overhear something. She said, "You tell Mary Niles I'm not taking any more medicine. If I want to go to sleep, I'll go to sleep."

No one ever called Dahlia a small woman. She stood no more than five foot three, but her hundred and ninety pounds countered her height. In her prime, even if she came home dead tired from having worked two jobs, she could pick my brothers up under her arms, kick my butt, and fold the laundry, all at the same time.

She sat in bed with her hands clenched together like a demanding prayer. Her eyes scanned me. "What the hell happened to you?"

"You know what happened to me. Why do you always ask what happened when you already know?" Pain rippled through my temples. "I don't remember you caring so much in the past."

Dahlia squeezed her eyes shut as if wishing I wouldn't be there when she opened them. I took my eyes off her because my anger benefited neither of us. Tears threatened to spill, and I bit my lip. I would have rather died than have her see me cry. Or let her in on how badly she'd gotten to me. Instead, I sucked my emotions back in.

"What were you doing in the storage closet?" I said, "Nelly told me they found you there this morning."

She grimaced. "I told you, they're trying to kill me."

I heaved a sigh. "No one's trying to kill you, Dahlia." She had been saying this for the last couple of weeks.

When I'd mentioned it to Nelly, she explained, "No matter how much we try to reassure them, they think we aren't taking good care of them. I guess they believe we don't care because we aren't family. And, even though many of them have family in Frytown, visits are few. Except for holidays, of course."

Dahlia interrupted my possible sympathy for the state her life was in. "What do you know about it, girlie? I haven't seen hide or hair of you."

I sighed again in exasperation. There was also anger and maybe a hint of martyrdom. "I've been coming almost every night for the last five years. *Five years*, Dahlia. I miss
three nights, and you complain?"

"I could be dead, and you'd never know it."

I wanted to encourage that idea but held back.

Nelly interrupted us. "Here we go." She held a syringe. "Let's make sure you get a good night's sleep."

Dahlia moved backward in her bed, seeing the syringe, but she had nowhere to go. She was trapped. She said in a low voice, "I told you I'm not taking no more medicine."

Nelly smiled sweetly and replied just as sweetly. "No, you told me to tell Mary Niles you weren't taking any more medicine. I'm not Mary." She gestured toward me. "You can see for yourself. Lillian's fine. Just like I told you." She pumped the air out of the syringe. "Turn over, dear."

I took this private procedure, or wrestling match, as a way out. "Gotta go. Nighty-night." As I left, I heard Dahlia say, "Nelly Crow, I don't want to go to sleep."

I was so eager to put as much distance as possible between Dahlia and me I almost ran into Edgar Pike. I knew Pike from my childhood home of New Liberty, Iowa, about a forty-minute drive from Frytown. Sometimes, no matter how hard you race to get away, in a small state like Iowa, your past keeps popping up. It's like your shadow on a semi-cloudy day. It can disappear for a minute, and you duck, thinking you'd outsmart it, but when you take a step in another direction, there it is, mocking you.

Pike was dressed in black pants and a black pullover shirt. His beer gut jiggled, and his beltless pants drooped from a lack of hips. He was the type that he'd order two fingers of the best whiskey the bar had to offer if you were buying. But if he was buying, whatever bottled beer would do. I doubt he ever bought a drink for anyone other than himself—not without wanting something.

I'd seen him recently at the Gas For Less gas station by Highway 218. He sat on the curb sucking a brown-paper-sacked bottle, looking like the world was ending. And while this wasn't an unknown habit of his in New Liberty, he wasn't wearing his usual "piss off" attitude. Instead, he seemed gloomy, as if he saw the apocalypse coming and didn't want to take it on sober. So I wondered what had brought him to Frytown.

I watched him shuffle across the street to where cars were parked. My jaw fell when he went up to a green car. He unlocked the door and got in behind the wheel.

The same green car that had nearly run me over this morning.

The car backfired, came out and away from the curb, and immediately made an illegal U-turn. I raced farther out, wanting to catch a better view. There was a dent on the back passenger side. The words WASH ME had disappeared. How many old green cars like this one could there be in Frytown? If Pike was starting to run people down, the state needed to snap up his driver's license before he killed someone.

After getting into my car to head home, I realized I was hungry and stopped at the Dairy Queen. Extravagant under the circumstances, but I qualified the stop by checking if they had any job openings.

The place smelled of raw meat and deep-fried onion rings. Lunch and dinner were the busiest times, and about a dozen people sat in the booths with white wrappers holding burgers and small red and white cardboard boxes stacked with french fries. Apparently, these customers had decided to eat in the air-conditioning rather than take their meals home.

Some sat across from partners. Others sat alone. A mother and three young children sitting in the back created most of the noise, the kids wrestling in the booth, and the mother, busy with a baby, too tired to care.

Others, like me, were opting for takeout. A couple of women stood by the pop machine with empty cups in hand, seemingly waiting for their orders before getting their drinks. Two teenage boys next to them were filling their cups and drinking as many refills as possible before getting caught.

I studied the menu above the counter. It offered the usual fast food: hamburger, cheese extra; double-double, meaning two meat patties, cheese extra; chicken strips; shakes; and cones. I gave each item some thought, even though I knew I'd ordered the chili cheese.

I was a creature of habit. If I ate in the restaurant, I'd order a cheeseburger. But if I took it home, I'd order a chili cheese because it was finger-licking good and horribly messy.

As I waited for my turn by the counter, I inventoried who else had come out for dinner. My eyes returned to the two women by the pop machine. I recognized one woman as Gloria Miller. Gloria worked for the school district. The other woman seemed familiar, but she had her back to me.

"Number one forty-three?"

No one stepped forward. The person in front of me, whom I recognized as someone who worked down at the pharmacy, began canvassing the area. Like me, she was probably hoping the person with that order number would hurry so the rest of us could order. The boys at the pop machine were checking their receipts. Gloria checked hers, too.

An older man in overalls, maybe a farmer out with his wife, treating themselves to dinner after coming into town shopping, stood up from his booth. Everyone else went back to what they'd been doing.

Gloria returned her attention to her conversation but caught a glimpse of me watching them. Her eyes widened. She motioned to the person standing before her, and the woman turned around.

Carol Carter's face was swollen, and her eyes were so red they appeared squeezed almost closed. Gloria gave her a slight push, encouraging her. Carol came over to where I stood.

"Hello, Carol. I am so sorry about what happened."

She startled me by saying, "I was going to call you tonight."

Gloria moved up beside us. "I told Carol she should call you. You'd be the right person to get this all straightened out."

"Straightened out?"

"Burt..." Carol said. His name brought tears down her already tear-ruined face. She wiped them away with the back of her hand. Her hair hung limply from the heat. Dahlia would say Carol looked "rough," meaning life was tossing her around hard. She said, "They arrested him a couple of hours ago. Handcuffed him like he was a criminal. They did it right in front of our youngest son, David. Lieutenant Manville says they're holding him on suspicion of arson."

Gloria put an arm around her shoulder. "There, there, dear. We'll get this all straightened out." Gloria turned to me. "The police are saying they found an empty gas can at Burt and Carol's campsite and that he could have driven from Carrolton and back without Carol knowing."

Carol's red eyes pleaded with mine. She choked back a sob. "Burt couldn't have left without my knowing."

Gloria nodded. "Stanly can't move an inch without me being aware of it."

I didn't know what to say.

Carol said, "You've got to help us." Then, after swallowing another sob, she said, "I need you to tell the police it wasn't Burt."

A hush settled over the room. Ears were stretched our way. Carol, Gloria, and the diners of Dairy Queen all waited for me to respond. "I can't tell them that."

"But you're an eyewitness."

I tried to explain to Carol, Gloria, and everyone else that I'd seen someone at the house, but was not good enough to identify them. I couldn't tell the police it wasn't Burt. Carol's misery turned into total despair. I added quickly, "But I'm sure he's innocent. Burt's a good guy."

Carol's despair exploded. "I don't care whether you think. He's a good guy. Why didn't you mind your own business? You shouldn't have said you saw someone if
you can't identify the person."

As I drove home, I heard the rumbling of far-off thunder. The sound echoed across the sky like the soft beat of a kettledrum. I knew the uncertainty and despair Carol was feeling. Her life was out of control, and she wanted all her troubles to disappear. I wished I could fix things for her. I considered going to the police station and giving Lieutenant Manville my statement. It was long overdue. But my account wouldn't change anything. I couldn't say it wasn't Burt even if I said it probably wasn't him.

Dealing with the police or personal problems isn't easy for any of us, but I think it was harder for people like Carol. I'm tougher around the edges. I didn't marry my high school sweetheart. I didn't come from a loving, supportive family. I understand being scared, helpless, and surprised by how easily life can bite you in the butt.

Shit happens and comes without warning, knocking you off your feet without caring one bit where you'll land.

The rumbling sounded again.

Where was *I* going to land?

I pulled over to the curb. The act of driving was suddenly too much for me to handle. Steering took too much effort. I forced myself to breathe. I thought of Dahlia. Was she scared, too? Was she telling herself two strokes weren't serious? Did she believe that a third wasn't around the corner? Was she fooling herself about dying, as she fooled herself about my father's drinking? She didn't fix him.

I couldn't fix my trouble. I couldn't fix Carol's. I couldn't fix Dahlia.

Dahlia and I may not be so different.

Had Dahlia hoped my father would die? Did she wish we kids never existed?

Like me, did she want a life she never got? A normal life.

That may be the greatest addiction for all of us, the want for a normal life—if we could all define normal.

CHAPTER FOUR
OVER WHAT WE WANT BUT CAN'T HAVE

I wanted my job back. I wanted a boyfriend, someone who'd take care of me. I wanted a normal mother, a typical family, a normal life.

When I got home, I fed Bacardi. I slipped into my PJs, turned on the TV, and began channel surfing. My head churned with thoughts and worries. How was I going to find another job? Hell, why had I let myself become involved with Charles? I promised myself what was now becoming a mantra: I don't need anyone.

Bacardi jumped up on my lap. "Except you, of course, sweetie." He purred. "What are we going to do?"

He looked at me with his little crossed eyes and meowed. He had no idea, either. I petted the frizzed-out hair around his head. "Don't worry. I'll figure something out. I always do."

Sleep didn't help. I dreamed of Dahlia again. Only this time, I was jarred awake before I could jump for the key and miss.

Noise. I sat up in bed. My first thought was Bacardi, but I spotted him at the end of my bed. He was awake, too, ears perked. I whispered, "What was that?"

Crash! Something broke. Bacardi leaped off the bed and crawled underneath it. I grabbed my phone. Dialed 911. Second shift dispatch operator DeLois Dexter answered. "Frytown Police, what is your emergency?"

"DeLois, it's me, Lillian Dove. Someone's in my condo."

"Can you speak up, please?"

"I can't speak up." Then, a little louder, "Someone's broken in."

She heard me this time and sent out the dispatch. "Three-o-three, a possible ten-thirty-one at three-two-four Riverside. The resident is in…" She came back on the line with me. "What's your location?"

"In my bedroom."

"Can you lock the bedroom door?"

"Yes."

"Do it. And stay where you are."

She went back to dispatch. "Caller is in her bedroom with the door locked. I am notifying sixty-seven for back-up."

Officer Dave Richards drove patrol car 303 on the second shift. Sergeant Corbin Wheeler crewed car 67. The numbers were assigned according to the cars' plates, and the identical vehicles were driven by the same officers each time unless shifts were switched.

I stood for a moment and listened. Then, not hearing anything, I opened the door and checked the hallway. A light showed beneath the bathroom door.

Was the intruder going to the toilet?

I pulled back into the bedroom and looked around for something to protect myself. Flip-flops, no bat. I grabbed a flip-flop holding it aloft as if it were thick-soled.

Still, no one was in the hallway, and the bathroom door was still closed. So I tip-toed to the bathroom. I put my ear to the door.

"Hell, Lillian, I thought you were told to stay in the bedroom."

I twisted around, "AH!" and threw the flip-flop.

Officer Richards stood with his feet shoulder-width apart. He ducked. His gun stayed thankfully holstered. The flip-flop bounced off his head.

"There's...there's someone in there." I pointed to the bathroom.

"Stand back." He waved me behind him. I hurried into my bedroom, stepped inside, and closed the door, all but a crack. After looking to make sure I was safe, Richards drew his gun. He ordered, "Come out with your hands up."

"Kitchen and living area are clear." Detective Jacque Leveque appeared in the hallway.

What was he doing here?

He said to Richards, "No doors breached. So what's going on?"

Behind him came Albert, the super. "People are coming out of their places wanting to know what's going on."

Richards grabbed the doorknob on the bathroom door and swung it open. I opened my bedroom door wider and stuck my head out into the hall. We all saw the shower curtain pulled back. The room was empty.

I came out. All three men turned toward me. "They must have got away."

Leveque announced to Albert, "False alarm. Tell everyone to go back to bed." Then, to me, he jeered, "Seeing things again, Lillian?"

Leveque had dark, brown hair, longer than regulation allowed, and a cocky attitude. A transplant from New York, he was a rogue child from a wealthy family. Well, Donna didn't actually say rogue or wealthy family. Instead, she said, "the Leveque family," as if they were the Rockefellers.

Leveque continued. "From what I'm hearing, Richards, Lillian here thinks she's more of an expert than us."

I clenched my teeth and wanted to growl. No, I wanted to take a big bite out of Charles for informing Leveque that Tim Johnson and I had a difference of opinion on whether someone was in the Carter house the night of the fire. Either Charles or Lieutenant Manville must have told him or given him a report copy. Whoever. It didn't matter who. Even if Leveque had a justified right to know, since he would be following up on the criminal aspect of the crime, his comment demonstrated his lack of objectivity.

"There was someone in the house," I countered, ignoring Leveque, thinking I needed to defend myself to Richards.

Richards didn't seem to be listening. He went into the bathroom and bent down to the floor. He scooped something up in his hand, then swung around, holding what he'd picked up. My ceramic soap dish, broken. He lifted it to show all of us. "It was probably left on the edge of the counter. You bumped it without noticing."

Okay, I could have left the light on in the bathroom, although I generally don't close the bathroom door after leaving. And it was doubtful the bugler needed to use the bathroom.

I twisted around to Leveque. Tim's pre-conclusion was right, and being wrong continued to infuriate me. I needed to be right about this. "How could I have bumped it? I was sleeping."

But Leveque stood smirking. He asked Richards, "Window up-locked?"

"No window," Richards said.

Okay, we could all see the bathroom didn't have a window. It was a small five-by-five bathroom with a shower tub, sink, and toilet. This was a senior condo, not a room at a Hilton.

Leveque's smugness became more cocksure. Finally, he asked me, "Any idea how your mystery intruder vanished this time?"

"EW! Get out of my way." I pushed past him and Albert and went into the living area.

There was a window in the bedroom, but I would have woken up if a strange man had come through. I wasn't drunk. There weren't windows in the kitchen because it was a common wall between Earl's apartment and mine. The only way someone could have gotten into the condo was through the front or patio doors.

I went over to the sliding doors. I'd been meaning to call Albert about the broken lock.

"Checked out there."

Leveque's certainty was more than annoying. "I bet."

The small table and two chairs on the patio seemed to be in the same position I'd left them last. Although, it'd been a couple of days since I'd come outside. Then I saw what I was looking for. Leveque wouldn't have known I kept added security. Sliding doors can be popped off their tracks and removed. Even when the lock worked, I used a stick in the door track as extra protection. It lay off to the side on the patio as if haphazardly dropped.

A doper might've thought I was still in the hospital and had something of value at home. Unfortunately, televisions, computers, and cell phones are easy to cash for someone who needs drugs.

A scenario played in my mind. He came in through the patio. He may have learned to pop yardsticks, and mop handles out of sliding door tracks. I'd probably find the same on Google. He came in through here, found nothing of value, and continued to the bedroom. That must have been when I heard him. He heard me and went into the bathroom to hide. Bumped the soap dish and broke it. Then when I searched for something to protect myself, he came out of the bathroom, went back to the patio door, shutting it, of course, and got away.

I came back into the condo thinking I would give Richards my theory.

Leveque stood, hands on his hips. His eyes raked my body. Albert stared, then twisted away as if embarrassed.

"Ah, Lillian." Richards motioned to me.

As I guessed, he and Leveque already exchanged opinions. I wasn't going to get any co-operation from him, either. But I wanted my opinion on record.

"He came through the patio."

Leveque snickered, glancing at Richards.

"Here's my stick." I held up my broken mop handle. "It was on the track when I went to bed. I'm sure of it." I was almost sure.

Now Richards started chuckling.

Ooooh…"I want the report to read that I found this," I shook it at them, "out by the patio wall. But, I repeat, it was in the track when I went to bed. So the intruder must have known how to…"

Leveque began cracking up.

Richards said, "Lillian." He pointed to me again. "Your pajama top is…"

I glanced down and found my pajama top half unbuttoned, gaping.

"Oh." My face, chest, and everything else exposed immediately turned crimson. I twirled around and quickly began buttoning it.

Albert said, "How're you doing, buddy?"

Thinking Albert was playing to Leveque's and Richard's childishness, I jerked around, ready to take on all three.

Albert was holding Bacardi. "We're old friends now that I fed you, hey?"

Leveque and Richards were still hee-hawing like teenage boys.

Sergeant Wheeler came striding into the condo. Leveque walked over to him, slapping him on the shoulder. "You missed the show,

Wheeler." He told him what happened and imitated me holding the mop handle and shaking it, which must have shaken…well, other endowments.

Okay, small endowments, but shaking would have occurred.

"I want this behavior in the report, too, Sergeant Wheeler. This is totally unprofessional. Sexist."

Wheeler grinned but said, "Sorry, Lillian. Knock it off, Leveque."

Leveque sobered a bit. "Sorry, Lillian. But it was funnier than hell." Then, he said to Wheeler, "This was a total waste of time, except for…" he walked away, snickering.

I might have given Wheeler my theory if I'd thought anyone would be listening to me.

"Waste of time and resources." Under control, Leveque came back to Wheeler. "I don't know about you, but I have bigger fish to fry." He looked at me, "Thanks for the entertainment, Lillian. It made my night."

"Ew!" I lifted the mop handle. If I hadn't been immediately arrested, I would have popped him a good one.

Officer Richards was the last to leave. He'd sobered and said, "You did the right thing, Lillian. It's better to call if you think something's wrong." But his words couldn't mask the good laugh he, Leveque, and Wheeler would have as soon as he caught up with them. He added, "Next time, I suggest waiting for one of us to get here or find something better to defend yourself with other than one of your flip-flops."

That did it. He walked out chuckling.

I'd hoped he hadn't noticed—more ammunition for Leveque.

Maybe Leveque was right. A horrifying thought. But, if Albert had left a note, the fork in the sink and the missing cat food would have been explained. And if Charles hadn't planted the idea I was somehow in jeopardy because I was an eyewitness, hearing a noise, I would have checked the bathroom myself. I wouldn't have called dispatch. Someone breaking into my condo would never have crossed my mind.

I couldn't stand the thought of Leveque being right. I put on a robe and flip-flops and went back to the patio. I had to know.

After pulling one of the patio chairs over to the wall, I searched on the other side, examining the ground. A flowerbed of roses and boxwoods lined the wall. It hadn't rained, and the condo complex adhered to environmental water-saving guidelines. The dirt was hard-packed—no distinct footsteps. But I saw something hanging from one of the rose bushes.

I climbed over the wall and pulled off a piece of black fabric. Whoever had lost it must have also received a couple of good scratches. It was an old rosebush with lots of thorns.

I investigated some more around the area but didn't find anything else. The outside lighting allowed me to give the fabric a good examination. It wasn't new or old. Not a deep-new-black or faded-gray-black from weather or repeated washing. It could have been unrelated to what happened. The gardener could have snagged his T-shirt while snipping off rose heads. It proved nothing

I went to hoist myself back over the wall and go back inside. The wall wasn't more than five feet, but my five foot five was too damn short. If someone came this way, they were taller and more robust than me.

I walked around the complex and went back in through the front entrance. Mrs. Ledbetter opened her door as I passed her condo.

"Oh, it's you, Lillian." A small woman, widowed, she pulled her bathrobe closer around her throat. "I thought I saw someone outside and, well, I heard there was a burglary in the building."

I didn't want her unduly frightened. "I was the one who called the police. I thought I heard something, but it turned out to be a false alarm. No worries."

"You called them? I thought you worked for the police."

"I answer phones."

"Oh." She then shut the door, and I heard the latch click.

When I got to my front door, I found it locked. I must have locked it after Richards left.

I went next door to Earl's and knocked. No answer. I knocked again. Finally, he answered, wearing his blue pin-striped pajamas, hair tousled and feet bare. "Lillian?"

"I locked myself out, Earl. Can you let me in?"

He glanced back inside. Was he with someone? This late at night? I never realized he had sleepovers. I took him for an afternoon-quickie kind of guy.

"Just a minute." He closed the door and was gone a minute. He returned holding the key.

"Sorry, I woke you up."

"The police woke me up."

"Sorry. I thought someone broke into my place."

"The police said it was a false alarm."

He came out, and I followed him to my door. "If you get scared again, remember I'm right next door."

Earl didn't impress me as the type who got into many fistfights in his younger life. And at his age, I could probably do more damage. But I hugged him. "Thanks, Earl. I just got spooked."

"Sleep tight." He hurried back to his place.

I considered the front door as having been the entry and searched for signs. No marks on the hardware. None on the wood. Of course, Richards and Leveque probably already checked.

Could I have bumped the soap dish, and it didn't fall immediately?

If you continue to insist you saw someone, it could mean you're an eyewitness to first-degree arson, a felony.

I wasn't ready to admit I hadn't seen someone at the Carter house, but my imagination might be getting the better of me.

When I woke up the following day, I could hear my name being bandied about down at the station. *Her shirt was wide open...*

I wanted my job back, but I'd never go back now. I could overcome embarrassment, the teasing, and the other guys would let what happened go, but not Leveque.

Maybe his New York upbringing caused him to be so...so annoying. Or perhaps his conceit came from the fact his family was wealthy.

Shortly after I refused Leveque's gracious offer, I slipped and called him Officer Leveque instead of Detective. He'd been giving me the cold shoulder since I wasn't interested in 'going out for a short one,' but this got him riled. *It's Detective Leveque.*

I couldn't imagine Sergeant Wheeler going into a rant if I had slipped and called him Officer Wheeler. Lieutenant Manville would have corrected me without yelling and talking about it all day. Frytown was pretty void of crime.

Someone needed to bring Leveque down a peg or two. And his arresting Burt Carter on felony arson charges put a cherry on his ego cake.

I'd love to "pop his cherry" someday.

Bacardi must have sensed I was in a mood. Patiently he waited while I filled his food dish. I poured myself a cup of coffee and began making another list. Clean the condo was on the top. Wasn't I always saying I'd give the place a good cleaning if I had the time? When Frank moved Dahlia, he'd packed up the New Liberty house and squeezed everything into this place. No sorting or throwing anything away. We weren't rich. Anything Dahlia had was old and getting older. When people in New Liberty talked about the Doves, it wasn't like mentioning the Rockefellers. The "Dove family" meant my father was passed out somewhere inconvenient to the public or nature. Another waste of human life and taxpayer's dollars.

I wrote on the list to *look for a job*. I made a notation, Internet. I'd heard good-paying career positions were advertised online. I didn't have more than a high school education, but I figured no one called to check on past employment. I bet many people put down they went to college but never spent a day on campus. Besides, it was time for me to jump for that damn key. Reach for something higher than answering phones or clerking. *Update resume* was next on the list. I could add five years as a communications facilitator for my time at the police station and five years as a sales executive for my work at Discount.

My bills were paid for the month, so I didn't worry about overdue charges. However, the tiny bit of cash I had left, especially after splurging at the Hy-Vee, wouldn't get me very far.

Running out of ideas for the list, my mind wandered back to what was being said about me at the station. There was only one person I could call, only one I could trust. I glanced at the kitchen clock. It wasn't yet eight-thirty. The phones wouldn't be busy.

"Frytown Police."

"Hi, Donna. It's Lillian."

"How're you doing, sweetie? DeLois said she sent a patrol to your place last night."

Of course, it was probably the hand-over-news DeLois gave her. Each time a shift changed, the those leaving handed over any necessary information—or scandal.

"I guess I got spooked."

"I've been spooked myself. It's hard living alone, especially after what happened."

Meaning...? My being laid off? "You could have warned me I would be laid off."

"What? Hon, if I'd known, I'd have told you to turn around and return home. Call in sick. I wouldn't have let you go in unarmed, not after that brave thing you did going into that burning house. I told Leveque that when he was laughing it up this morning about you thinking someone broke into your place and was hiding in your bathroom. I said, 'When did you run into a burning house, Leveque'?"

I yelled a silent *yeah*. But what else had they been laughing it up about? He wouldn't be forthcoming about my undressed appearance. Not at the station. Would he?

Donna said, "Of course, the city was on the chief about being way over budget, but what do they expect? There's not enough of us to go around as it is. If they'd had said something to me, I'd have told them they should cut back on some of those council people's projects. You know, like Richard Brenner's cowboy museum. We don't have a rodeo in Frytown, for god's sake. The rodeo is in Carrollton, and they have their museum."

She must have been drinking coffee or eating watermelon. I heard a slurp, then she said, "Just because his son won second place in steer roping two years ago, Brenner thinks the city needs a public place to hang his kid's photo." She concluded I'd heard her come to many times before. "Some people are just plain stupid."

I knew a lot of people from working my two jobs, but I hadn't made a lot of friends. Donna was number one on my list for having invited me over for dinner the first week I came to work. I knew her type and figured she wanted to check me out. But she never asked me anything more personal than if I'd been married. As our friendship grew, she confided she hated her mother, too. And she greeted me each morning as if my coming to work added to her day.

"Thanks for sticking up for me with Leveque."

"I meant what I said. He's full of himself."

She then informed me she was handling both the office calls and dispatch. I didn't ask, but she said the chief had been in a grumpy mood since I left. She said she heard he was making a big stink down at city hall, especially with everyone at the station calling in sick with the flu. This prompted me to say, "The chief must be glad the Carter fire is solved."

"Solved? Who said it was solved? It's a big mess if you ask me."

But I couldn't ask. Then, a call came in, and she put me on hold for a moment before coming back on the line. "You still there?"

"I'm here."

"Listen to me, Lillian. Burt Carter didn't burn down his own house. I don't care what anyone says."

I mentioned bumping into Carol Carter at the Dairy Queen, and Gloria Miller telling me Leveque had found an empty gas can at their campsite.

"Uh-huh. That's public knowledge."

Had someone come into her office? "Can you still talk?"

"Yes, please continue."

Someone must've been within hearing distance. I continued, carefully wording what I said so she could reply without getting in trouble. "Gloria said Leveque said Burt would've had enough time to set the fire and get back to Carrollton Lake before Carol noticed he was gone."

Her response was louder as if it were safe to talk again. "It's not what Burt did but what he didn't do. You can't buy his kind of insurance. Leveque will look like a fool when it all gets said and done."

Insurance? I wanted to hear more, but Donna had to take another call. When she came back on, she said, "That was Richards. He's calling in sick for tonight. I've been praying to get some of this crud myself. I bet I could lose ten pounds if I became ill. I took an Ex-Lax once and lost five pounds overnight." She stopped and took a breath or a piece of melon. "The chief won't like hearing another of the men called in sick. Garth's still out. Miner's come back, but he's not looking too good around the gills. And the chief looks like a walking flu-stricken zombie. He's sicker'n hell, too. And it ain't even flu season yet."

"Is that why Leveque showed up at my place last night?"

"Yep. He's working first and second shift." A pause, "You feeling okay?"

Before I could answer, another call came in. "I got to go, Lillian. The phone's lighting up like a Christmas tree. Damn weather. It brings all the troublemakers down to the lake." And then, in a rush of words, she said, "Don't put a broomstick between you and Charles because of what happened here at work. The man hasn't let himself have a life for years."

She hung up.

I rinsed out my coffee cup and added kibble to Bacardi's dish. Then, I pulled a broom and dustpan from the closet. What did Donna mean by saying not to put a broomstick between Charles and me?

I gave the broom a hard consideration and put it back. I hate cleaning. It's not on my addiction list. And I put nothing between Charles and me. He did.

I changed into jeans and a T-shirt and slipped into sandals. I called the station again. Donna said she had five lines on hold and put me through to Peggy. I got right to the point. "Have you mailed my check?"

She reminded me I'd rushed out without taking it. She said she returned it to the fiscal office in the courier package, meaning Officer Davis had dropped it off at the end of his shift. The fiscal office would then mail it out officially. However, she did say if I was desperate and couldn't wait for it to come in the mail, I could probably pick it up if I went down right away this morning.

I told her I wasn't desperate and the mail would be fine.

"Sorry about everything, Lillian."

"It's probably for the best. I wanted to look for something full-time, anyway."

I called the city fiscal office as soon as I hung up and checked if the check was still there. I told them I was coming to get it.

I saw Earl as I headed out. "Sorry about waking you up last night. Twice."

"No problem. As I said, you can always call on me."

"I forgot to ask, how was the funeral?"

"Susan's daughter served a lemon cake at the reception."

"That was nice. I'm sure you'll miss her."

A cheery voice called out, "Earl?"

Alice Steward came skipping towards us. I could smell freshly baked chocolate chip cookies.

"Life goes on." Earl grinned.

It was hot outside, but it felt cooler than the day before. But, of course, it wasn't noon yet. So things could still heat up.

The courthouse was located smack in the middle of the town square, and all city departments were in the courthouse—all except for the police station, which had relocated to a newer building out by Highway 218.

The girl in the fiscal office tried hard not to stare at my penciled-in eyebrow and the large bruise on my forehead. It's the innate inability most of us have to keep ourselves from staring at what we're trying not to notice.

My check totaled two weeks' pay, with a severance kicking the amount to four weeks. Plus, I had a week of vacation time coming, which was added to the total. It paid to be union.

Taking a good guess, Charles didn't change any of the paperwork after I insisted on quitting. I asked about unemployment. Instead of answering, she supplied me with the forms.

I then went upstairs to the City Parks and Streets Department, where Burt Carter worked before being laid off. Maybe I was feeling an affinity to others on the bad-luck cross. Nah, I was being nosy. Town chit-chat is addictive.

Donna's mentioning insurance stuck in my mind. An insurance policy on the house would be a good motive for arson. The house was old and needed a lot of updating, and was probably worth more in insurance than the housing market. I also remembered Sylvia at HyVee saying the Carters were thinking about moving away before the fire.

Could Burt have set the fire for the insurance money?

When the first snow comes, people call the police to know when the plows will be on their street to dig them out. Of course, people can always contact the street department directly, but when most people are frustrated, they call the police first. Like Officer Mitch Miner once said, "The police are the first to arrive and the first to be blamed."

Jim Johns was the supervisor of the department. "Hey, Lillian. Sorry to hear about the pink slip."

I put a hip to his desk. "Yeah, like the flu bug, it's going around."

"You can say that again." Late forties, married, he pointed to the chair beside his desk. "Take a load off and BS for a couple of minutes. Nothing is going on around here. I had to call the street crew back in this morning. It's just too damn hot. Yesterday Morris

Cleaver, you know Morris, young kid, he started with us last year after graduating?"

I nodded. High school basketball hero.

High school football and basketball are the entertainment highlights of Frytown.

I picked up a booklet entitled *Street Regulation* from off Jim's desk, figuring it'd been there for a while. I began fanning myself with it. Apparently, the city fathers were cutting back on air-conditioning budgets, too.Jim had a story to tell. So he settled into the telling. "The crew was pouring asphalt yesterday, filling a couple of holes on Church Street. Morris keeled right over. If Dan Burke hadn't been standing right next to him, Dan says Morris would have fallen right into that asphalt."

I pointed my fan at my head. "Glad to hear he wasn't hurt. I know how it would have felt."

"Yep, I heard about you coming across Burt and Carol's fire. I also heard you saw the person who started it."

I stopped fanning. "I didn't exactly see them. I couldn't pick them out of a lineup."

"Sorry to hear that. Ol'Burt could use your help."

His comment allowed me to move on to why I'd come to see him. I started fanning again and said, "I can't tell you for sure, but I don't think it was Burt. I can't think of a good reason why he'd want to burn down his home. Can you?"

"You're not the only one who feels that way. All of us around here are saying they got the wrong guy. I heard the police were waiting for you to make some sort of statement before officially charging him."

"I'm supposed to give an official statement to Lieutenant Manville. But I've already told Chief Kaefring I can't say it was or wasn't."

He seemed to like the clarification. "Burt's a smart guy. If he'd toasted his house, he'd have been downright stupid to keep the empty gas can, as the police found. He might be a lot of things, but he ain't stupid. Plus, I heard tell he'd left his gui-tar at home." He stressed the first syllable guit-tar. Jim played weekends in a blue-grass band over in the Oxford area. He said, "If he were going to burn his house down, he'd have taken his guit-tar."

"People do desperate things in desperate times. I heard Carol was worried about the school handing out pink slips."

"True enough. But Burt wasn't that desperate."

'If the house was insured, he could have bought a new guitar."

"Burt and Carol rent. Besides, a man might get himself a new wife, but he doesn't get rid of his guit-tar, no matter how old."

I leaned further back in my chair. Just two friends BS-ing about the latest town news. "Who owns the house?"

"What do you mean?"

"You said Burt rented the place. Who owns it?"

The question unsettled him. He sat up. He searched his desk for something, then spied it in my hand. "There it is," he said, pointing to the booklet I was using as a fan. "I'm going to need that." He glanced at the clock on the wall and double-checked the time with his watch. "Sorry to have to cut this short, but I got a meeting coming up." He pulled out his cell phone as if checking for messages. "Hell, I'm going to be late."

Suddenly he had a meeting. "What's the deal, Jim? Who owns the house?"

"Not sure. I... I've got to go. I've got this dang meeting." He pulled out his file drawer and began fingering through the files. I took the hint.

My leaving grabbed back his attention. "What's your plan now, Lillian?"

"About what?"

"Your job?"

I shrugged. "I'm tired of this part-time stuff. It's time I figured out what I wanted to be when I grew up."

Having forfeited my hamburger the night before, I stopped at the Dairy Queen. The lunch crowd wasn't in yet. So I ordered a double cheese and fries and held the chili because I was heading to Discount afterward. I asked the sixteen-year-old wearing a tag identifying her as the manager if they were hiring.

She stared at my head and then said I could put in an application, but she didn't think anyone was planning to quit. "You might have some luck after school starts."

While I was eating, I thought of the peanut butter and preserves back at the condo. So, to compensate for my burger extravagance, I took advantage of the free refill for my Pepsi and stuffed a handful of ketchup packages in my purse.

"It doesn't seem so bad today," Clarence said as the bell jingled me into the store. The fan was running but humming low.

"I haven't checked the temperature, but it seems cooler," I agreed.

"I mean you. You've got a smile on. There's a hop in your step. And do I see an eyebrow?" He chuckled.

"You're right." I laughed. If you can't laugh at yourself, then you become the joke. I pulled the payroll envelope from my purse and held it up. "I got my severance check." A ketchup package fell to the floor. I didn't bother explaining it. "The amount was more than I expected."

"Good for you. You know what they say, don't you?" He was full of old sayings. I shook my head, and he said, "Live it up while you can. Life is a smorgasbord, and most poor suckers are starving to death."

I laughed and patted my purse. "I'm not starving yet, but I think I'll keep it to the Dairy Queen until I find other work."

He became serious. "As I told you, I can give you more hours if you need them. I know a part-time job isn't worth much."

I tried a Little Orphan Annie saying, "The sun will come out tomorrow."

He looked out the window. "Out today, too."

I tried again. "I heard bad luck comes in threes. I've had mine."

"I had bad luck three times." His smile took its time, letting me know there was more to come. "The first time was when my first wife left me. The second time was when my second wife left me." He paused. "And now my third wife won't go." We both laughed. As far as I knew, Clarence hadn't ever been married.

Officially I was on the clock, but the street was quiet outside, and Clarence didn't seem to be in any hurry to leave. So I asked, "What do you know about the Dillard fire?"

"You mean the Carters' house?"

"No, before that. The Dillards'?

"About as much as anyone as old as me."

"How old are you?"

"How old do you think I am?"

I figured he was somewhere in his seventies, but I could be wrong. The Iowa sun is brutal on people and can quickly put on five years. "Sixty-five," I guessed.

He barked a laugh. "Off by a good ten, but I'll take'r. What do you want to know?"

"Just curious. It's pretty weird. I mean, with the same house burning down twice."

"It didn't burn completely down the first time, but it killed every-one."

"It was arson, too, wasn't it? Were there suspects?"

"Policing back then wasn't like it is today." He scratched his head. "I think the Dillard fire was set by gasoline or kerosene, something with an odor. Gertrude Dillard, Horace's wife, she and the girls got trapped in an upstairs bedroom. They died from smoke inhalation, most probably. People normally say the fire killed them. But some-one put a bullet in Horace Dillard's head."

I'd heard bits and pieces of the Dillard tragedy. Human tragedy sticks to a town like gum on a shoe. But this was the first time I heard Horace Dillard was shot.

"Shot? You sure?"

"I am. But if you're wondering by who, you wouldn't have to hand out invitations for the suspect list. The man wasn't liked. He was as mean as a bull spotting a farmer coming at him with a rubber band and a sharp knife."

Rubber band? I let it pass. I didn't want him to get off point. "You know they arrested Burt Carter. They think he set the fire."

"Heard that."

What had he heard that I hadn't? "Jim Johns says Burt and Carol don't own the house. They rent. So, if the place had no insurance, what motive would Burt have? Who owns the house?"

"People talk too much. Some of them need to learn to shut their mouths."

My face immediately reddened. It wasn't like Clarence to give a reprimand. He walked into the backroom, got his hat, and cane, and came around the counter, heading for the door. "Guess I'll call it a day. You probably won't be too busy this afternoon."

He opened the door to leave and stopped as if he'd forgotten something. He glanced back at me. His face, solemn. "You be careful, Lillian. I wouldn't want to hear you'd been cornered by someone meaner than Horace Dillard." Then, as an afterthought, he said, "And it might be best you're not working for the police. I'll give you more hours until you can find yourself another job." He paused, then said, "I heard you and Charles were seeing each other. You'll end up getting hurt. He'll never leave Rita."

CHAPTER FIVE
OVER WHAT I HAVE BUT NOT THE WAY I WANTED

R ita? Was Charles married?

Clarence had to be wrong. But he'd lived most of his life in Frytown. Or he grew up here and came back. Maybe Charles had been married, but Clarence never heard he got divorced. Only a divorce in town is too juicy to stay secret. Donna told me when Linda Mae Sharp decided to divorce her husband, Mac, he hadn't thought anything was wrong with his marriage. The process server stopped to get his hair cut before delivering the divorce papers, and he and the barber got to talking. Mac's name came up along with the word divorce. Mac's cousin was sitting in a chair waiting for his turn. The server had to chase Mac all over town.

No one had mentioned Charles being married. Especially not Donna. *Don't put a broomstick between you.* A wife is one hell of a broomstick. I may have done a lot of things I am not proud of. I may have failed in romantic relationships, but I have never knowingly had a relationship with a married man.

And why hadn't one of the other officers mentioned a Mrs. Chief? Leveque would have said something, especially after catching the chief and me together. Maybe that's what pissed Leveque off. That I was dating a married man, go figure. From Donna's viewpoint, he had no stand on morality.

A Mrs. Kaefring had never called into the office on my shift. Peggy had never mentioned her. We didn't have Christmas parties, but I'd met Garth's Mary Jo. I'd met Miner's wife, Sue. Lieutenant Manville's wife and kids stopped by the station now and again.

Wouldn't I have seen a woman's touch at his place? No photos were on the bed stand. Not that I was looking for any. I could have missed them, but I was pretty sure there were no clothes over a chair, perfume in the air, a hairbrush on the dresser, shoes toed off in a corner. Hell, his sheets were ugly- average. Not the type a woman would buy.

My head reeled with what-ifs all afternoon. It was slow enough at the store for a lot of thought. There were only three sales the entire afternoon, and the clock ticked slowly towards six.

Finally, I decided to owe Clarence a half-hour and left at five-thirty. If I hadn't received my severance check and the extra money, I might not have felt so whimsical. But there was someone in town who may have had answers to my Dillard questions, and that person would be closing the doors at the stroke of six by city regulations.

In a couple of weeks, the Frytown Library would be full of kids who did not want to go home and used the library as their excuse not to do so. Town libraries were still meet-ups for those without driver's licenses. Only one person sat at the bank of computers set aside for those who didn't have own a PC. At the check-out counter, a teenage helper stamped a lone woman's books with boredom.

I walked around to the research desk, and not finding Amanda Keiff at her computer, I began looking in the stacks.

Amanda Keiff and Clarence were about the same age. She was married to Reverend Keiff, a First Baptist minister. One cold winter day, she and I became quick friends when I discovered her alone reading a romance novel in the library. When she noticed me noting the book's title, she said, "Nothing wrong with reading about the sins of others."

I found her kneeling on the floor with several small piles of books. "Are you praying or reading, Amanda?"

Her small, bird-like eyes peeped up behind gold-rimmed glasses. She brushed her hair away from her face. "I'm praying someone will start teaching these young people how to count. They never put the books back into the right places."

"I doubt they teach Dewey-decimal math."

"I'd be happy if they'd just get the six-hundreds back in the six-hundred and not the nine-hundreds." She struggled to get up, using a shelf to give herself leverage. She then leaned over and picked up a small mound of books. She took one from the top and showed me the spine. "It's clear as a bell, three nine-ty-two-point-o-eight. What's it doing over here in the autobiograph-ical section at ninety-eight point two?"

I guessed the other groupings on the floor were sorted for the correct areas. She put the book back in place. "What are you up to?" She was panting slightly from getting up and her bout of annoyance. "I heard about you playing at firefighting." She glanced at me. "You don't seem to be harmed much."

I pretended to be affronted. "What? My hands got burned, and I lost an eyebrow." I pointed to my penciled-in mark and my stitched-up forehead.

She moved closer to take a good look. She smelled of lavender mixed with the dust of printed pages. Until now, I hadn't noticed the small freckles across her nose. They gave her face the hint of youth gone by.

"Hair and skin will grow back."

I stooped and picked up the remaining books, carefully keeping them organized. "I keep threatening to start a new trend."

I followed her to the front, where she put her stack of books down on the checkout counter. I separated mine into the presorted sections. She asked the teen helper to shelve the books before going home. He gave a frantic glance from the books over to the large grandfather clock. "I'm off in ten, Mrs. Keiff."

Amanda checked the clock. "Where has the day gone?" Again, she swiped her hair back away from her face. "Okay, put them in order and re-shelve them tomorrow when you get in."

She turned to me. "What are eyebrows good for, anyway? Unless you're Mark Twain. He had enough to provide shade on a sunny day." The teenager rolled his eyes. Amanda chuckled.

I asked, "Got some tea in the back room?"

"Never out. Let me get the front doors locked first." She called over to the computer bank. "We'll be closing in about five minutes, Claudia. Steve here will lock up behind you." She instructed him, "Make sure the computers are all off before going. I'll see you in the morning." She went over to the doors on thin, bird-like legs sticking out beneath a summer cotton skirt. She put a key into the old doors, made sure it moved the locks, left the key there, and returned to the circulation desk.

Together we headed toward the back of the library, where she kept a small office. Inside was a desk cluttered with papers and books in an organization only Amanda might've understood. A photo of her husband without his clerical collar rose above the melee. She was using a King James Bible as a paperweight. Not far from the desk stood a file cabinet heaped with files. A wooden swivel chair was behind the desk holding a well-worn, red pillow in its seat. Across from it, there was a club chair with the same worn look. On its seat was a book turned upside down to hold its place. There was a small table big enough for a couple of cups, a box of sugar cubes, a paper cup full of stirrers, an assortment of tea bags, and an electric tea kettle. Amanda tested the pot, found it cool, and shook it to see if enough water was left in it. She turned it on.

I picked up the book on the chair, taking notice of the cover. "A new Danielle Steel?"

Amanda grinned. "Now, don't you be giving me a hard time. It's my job to read the books I put on the shelves. How else will I recommend a book for you to peruse through the lonely nights?"

I turned the corner down on the page so she could find her place. Why did everyone think I was lonely? Did I look lonely? I went over and put the book on the desk. "Let me know when you're done so I can check it out. Vicarious romance saves a lot of trouble and heartache."

"It doesn't warm up the bed much."

"Amanda, you're the strangest minister's wife I've ever run into."

"Run into many?"

I shook my head. "I gave up church for Lent."

She shrugged. "There are a lot of people who come to church every Sunday and nod their heads to the sermon, but when they go to work on Monday, they aren't much changed. And some never come to church, or maybe they don't step inside except for Christmas and Easter, but they move through their day as if they're next in line to be judged."

She settled onto her red cushion, straightening her skirt so it wouldn't wrinkle, and rested her hands in her lap. "So, are you here for a reading list, a good sermon, or is there something else I can do for you?"

"Tell me about the Dillard family."

"The Dillard family? The Dillards are long gone."

"You heard they arrested Burt Carter for setting the fire?"

She nodded, waiting for me to get where I was going.

"Some are saying there may have been insurance money on the house. But when I talked to Jim Johns, he said the Carters rent the house. So, I can't figure out why Burt was arrested. If there's no insurance, there's no motive. I heard the Dillard house was set with gasoline, the same as the Carter house. I think that's interesting and wondered what else I didn't know."

Her hands clasped together. "You've been hearing a lot."

"You know how it is. People talk. They're curious. I'm curious. After all, I was the one who called the fire in."

"I heard you saw someone. That you're an eyewitness."

I shook my head. "Now that's just talking."

"You didn't?" Was she confirming a rumor, or did she think someone could have been at the house?

I nodded, "No, I'm fairly sure I saw someone, but I never got close enough to identify them. Or they were a ghost. Tim Johnson swears no one could have made it out of the house alive. They didn't find any human remains. And if the fire department hadn't arrived when it did, I wouldn't be sitting here thinking about reading another romance novel."

"Good."

"Good, what? My reading romances?"

"No," Amanda said. "Good about you not being able to identify the person you saw. I'd hate to think you'd seen Burt Carter."

Amanda was hard to read, and she wasn't one for gossip. Yet, I didn't come to the library for rumors. "If anyone knows the history of Frytown or the Dillards, it's you, Amanda."

"Not much to say about the Dillards. Most everyone knows Horace Dillard Sr. was a large landowner in this area."

"They were rich?"

"Bigger houses are built today, but back in 1920, the Dillard house was one of the biggest. Well, you saw it. Large, two stories. There were two stairways, a fancy front one for the family and a back stair for servants. Horace Dillard Sr. had it built. Some of the materials used came from New York. They had servants, a cook, and a housekeeper. That alone made the Dillards richer than anyone else. Most around here, especially back then, prepared their meals and washed their clothes."

"I am more interested in Horace Jr."

"He had money, inherited."

"The Dillard fire was in nineteen-forty-nine?"

"November seventh, nineteen-fifty-four. It's just going on for sixty years."

" Everyone died in the fire?"

"Not all. They kept a live-in housekeeper, but she was away."

"But they all died in the fire, right?"

She cocked her head, "What are you getting at?"

"Clarence said Horace was shot."

She appeared startled. "Clarence said that?"

Amanda was a forthright woman. Small, but if she asked for quiet in her library, not another peep was heard. More than one high school football hero and cheerleader had been thrown out for doing more between the stacks than searching for a book. Her jaw clenched, and she stared beyond me. I hadn't expected Amanda's reaction. I got the feeling she didn't appreciate Clarence talking about the Dillards.

"Did Clarence get that part wrong?"

"Clarence wouldn't have said it if he hadn't known for sure." Her voice was unsteady. "Why do you want to know, Lillian? Are you sure you're just curious about the history of the place, or did you see someone besides Burt? Are you trying to figure out who it might have been?"

I shook my head. "I'm interested in the history for my own state of mind. Unfortunately, I'm not that good at figuring things out. You know how my life has been a series of wrong moves."

Amanda was the only person in Frytown to whom I'd confessed my drinking addiction and other misshapen personal histories. If others, like Charles, guessed, well, that's all they had, a guess. Not even Dahlia knew how bad it had gotten for me.

I scooted my chair towards Amanda, wanting to shorten the distance between us. "There will be an investigation into the Carter fire whether the charges stick to Burt or not. The state fire marshal's being called in. Chief Simms thinks it was arson. I'm being called an eyewitness, even though I'm not a good one. What I do know is that someone was in the house. Was it a ghost? I don't know. But I saw something."

Amanda spat, "It's the Simms family. They're still brooding. They didn't go along with my father's decisions back then." She grimaced, "Gilbert Simms better think carefully about what he might set off."

"What decisions?"

She sat for a long time, staring at her clasped hands. Then, finally, her eyes came back to mine. "My father was a prominent doctor in Johnson County. He knew most families around the area. And because of his practice, we knew many of them, too. He was a good man. He made decisions because he thought they were the right ones to make." She held up a hand. "I'm not saying he didn't make mistakes. Who doesn't? But I can't think of a decision he made so that his life would be better than another man's.

"Many families couldn't pay for a doctor. My father never refused anyone. He'd go out in the middle of the night to tend to someone sick, help bring a child into the world, or sit with a family while one of theirs was dying. Most of them had little if any money. Some paid him in the summer when they harvested their vegetable gardens. Some would bring over canned goods. Fresh eggs. A side of beef or a pig. Folks don't like to take charity around here, and most are honest. They pay their debts, one way or another."

I nodded. I couldn't figure out why she felt the need to explain her father's decision-making to me. What action did he take that the Simms family was so against?

"I can't tell you anything about Gertrude Dillard. I think she came from somewhere in Michigan. Or was it New York? Wisconsin? What I do know is that she was much younger than he was.

"Horace Sr. made his money on the railroad by purchasing the real estate along the routes. He got the land cheap. Some say he took a little more than he had coming. I think, in the end, he was involved in other businesses besides the railroads." She paused and then said, "People who have a lot of money always want more money, don't they?"

I nodded. "Why is that? Poor people never want more poverty."

She gave a faint chuckle. "You're right about that. Some are poor, and some are poor and only think about what they don't have instead of what they do."

It sounded like a sermon topic for her husband.

I wanted to get back to the Dillard story. "So why do folks around here get a bit edgy when the Dillards are brought up?"

"People don't like to talk about bad things that happened. They think when something bad happens where they live, it says something bad about them."

"But the Dillard fire was years ago. How could it hurt anyone today? And whether they want to talk about it or not, the media is picking up the story. Bobby Bowen is doing a whole show on the Dillard tragedy."

She shook her head. "I hadn't heard, but I'm not entirely surprised. Even though my father did what he thought was best under the circumstance, I've wondered if what happened to Horace would come back to haunt us one day."

She used the arms of her chair to stand. "Why don't you make us both a cup of tea while I check out front to make sure the doors are locked?"

When she left, I went over and touched the tea kettle. Hot. I wondered if she really wanted to check on the doors or if it was her way to hint that our visit was ending. Surely she wouldn't leave me hanging about why Horace Dillard would come back to haunt his house. Could I have seen his ghost?

I fixed two cups of Earl Grey. I added a sugar cube to mine but knew Amanda liked hers, black and strong. The library was tranquil. So much so I could hear the tick and tock of the grandfather clock.

Sipping my tea, I walked around the office. A purchase order on her desk showed the library had just taken in several new books. *Sins of the Mother,* by Danielle Steel. Then, the novel I'd found on the chair, *Family Ties.* Two I'd read before by Jill Churchill and one by Dorothy Cannell. And someone new. Someone I'd never read. Gillian Flynn, *Gone Girl.*

I picked up *Family Ties,* sat back down in the chair, overstuffed and comfy, and began flipping through the pages.

But my thoughts returned to the empty gas can found at Burt's campsite. Jim Johns was right. Burt wouldn't have kept the empty can. He'd had seen too many cop shows on TV to be that naïve. If the Carters didn't own the house, then they wouldn't have purchased fire insurance. If they had renter's insurance, they'd have canceled that insurance after he was laid off and since Carol's job was also being threatened by layoffs at the school. Insurance is among the first things to be dropped.

There had to have been a logical reason why the can at the campsite was empty. Maybe the boat's tank was empty, and he'd filled it. Or maybe one of the kids, in their excitement to get out on the lake the next morning, wanted to get the boat ready and didn't say anything about filling it with gas. That seemed possible. But wouldn't Leveque have already thought to check these possibilities? And wouldn't one of the boys have told him they filled it?

Amanda came back carrying a book. On the front cover was a picture of city hall and the words, *Frytown, USA*. She glanced down at the Danielle Steel novel I held and said, "Isn't it about time you got out there and found yourself a guy instead of reading about one? Risk a little bit, Lillian. It makes life more interesting." She exchanged the Steel for the book she held. "Turn to page two hundred and three," she instructed, then moved to the small table to get her teacup.

"Yours might be cold," I warned. I flipped through the pages until I came to the requested page. I saw a photo of a large man wearing coat and trousers on it. On his head was a Stetson with a wide brim, and on his face, a large, handlebar mustache. Something about him looked familiar. Horace C. Dillard, Dillard Stock, and Rail. In parenthesis were the letters DS & R.

There had been a DS & R office in New Liberty.

I flipped to another page. There was a family portrait. Horace Dillard, Jr.

"Take a good look at the man," Amanda said.

I found her standing with her tea watching me. She leaned over slightly so she could see, too.

My eyes went back to the page. What did she want me to see? The man appeared to be somewhere in his forties. He'd taken after his father in looks. Gertrude Dillard looked younger than her husband. Their oldest child, eleven? Twelve? I turned another page. There were no other photos. And more interestingly, there was no page dedicated to the fire or their deaths.

Amanda said. "Dillard Sr. was said to have been associated with gangsters, men like Al Capone. There's one story claiming it was the mob that killed him." She went over and set her teacup on the desk. "Horace Jr. inherited his father's railroad holdings and money and was also said to have dealings with influential men and didn't always keep to the straight and narrow."

"Why isn't there anything about the fire here?"

"A small town like ours doesn't have much history, Lillian. Not the kind they put in books. These books are a series. A Midwest publisher recorded what the citizens wanted to be shown about their hometown." She paused. "Most people around here don't believe in airing their dirty laundry. So you need to be careful."

She came over, took the book out of my hands, and put it on the filing cabinet. I was confused. Judging by the length of time it took her to go out, check the doors, find this book, and then come back in. I was pretty sure she'd spent the time deciding whether or not to tell me the truth about the Dillard history. But now, it was as if she regretted the decision.

She said, "If Gilbert Simms isn't afraid to stir up cold ashes, I am. I don't care what evidence the police say they have on Burt. He wouldn't set a fire. It's not in his blood."

I got up and set my cup on the table beside hers. "Amanda, are you saying you may know who set it?"

She appeared emotionally shattered. "Please. Let it be."

I hadn't driven more than a block away from the library when colored lights flashed in my rearview mirror. I glanced down at the speedometer. It showed a speed slightly below the twenty-five miles-an-hour limit. Not that I never broke traffic laws, I just hadn't accelerated yet. So when the cop in the patrol car got out and came into view, my blood raced—Detective Leveque, my nemesis.

He lifted his belt higher on his hips and glanced around with authority before striding toward my car. He was checking everything out as if he'd just heard on his radio that a bank robbery had taken place, and a sunny brunette drove the getaway car in a bullet-ridden convertible.

I had to admit that he did fill out his uniform nicely. His curly hair tumbled onto his forehead from the slick heat of the day. The curls continued to ring around and below his ears, coming just short of his collar, producing an effect of a little boy dressed up in a man's uniform.

"Window down," he ordered, coming beside my window. He made a circling motion with his index finger. He shifted his hip, taking the load off his gun.

I kept the window up and clicked the locks.

"Your window? I need you to roll it down." He said louder.

I did as he instructed. I do respect the uniform. I lowered my window a few inches and said through the opening, "It's a shame about all the cutbacks. I see you've been bumped to patrol."

His lips pulled back, exposing his straight, celebrity-white teeth. He narrowed his eyes and made the finger motion again. "All the way, please."

He said please, but I knew he didn't mean it.

"I believe I am within my rights to keep my door locked and stay inside my car until a woman officer is present at the scene."

His grin pulled wider. "Well, now. Aren't you an avid reader of the law? You're right. If I asked you to step out of your car and you felt in jeopardy, you could request a female officer. And I'd be happy to assist you if we had a woman officer. But, unfortunately, we don't." He pointed back toward his patrol car. "See that small camera hooked onto the side mirror? It's a new acquisition. Not as big and tech-savvy as the cameras the state police have on their cars. We have to turn ours on when we make a stop. But it makes a video just the same. And I think if a judge looked at this video after I arrested you without a female officer present, I think the video would show you were not in any jeopardy. In fact, a judge would see it my way. You were evading a police officer's lawful request."

"I'll take my chances," I snapped. But he was right. If he'd bothered to turn the camera on, which was a big if. I wasn't in the mood to play games. "What do you want, Leveque? My driver's license?"

"It's still Detective Leveque."

"Ah, huh. Did you pull me over to smear mud on my face? Are you happy I've been laid off?"

"Laid off?" His tongue poked his cheek in thought. Then he smiled huge, exposing both dimples. "Laid off?" He cocked his head as if needing to contemplate the term. "Honey, you weren't laid off. You were fired." He leaned down, his face an inch away from the glass, one hand holding the outside mirror to brace himself. "Now roll down this window."

I let his "fired" comment blow past me, although, a piece of shrapnel did penetrate my pride. I rolled the window entirely down but avoided looking at him. Nothing in the law stated I had to look at him.

Aftershave, musky, and a sensation of power. No, not strength. Assurance. No, not right yet. He had a sureness about himself. He not only thought he was cool, he thought he was the coolest. Disgusting.

He cooed, "I guess the chief wanted to get to know you a little better first before he decided to find someone who could do the job."

I put the Mustang into gear. "Either give me a ticket or get out of my way, Leveque."

He didn't move.

I stepped on the accelerator, throwing him off balance, and burned enough rubber to award me another ticket. I hope he got it all on video.I couldn't afford new tires, but I'd be damned if Jacque Leveque was going to push me around anymore.

By the time I got to Oaks Manor, it was almost eight. I switched off the motor and sat. The truth was I wasn't sure I could handle Dahlia on the backside of Leveque. I felt beaten and emotionally damaged. But if I didn't go inside, it would've meant Leveque won. Charles won. Dahlia was winning.

For once in my life, I wanted to be successful at something.

I pushed my pride out of the way and finger-combed my hair.

Mary was at the desk. "Hey, Lillian. How are you holding up?"

I put a false cheer into my voice. "Can't beat people like me down, no matter how much some people try."

"I hear you." But, of course, Mary Niles heard me. She was the first in her family to get a high school diploma and a nursing degree from Mercy College. She probably thought I was talking about the lay-off. "You're late tonight," she said. "Your mother was asking about you."

"Where is the old girl? Did you put her away for the night?"

"I think she's still in the living room. The Betty White show is on. You know, the show where old people play practical jokes? Did you see the one where the old man sits down on a city bench next to this young girl and begins farting? I thought I'd die." She slapped the desk, laughing. "I don't know what he'd eaten beforehand, but that girl kept moving over on that bench until she about fell off. And the expression on her face."

Nothing funnier than old people farting. "I guess I missed that one."

"The show's a hit here. Standing room only."

I headed to the television room, finding Mary hadn't been exaggerating. The room was full of patients and what looked like most of the attendants. Every head was turned toward the large flat screen. Glancing at it, I saw an older man with a hairy chest, and a bald head, smoking a cigar, and wearing a Speedo. He was speed-walking along a sunny beach, probably in California or Florida. The cameras panned the faces of incredulous onlookers.

Everyone in the room was wetting their Depends.

Non-sociable Dahlia was not in attendance.

I searched for her, figuring she must have gone back to her room. Dahlia wasn't a fool, and she also wasn't the type to sit and watch people make fools of themselves.

The same scents of food, medicine, and older people filled the hallway with an added heaviness of illness. The flu was marching through Oaks Manor, taking casualties. When I got to Dahlia's room, the bed was made, and the room was vacant.

Where was she? Had she gone out onto the patio? It was a warm night. If so, there was no way I was going to be able to maneuver a path through Betty White fans.

I went to leave, moving back out into the corridor. I stood, listening. And heard voices.

I continued, rounding a corner into another hallway. An abandoned dirty-linen trolley sat heaped with soiled sheets. This hall was shorter than patients' corridors and offered storage rooms and other working areas.

At the very end of the hall, an emergency exit door held a dimmed red neon light. Below it was Dahlia, sitting in her wheelchair.

A man stood before her. His back was to me.

I made my presence known. "Are you all right, Dahlia?"

Edgar Pike rotated his head without moving his body. He had a disproportionate appearance, with his long torso and stumped legs.

"There she is," He said. "We were just talking about you." He circled around behind Dahlia and grunted as he pushed her wheelchair. "I told your mother how lucky she is to have you live so close."

Dahlia's eyes were narrowed. Her lips turned down at the corners. She didn't look at all happy.

He wheeled her slowly toward me. His eyes were embedded in swollen pillows of skin, and the discoloring made his eyes look like overly poached yokes in an egg. He wheezed, "We were talking about the good ol'days. Before you were born, of course."

He said it like *of coooorse* with a rasp and a slur. I could smell the cheap booze on him.

"Shouldn't you be in bed, Dahlia?" I asked.

She said, "What am I, a child?" She grabbed the wheels of her chair and tried to maneuver them herself, a feat she was very capable of under different circumstances, but Pike had a firm hold. "Leave me be, Pike."

"I think my mother would like you to let her go."

There was something about him that didn't seem right. It wasn't just his drunkenness. I'd been around alcohol-saturated scum like him most of my life. But, no, it was something else. Something dark.

He tilted his head. "Did you know your mother was a sweetheart of mine?"

Dahlia soured more and didn't meet my gaze.

He gave a low chuckle. "Oh, not now." He came around to stand at the side of her chair. "We're too old for all that tom-foolery. But your mother was a stunner. Did you know that? Seen pictures of her? Why? She could have had her pick of any man in New Liberty." He turned to Dahlia. "I heard around she was like Elvin, but she's as beautiful as you were, Dahlia." He put his hand on Dahlia's shoulder and addressed me again. "It's sad but true. Your mother didn't choose well when she married your father."

Dahlia slapped his hand off her shoulder. She put her hands on the wheels again, but they wouldn't move. This time, Pike wasn't holding her back. The chair's brake had been set.

I moved a few steps closer, unsure what was taking place. I didn't like Pike, and I sure as hell didn't like his comment about my father. Who did he know that could tell him anything about my life? I didn't care enough to ask. So instead, I asked her, "Are you ready to go back to your room, Dahlia? Do you want me to take you?"

She pulled her arms into her body, lowered her shoulders, and tucked her neck down. She sat solidly as a rock.

Pike ignored my attempt to get Dahlia away from him. "Yep, we dated back in high school before she met your father." He guffawed. "Just think, I could have been your da...aaddy."

Wonderful.

"But your grand-daddy didn't cotton to me. No, sir. He thought I wasn't good enough for his daughter. His shit didn't stink, but mine did." He looked down at Dahlia. "I told your mother when she broke up with me that she was makin' a mistake. I told her someday my ship was gonna come in." He leaned over. Dahlia turned away. "Didn't I, honey? Didn't I tell you someday I would be a rich man, and you'd be sorry you didn't marry me?"

Dahlia blew air between her lips. It was her only answer.

Spittle dripped from his lips and down his chin. He slurred, "You married that god-damn Elvin Dove. Where'd that get you?" His body lowered even further so that his face was right next to hers.

Dahlia took a swing at him and missed. But he backed away.

"Okay, enough," I said.

It was one thing for me to put down Dahlia and complain about my father's drunken behavior and quite another for someone from outside the family to offer condemnation. Someone as despicable as Edgar Pike.

In two steps, I was around her chair. I found the brake locks and flicked them off. "Come on, Dahlia. I've heard enough of this. I'm sure you have, too."

Dahlia took another swipe at Pike as the chair moved past him, her hand making contact this time. She raised her fist and shouted, "Stay away from Lillian, do you hear me, Pike? You come anywhere near her, and you'll be sorry."

I was stunned. Was she defending me?

Pike roared back, "You better be the ones who stay clear. Keep your mouth shut, Dahlia, or I'll have to shut it for you."

I wheeled her into her room and set the break. "What was that all about?"

She pushed herself out of her chair. "Nothing. He's a crazy old man." She stood unsteadily and mimicked his voice, "My ship'll come in." Then, she spat, "Hell, there's not a ship out there anywhere with his name on it. He was born a bastard, and he'll die a bastard."

I offered to help her to her bed, and she let me. Dahlia and I didn't touch much, and her arm was softer than I remembered. Then, she leaned on me, and something I thought I'd never allow her to do again.

Her body sagged into the mattress when she sat down on her bed. The confrontation had taken more out of her than she wanted to admit.

I said, "I'm going to tell Mary Niles about him. We should call the police. He was drunk."

She waved both statements away. "When was the man ever sober? Elvin was twice the man he ever was. Leave it alone, Lillian. You stay clear of Edgar Pike."

I wanted to ask her why and what he meant by saying she should keep her mouth shut? What was it she was to stay clear of? However, her exhaustion caused me to hold off on questions until later. "I'll go get Mary to help you get in bed."

"Don't go bothering her. I'll sit here until they come to help me get ready for bed. They'll be along shortly."

There were very few times I saw the vulnerable Dahlia. She was a good chameleon. I searched for her robe and gown in the closet, thinking that I could have her nightclothes ready. Then I worried, what if they didn't come soon? Should I help her get ready for bed? I prayed Connie, her attendant, or Mary would come in and take over. I didn't want to offer Dahlia any further demonstration of my inadequacies.

I turned around, nightclothes in hand, "Do you think…?"

I found her lying down on top of the covers, asleep.

I covered her with her bathrobe to keep her warm, then stood trying to figure out how I could have come from this woman's body. Her blood was mine, and yet we were nothing alike. I didn't understand her.

If it was true, if she could have had any man in New Liberty, why had she picked my father? Was he different when they were younger? Or had her parents pushed her toward him? I didn't know the maternal side of the family. Both grandparents died, and Dahlia's sister, Aunt Janice, moved back east somewhere. Dahlia never visited, and her sister's name wasn't mentioned much. We didn't get to know my father's side much either, especially after my grandmother died and he began to drink heavily.

Had Dahlia loved Pike?

When I was little and complained about Dahlia, my father said you only get one mother in life, and you should thank her for everything she did for you. I wanted to ask him if that included thanking her for forcing me to help him into the house when he was drunk. Clean up his vomit? Change Frank's and Patrick's diapers when I was barely out of them myself? Was I supposed to thank her for threatening me that I'd better get my butt home straight from school and clean the house and make dinner so she could work a second job? Thank her for when the kids at school called my father a drunk behind my back if I was lucky because they usually said it to my face. They said I was white trash. Adults warned me I was going nowhere fast and seemed to run toward more ruin.

I left her sleeping in her clothes.

But I wasn't about to leave without telling Mary what had happened and demand Marilyn Yoder to do something about Edgar Pike. However, when I told Mary, she was more than shocked.

"What do you mean he was here? Marilyn told him not to come anymore."

"Why?'

"He was upsetting your mother when he came to visit her."

The following day was Friday. I called and asked Clarence for the afternoon off. I told him about the Bobby Bowen show. He kidded me about becoming a big celebrity. I said, "They offered me two hundred dollars."

"Beats what I can offer unless you did it, Lillian. I can swing giving you a loan."

"You give me more than money, Clarence. You know that." I told him about leaving early the day before and the time I owed. He said he'd start an IOU on me.

I wasn't entirely honest with Clarence. Besides getting ready for the Bowen show, I was also planning to check out the job situation in Iowa City. Maybe I could get a full-time job and start a career. It's never too late, right? Of course, I wasn't forty, yet.

I spent the morning on the Internet, and I found a job listing for a company called Messer Corporation that was looking for an account executive. The job description said the person needed sales experience. I pulled up my resume and tweaked the Discount experience to read sales associate. Another position read *Needed Immediately*, senior center manager. I figured I could do that. I'd been managing Dahlia for five years. Well, maybe not controlling, but I was doing time. I tweaked the resume to show I was a senior manager at Oaks Manor. If I gave a heads-up to Marilyn, she might give me a recommendation. I noticed one more position because I had lots of experience: *Buyer, Hof Brewery*. The job offered benefits. Again, I tweaked the ol' resume. I had many years of experience in alcohol. I put down fifteen—skipped adolescence.

I jotted down the addresses for each company. I figured people today counted on the computer to do their legwork. How many people would drop off their resumes? I was going to show determination.

I fed Bacardi, showered, and tried on three or four outfits, not knowing the proper interview apparel. Then, after selecting an outfit I thought was appropriate, I headed off.

The air conditioner was still blowing heat, so I put the Mustang's convertible top down. After thirty minutes in the humidity, my hair whipping in my face, I pulled the car over. My fingers tried combing my hair, but the mousse I'd used adhered like glue. I rummaged in the glove box for a rubber band, found one, and pulled my hair into a ponytail. The bruise on my forehead was still prominent, and I'd tried to cover it up with make-up. Now, however, the makeup was weeping from the heat and wind.

I got out to put up the top. I figured it was better to be hot than look a mess. I wanted to make an impression on whomever I left my application so that the person might pass it on to someone or something other than the trash can. But no matter how much I tugged, levered, and cussed, the top refused to unfold and go back into place. It was as if its stupid hinges had rusted in the humidity. It was an automated top, but the automation hadn't worked when I purchased the car. Desperate as I was now becoming, I gave it another shot. No, go. Not even a whine of power.

I stopped at the first Dash and Go at the first exit into Iowa City. A pimply-faced girl at the counter gave me a smug expression when I asked for the bathroom key.

"Customers only," she said.

I told her I'd buy a Coke when I came out.

"We have Pepsi," she said.

"Even better."

She reluctantly handed me a key attached to a ruler.

The bathroom was unisex and smelled like a stockyard. Checking in the mirror, I understood the counter girl's hesitation. My sunglasses had created white bottle rings around my eyes. The bruise, hidden by the foundation earlier, appeared more prominent than when I was in the hospital. The penciled-in eyebrow was long gone, and my nose was beginning to blister.

I took a rarely used compact out of my purse and did what I could to blend in all the shades. Finally, I penciled in another brow and added a little lipstick. Lipstick can make a day seem a whole lot better,…or not. First, it'd melted in the tube, and not only did it smear on my fingers, but it melted into the corners of my lips, causing them to bleed out like a clown's smile. Then a piece of the lipstick broke off and dropped onto the white blouse I'd chosen to appear clean and tidy.

There were no more clean paper towels, so I took a used and wadded up one on the counter and dabbed at the reddish pink. After checking out the stall, I skipped a pee. I went back out into the restaurant and handed over the key. The girl gave me the same smug expression. Either it came naturally to her, or my handy make-over didn't do the trick. As promised, I bought a Pepsi, then asked her for directions to my first job address. She scratched instructions on a paper napkin, correctly figuring I knew very little about Iowa City's streets.

At least there'd been hot air blowing on me on the interstate. Inside the city, no breeze was offered. Instead, the street tossed up a wet sheet of heat as if it'd just rained—no rain in sight. People walked with shoulders stooped. A child holding his mother's hand blubbered at a stop sign while waiting for the crosswalk light to change.

On Interstate 80 to Highway 1, I got off at Oakdale Boulevard. There were four large buildings, each three floors high. I may have bitten off too much from the employment cookie on this one. Messer Corporation wasn't hard to find, for the sign with the company name was a floor high.

I drove into the parking space marked GUEST. I hoped I wouldn't be asked to give an interview, not with the pink stain showing on my blouse. But, inside, just the promise of as much air conditioning as I could stand said this might be the company for me.

The twenty-something at the desk asked who I was there to see. I stood sideways to the desk so she wouldn't notice the stain. I told her I was there to drop off my resume for the account executive position.

She asked, "Hot outside?"

I guess I was sweating a bit.

She told me the company only accepted resumes online and suggested I email it per the instructions. I guess those instructions had been at the end of the job listing, but I never read to the very end.

I said I would be sure to do that, then asked if she could give me directions to Pathways Avenue. Maybe she figured out I was a virgin on the career circuit. She pulled up a city map on her computer, saying I needed to continue taking Highway 1 further out.

She didn't say it was three miles.

I was ruined by the time I pulled up to Hartfield Center for the Elderly. Sweat had smeared my mascara. My clown lips had only an outline with a shade of the lipstick on my lips. This was getting to be another fucked up day.

Hartfield was a one-story building painted hospital green. The woman behind this desk took my enveloped resume. "We really need someone," she said. "We haven't been able to fill the position."

I told her I was the right person for the job.

She made notes on the envelope and asked if I could start immediately. I knew Clarence wouldn't like losing me, but business hadn't been that good lately. It might come as a relief if he didn't have to keep me on. So I told her sure I could start right away. She asked for a reference, and I gave her Marilyn Yoder's number at Oaks Manor. I hoped she didn't call until I'd gotten ahold of Marilyn. And then, she asked me if I had experience with the elderly or only with managing.

I kept my response short. "Managing the elderly is easy to do if you remember you're going to be old one day." She seemed to like that and said they would get back to me.

Her eyes did stray to the stain on me, but she didn't mention it.

Having succeeded with potential employer number two, I headed back on Highway 1, which I knew ended in the downtown area. I glanced in the rear-view mirror while at a stop sign, sweat trickling past my sunglasses, stinging my eyes. Mascara running down my cheeks. Face powder becoming war paint. The pink patch still showed above my left breast. And now, a wet circle was forming under my armpits.

I was not ready for showtime. It was almost four o'clock. I decided I shouldn't chance going to Hof Brewery. I wasn't afraid of working for a brewery. I didn't think it would backslide me out of recovery, but I wasn't ready to stake my life on it. Selling booze at Discount had more distance from opening a bottle than walking around a place where they offered free samples.

Before going to Burlington Avenue and KETV, I thought I'd clean up.

I circled, looking for another Dash and Go or something similar, and found the bus depot/ Amtrak station on Court Street. The inside felt like a refrigerator. So far, Iowa City was very promising. Like Messer and Harford, Greyhound apparently had no economic slump.

A scattering of folks sat on benches, their luggage stacked in front of them. They could've been pretending to be traveling just to get inside somewhere cooler than their places.

But because I was there, I went over to the ticket counter and asked if there were any job openings. The man behind the counter yawned. He was taking a break between buses, I guessed. He said offhandedly, "Check the computer. Employment's listed on the website." He eyed beyond me as if I were taking up his valuable time. No one in line. "You buying a ticket or what?"

It was the "or what."

I toured the bathroom and found it clean. I washed and remade my face. I tried rewashing my blouse, and the pink thinned a bit more and was barely noticeable unless you weren't blind. I hit the snack machines next. My morning PB & J was wearing off. Chips and another Coke, no Pepsi. Call it dinner.

Back outside, it took several turns of the motor before the Mustang agreed to get up and go. Not that it always started on the first twist of the key, but this time, it took some floor-stomping encouragement to get out of the parking lot.

I found a Walmart, took one of my credit cards with some room on its limit, and purchased another white blouse. If TV cameras added five pounds as people say, I figured my boobs would grow to where the spot on my shirt would become a bullseye. I am not sure why I thought it would be my boobs that would take on pounds. Maybe I was hoping my desire for more cleavage might be fulfilled. Besides, I was going to need interview clothes. I tossed a Hershey bar on the tab, too.

The Mustang started right up this time.

I was wearing a new blouse. I was feeling better. Refreshed.

The candy had been solid when I purchased it. Within minutes of its unwrapping, the chocolate stuck to my fingers and smeared the steering wheel. My bites became larger. Finally, I pushed what was left in my mouth, wadded up the wrapper, and let it fly.

I smiled at my quick thinking, getting rid of it before something terrible happened. Then I felt guilty for littering. I looked into the rearview mirror. Chocolate coated my gums and teeth.

Stopping at several fast-food restaurants and a gas station with a PERSON WANTED sign, it wasn't until I started into the TV station at a little after five-thirty that I noticed the dark chocolate stain on my new blouse. With no more time to do laundry, I grabbed the pink-stained blouse from the back seat. I'd let those in charge choose the worst-case scenario.

Randi Quince of KETV was in a real snit when I checked into the lobby. She was one of those tall blondes who never eat and can balance on five-inch- heels. She claimed I was late. When she saw the brown stain on my blouse, she became unnerved. I offered the other pink-stained one, and she screamed.

Television production must be a very stressful job.

She led me into a room and informed me someone would be right in to do my make-up. "God, I've got to find something for you to wear."

The makeup person came in and powdered me up, frowning as she did so. She said something like red is the worse to cover. My face had gotten sunburned. She put so much powder on my face that I felt like a mime. If it hadn't been for the money I was getting, I might have walked out right then and there. But instead, I asked the make-up girl if they were doing any hiring.

"Any experience?"

The look of horror she was wearing on her face while trying to do something with mine forced me to admit I might not have enough bluff to get me through this type of career.

Randi found a blouse without stains. She'd looked like the resourceful type to me. She led me into the studio to an area where stage lights were mounted overhead. Cameras stood on small-wheeled cranes. And there was a green screen. *Here's Johnny.*

A young guy in a T-shirt and jeans came over and held out what he said was a microphone. Randi left while he helped me hook the small black box onto my waistband and a tiny microphone on my lapel.

The staged area held a couch and desk. Sitting together on the sofa, Chief Simms and Tim Johnson watched as I got wired up. Both were wearing their uniforms. When Randi came back, she led me over to Bobby Bowen, who stood off to the side of his desk chatting with the crew on the couch. She made the introductions. He gave me a looking over, and then he pulled Randi off to the side. I heard him say something like, "Best you could do?"

Bobby Bowen was no Brian Williams. This was small-town television even though Iowa City holds a population of seventy thousand.

Someone said, "Two minutes."

Bobby Bowen hurried over to his desk. A different make-up person came out to swab the sweat from his brow. Randi led me back over to the side of the stage. At first, I thought maybe they'd decided not to use me. Then, I wondered if that meant I wouldn't be paid. Could I return the new blouse at Walmart?

Randi started giving me instructions. "Mr. Bowen will bring the audience back."

I asked, looking around, "What audience?"

She ignored my question. "He will introduce you. Then, you will walk out onto the set. Mr. Johnson has been instructed to stand so the two of you can hug. He and Chief Simms will then move over so you can join them.

"Ten, nine, eight..."

She gave me a big push. I headed over and tripped on one of the camera cables. Tim Johnson stood and grabbed me before I could fall.

"Almost had to save her again," Bobby Bowen said, chuckling, as Tim and I uncomfortably embraced.

I stared at the camera as if it'd confirm or deny my stumbling incident was caught for the entire world to see. Then, as instructed, Chief Simms and Tim scooted over on the couch. As told, I sat down beside them.

Bobby said, "You must be thrilled to be here to thank Mr. Johnson for saving your life."

He waited for me to respond. I turned to Tim, keeping my face visible to the camera, "Yes, I am. Thanks, Tim."

"No problem. It's part of the job."

Evidently, neither one of us had been given a script.

Chief Simms edged up a bit on the couch so he could see Bobby around Tim and me. "We drill for victim rescues such as this," he explained the procedure. But, after about twenty seconds, it seemed he had nothing to say.

Bobby said, "I understand you entered the burning house because you saw someone in an upper window."

I nodded, but nodding doesn't work on television, so I said, "Yes."

"This was a lucky break for the police."

"What do you mean?"

"An eyewitness isn't always available when a crime takes place."

I said to those same cameras, "Well, I didn't see the person clearly."

"Meaning?"

I wasn't sure what he wanted. "I couldn't see them very well."

He frowned, and his voice took on a more dramatic tone. "Are you aware, Ms. Dove, that the house has a history? As I discussed before you came on the set, the Dillard family died when the house burned in 1954. You are a lucky woman to have gotten out alive."

I said, "Thanks to Tim." I didn't like being the center of attention. Tim looked over at Chief Simms, who rescued us by saying, "Frytown's fire department is one of the best in the state." Then, he started explaining more about the station and a firefighter's responsibility to the community.

When the primary camera's red light went off, Randi hurried over. She instructed the three of us to go around and stand behind the couch. I thought I'd be done with the show by this time. I said as much to Tim, who said he'd been told he'd be needed for only about ten or fifteen minutes. So together, we stood to wait behind the couch next to Chief Simms, who didn't seem to mind staying around a little longer.

Just then, Randi led Carol Carter into the wings. Along with Carol were her two sons, Darrell and David.

A cameraman yelled, "Thirty seconds."

Bobby, who'd been in a conversation with another cameraman, quickly sat behind his desk. He said, "Please join me in welcoming the Carter family." He stood, clapping.

The Carter family walked onto the set. First, Carol Carter stopped to say something to Chief Simms and Tim. Then she came over to me. "Thank you," she whispered. I wasn't sure what I was being thanked for, but I told her it was no trouble. She didn't seem nervous at all.

"I'm sorry your husband isn't here with us," Bobby Bowen told her. Carol made no reply. Clearly, Bobby wanted to be diplomatic about Burt's arrest. All three sat on the couch. The story of their having gone camping was retold.

There was no dead air with Carol. She and Bobby got along famously. She confirmed everything in the house was lost and thanked the Frytown Women's Club for the sale they planned to have down at the lakeside. "Saturday from nine to seven."

When Bobby seemed to have run out of questions for her, and after the boys had given their ages and grades, with David yelling "Go, Cougars," -- the Frytown football team-- I again thought we'd come to the end of the show. Or, at least, this time, the commercial break would allow those of us standing to move from the set.

But Randi was at it again. This time, she was leading a woman walking with a walker. She seemed to be around Dahlia's age but frail. Behind her came Edgar Pike. He was wearing a dark, ill-fitting suit and a shirt with a collar so small that it choked his neck. His face looked red but not the bright red from drinking. No, Pike was sober.

Darrell leaped off the couch and hurried over to the woman. He slipped between Pike and her and took her arm. The woman gladly accepted his help, leaving Pike to tend to the walker. I couldn't help but notice how Pike scowled and glanced around as if he hadn't been instructed on what to do should something unplanned occur. Each of the Carters hugged the woman, and then Carol and the two boys joined us behind the couch. It felt like we had a family portrait taken. Carol didn't look like she had been forewarned about the guest. She and Darrell whispered together.

Bobby helped the older woman sit on the couch. Pike was just about to sit down beside her when Bobby Bowen held his hand out.

Pike shook it. He whispered to him and led Pike around the couch to stand in back with us before Bobby sat down on the couch.

During the break, the cameraman Bobby talked to came out with a shoulder camera. Randi looked on nervously. Everyone seemed unaware of what was occurring except for the cameraman and Bobby. Finally, the cameraman brought his camera and knelt so that only Bobby and the woman filled the lens.

"Thank you for coming, Ms. Dillard." Then, he said, "I would like to introduce Margaret Dillard, the only surviving child of Horace Jr. and Gertrude Dillard."

Margaret Dillard was dressed in a navy-blue dress with a Peter Pan collar, a style of yesterday. White kid gloves with small pearls at the wrists covered her hands. She carried a large, black, shiny purse. "Please call me Meg," she said. "Everyone does." She sat primly, taking her eyes off Bobby Bowen only to quickly glance back at Pike.

I glanced over at Tim, who looked as puzzled as I was. Chief Simms, however, had an entirely different expression. Shock? Surprise? Dazed? Disgruntled? Whatever. He wasn't happy.

"I am so sorry about your loss," Bobby said to Meg, making it sound like the Dillard fire had happened yesterday instead of sixty years ago. "I understand you have never appeared in public. Until *today*," he emphasized the word today, his show, "many thought you were killed in the fire."

She nodded and glanced back at Pike. Or was it Chief Simms? The two were standing uncomfortably next to each.

Bobby said, "We're grateful for Mr. Pike's help locating you. I understand he is your half-brother?"

"Yes. He is my brother." Her voice was tender and quivered, probably nervous at being on television.

The Carters, placed in the middle, stood directly behind where Meg sat. Darrell reached out to touch her shoulder as if offering support. Carol said something comforting to her. I noticed Chief Simms edge away from Pike, and Pike moved slightly to where I could see him. His hands gripped the back of the couch as he roared, "My father was Horace Dillard."

Randi was pacing back and forth in the wings. She held both hands, fingers spread, notifying Bobby he still had ten minutes to commercial.

Bobby moved slightly closer to Meg. "I understand you have also been like a family member to the Carter family." The woman twisted around, giving all the Carters a smile, which they warmly returned. Bobby followed suit. To Bobby, she said, "They call me Meg."

"All right, Meg." He reached out and took one her of gloved hands in his. "Can you tell us what it was like hearing your family home burned for a second time? Again, arson?" She looked toward the cameras. "You do remember that day so long ago, don't you? Isn't it the reason why you have remained hidden?"

A shadow of worry crossed Meg's face. "Hide? I live in Frytown, next to my daddy's house. I've always lived there." Her words were simple, her thoughts not complicated. "I moved there when Mandy's mom and daddy died."

Mandy? Amanda Keiff, the librarian?

Meg patted Bobby's hand. "Edgar and I talk about Daddy all the time. Edgar's like him, you know? My daddy was a strong man, and Edgar has his eyes." Then, again, she glanced fondly back at Pike.

I leaned over, trying to get a gander at Pike's eyes. They looked red-rimmed and bloodshot to me.

"I miss my daddy." She took back her hand from Bobby. She opened her purse and pulled out a much-used Kleenex. Although she didn't seem emotional, she dabbed at her eyes and took a deep breath. "When my mommy and daddy died, they took me to Dr. Hayes' house. Dr. Hayes said I was going to live with them. They were nice to me."

Hayes was Amanda Keiff's maiden name.

The memory of it seemed to make Meg happy. "I miss them. I miss Mandy, too. She doesn't come to see me hardly at all anymore."

Bobby said, "The Carter fire must bring back all those emotions you had as a child."

"I was twelve." She looked at the camera, her eyes wide and blinking. Her voice got louder, a bit frightened. "My daddy was Horace Dillard."

Bobby again looked to the wings. Randi shrugged. Carol jumped in. "It's okay, Meg." Darrell echoed, "It's all right, Aunt Meg." David was texting someone on his phone held low and out of sight.

The atmosphere became sullen. Bobby tried to change it. "We don't mention ages on television." He put his hand up to his face, in an aside to the audience, "Especially mine."

Pike moved from behind the couch and sat down, shifting Meg closer to Bobby, forcing him off-center. "Like I told your assistant," Pike said, a bit roughly, "Meg isn't much of a talker. She never aged much beyond twelve." He pointed to his head. "If you know what I mean." He lowered his hand and went on. "Once I knew who I was, I wanted to help my sister. Family needs to take care of family."

"I don't understand."

Pike seemed embarrassed. "I knew who my daddy was since I was a boy. But my ma wouldn't say for sure." He grunted. "Others told me I was crazy. But I'll show them. I have proof Horace Dillard Jr. was my blood relation. I've come to take care of Meg, my sister. As is my right."

He reached for Meg's gloved hand and held it. "We both lost a daddy and sisters. We're all we have now."

"Incredible," Bobby said. "The two of you, after all of these years, find one another. How long have you been caring for your sister?"

"A couple of months. But I'm taking care of it legally with a lawyer to ensure no one can keep us apart now." He got Meg's attention, and she nodded.

Pike began chewing his lips as if he held back deep-seated emotion. "I wish to hell I'd have gotten the chance for my daddy to have known me. If he had known me, things would have been different."

Bobby tried to bring the conversation back to Meg. "I understand no one was brought to justice for your family's tragedy."

Pike jumped back in. "No, Sir. But you can be damn sure we plan to find out who did it this time." He glared back at Carol Carter.

Meg said, "I'll never forget."

Bobby concluded, "I am sure what happened is etched in your memory."

Meg opened her big, black, shiny purse. But Meg wasn't rummaging for a Kleenex. Instead, she pulled out a small folded paper and handed it back to Carol. "Mandy helped me get it for you. It's a present."

Carol unfolded a check. Her eyes widened. "Fifty thousand dollars?"

David peeked over her shoulder, giving a thumbs-up before his thumbs began hip-hopping on his phone. Darrell hugged his mother. She was crying. She hurried around the couch, helping Meg stand. She hugged her.

And Edgar Pike? His eyes darted from the check Carol was holding back to Meg. He had such a black look on his face that I think he wouldn't have hesitated to shoot us all if he had a gun in his hand.

I changed back into my clothes and left the station. It wasn't long before Pike came out, hurrying Meg Dillard along. She stumbled, her big purse causing her to be off-balanced. She said something to Pike, and he stopped and stared stonily at her and gave her a shove. She stumbled backward. Her walker fell over. Her purse fell. She would have fallen if Darrell hadn't come out the doors at that exact minute. He ran out so quickly, he must have been watching them from inside.

He yelled something at Pike, holding up his arms to give Pike a push. Pike came to him, arms stretched out, fingers splayed. Meg gathered herself and said something. Darrell backed away from Pike. Pike took Meg in hand but not as roughly and led her to his car. He opened the passenger door and helped her in.

Darrell and I watched them drive away. Darrell smiled. He looked up and down the street, then he noticed me. I started to get out of the car, wanting to commend him for stepping in as he did and maybe to ask a question or two. But he rushed off, moving away from me. He turned a corner and disappeared around a building.

David and Carol came out then. I got out of the car. "Congratulations. You knew one of the Dillard children survived? That she'd be on the show?"

Carol could hardly talk she was so excited. "I had no idea. We know Meg, of course. We rent her family's house from the trust. She lives next to us in one of the small houses on the original estate. My children have always called her Aunt Meg." She grabbed me, needing something to hug, I guess. David was preoccupied. He seemed to be taking pictures of himself. "I never expected this," Carol said. "So much money. It'll take care of everything."

Fifty thousand dollars. Not a small bit of cash. Not to a third-grade teacher and a city employee who'd recently been laid off. There was no doubt in my mind the fifty thousand came as a complete surprise to the Carter family. Or at least, it came as a surprise to Carol and the kids. Was this insurance money from the house? But, if there were an investigation, the insurance company wouldn't have paid off until a cause had been established. Was Meg Dillard still rich? Had Burt known Meg would give them money if they were in trouble? A house fire would trigger memories of her own ruined home. How did she survive? And why had her survival been a secret?

Burt could have driven back to Frytown, only a little over an hour's drive. Carol and the kids could have been so tired they didn't hear him leave and come back. I remembered what Burt said to Bobby

Bowen the day of the fire, "Why would anyone think we'd set fire to our own house?"

Fifty thousand dollars may lead people to believe just that.

I reflected on Pike's rage when Meg gave Carol the check. He hadn't known about it. Was he expecting Meg to give him the fifty thousand?

What had Dahlia said? "He was born a bastard, and he'll remain a bastard." I didn't think she'd meant it literally.

Amanda Keiff had shown me the photo of the Dillard family, but she failed to mention how the oldest daughter survived. Apparently, Meg lived with the Hayes family. Amanda was Mandy. Why had she wanted to keep that secret from me?

Clarence also had to have known. Hell, I bet his whole generation in Frytown knew Meg had survived. I remembered Amanda saying, "The Simms family didn't like the decisions made at the time." So I guessed those decisions had to do with Meg Dillard.

An even bigger question popped into my mind. One Clarence planted. Amanda had echoed. Clarence said to watch out for someone meaner than Horace Dillard. Did he mean Edgar Pike?

"This will take care of everything," Carol said about the check. But did she mean the money would let them rebuild? Fifty thousand was a lot of money, which reminded me that I would soon be out of money. I received the two hundred from the show, and my severance check wouldn't last.

Traffic can be heavy between Iowa City and the smaller surrounding towns. Many people commute to work at Mercy Hospital or the University of Iowa. Companies such as Walmart offered more employment than local hometown retail stores. Damn, I didn't ask Walmart if they were hiring. The company may have helped Midwestern businesses dry up, but a lot more people could work because of them.

I needed to keep my focus back on job hunting, but I wouldn't email my resume to Messer Corporation. It was too big for me. But I could do the senior manager's job. I needed to call Marilyn as soon as I got back in town.

I was tired from the long day. My thoughts moved from my worries to Cressie. She'd shown me sobriety was possible. She told me there was life after the next drink. I hadn't expected Frytown would become my life, but it was what I'd been given. Given? Forced into. But it was okay for now. I still carried guilt about Cressie's backsliding after so many years.

She'd called me the night she died. She said, "Let's go to a meeting, then pop some corn and watch a movie." Of course, I'd turned her down. You never want to go to a meeting when you need one. The hardest thing about recovery is showing up.

If I had agreed to go with her...would Cressie still be alive? It was torture thinking my decision rippled across the pond of probabilities and ended up causing her to make a wrong decision. A deadly one. What ripple did those in Frytown cause by keeping Meg secreted?

The commute seemed too far. I was overthinking. Not everything has an easy answer, I've learned. I wasn't in the mood for sucking in the exhaust and exited as soon as I saw the sign for Highway 6. The sky, only partially cloudy when I'd left KETV, grew darker with heavy, lumbering clouds moving fast. I drove past cornfields beginning to look more yellow than green. The crops needed a steady, nourishing rain. The exhaust from the highway was replaced by grit and dust on this minor road. The dryness caught in my nose and throat. The thought of the shower I'd take as soon as I got home made me step on the accelerator.

When I reached the crossroad of Black Hawk and Rohert Road, a flash of lightning scored a brilliant streak across the sky, lacing strangling fingers from one darkened cloud belly to another. A blast shook the air, so close my car vibrated, and the rumbling sound of the explosion moved farther and farther until it finally rolled to a stop.

I had to find cover. I could go left toward Charles's farm, which was closest. It was the choice I wanted to make, but I didn't always make good decisions. Somehow, I needed to change that. I turned right.

Lightning hit the road in front of me, and the hair on my arms sprang straight up. Hell, the fuzz in my navel popped with the electrical charge. Damn convertible top. And then it began to hail. Not tiny ice flakes like the shavings in a snow cone at the state fair. This cloud's belly slit open, and God tossed out frozen golf balls. I got hit, not once but several times, no matter how I ducked. Then I saw something on the road. Two somethings. Sam Roe's cows.

The cows were living up to the saying, *dumb as a cow*, standing in the middle of the road, chewing their cud, as if having no more sense than a…well, a dumb cow. I got out of the car and tried to shoo them off the road. Unfortunately, I slipped on the hail and fell. I got back into the car and honked the horn. The only reaction came from one of the cows, which raised its tail in a high arch and began to defecate.

Miraculously, the hailing stopped just as quickly as it started. Another sharp jolt of lightning lit the area, but farther and at a safer distance. Yet, all was not over. It began to rain. It rained as if God had been collecting all that damn hail, melted it, and saw me sitting in a fucking convertible behind a cow shitting on the road.

God must be a man.

The inside of the Mustang flooded. I was immediately drenched.

Thankfully, Sarah Roe opened the door of her house at my first knock. "My lands," she cried, wiping her hands on a dishtowel. "What are you doing out here in weather like this?"

I asked, "Where's Sam?"

"He's sitting in the room there, reading his paper. I was just finishing washin' up the supper dishes." She opened the door wider. "Come in, come in. You're wet through. Let me get you a towel."

While Sarah searched a towel to stop me from dripping on her carpet, I stepped over and glanced into the living room. Sam, as she said, was reading his nightly paper. Obviously, he was unaware his cows were out for a nightly stroll.

"Sam," I called. No movement from behind the newspaper. I tried again, a little louder this time. "Hello? Sam?" I was a touch pissed.

Sarah came back carrying several towels. She put one on the floor and handed me one. "Sam," she called. "Look what the cat brought in."

I swear, her voice wasn't any louder than a conversational tone, but Sam dropped his newspaper and looked over. "Is that you, Lillian Dove? It's pretty stormy to be out and around tonight. They're claiming on the radio that we could get severe weather."

I was standing on a towel. Sarah tried to dry my arms while I tried to dry my hair and face. "Sarah," I said, "tell him the cows are out on the road. People can't get through."

"Cows are out, Sam," she called over to him, not missing a wipe. Then, she asked me, "What happened to your head?" She finished drying me off, and then satisfied, she said something about having baked a pie, and she'd go cut me a piece.

Sam got up from his chair, carrying his newspaper in both hands so as not to lose his place. He glanced out the window. "Yep, they're out all right." He went back to his chair and sat down.

I yelled, "Aren't you going to do something?"

He didn't answer. The newspaper didn't even ripple.

Sam and Sarah are somewhere in their late seventies or eighties. Undistinguishable ages. She kept her hair dyed and curled, and he was usually dressed in overalls. I walked over to him.

"Sam," I said louder. "Don't you think we should get the cows off the road? There could be an accident."

"Hey-yeah. Dangerous out there."

"No, the cows." I reached out and rattled his paper. He lowered it and gave me a disgruntled look. "The cows are on the road," I said each word distinctly. "They could cause an accident."

He chewed on that. "Get to'er soon as the storm moves on. No one in their right mind will be driving around in this weather." He went back to his reading, turned a page, and mumbled, "I hear Sarah rumbling around in that there kitchen of hers. Why don't you go on back and get yourself some pie?" He said, "When it's done rainin', I'll go get the cows in."

I couldn't get anywhere until the cows got off the road, and the cows wouldn't get off, it seemed, until Sam finished reading his paper. So I looked for Sarah, thinking she was someone I could reason with.

She was putting a nice, big slice of berry pie on a plate. She set it on the table with a napkin and fork and poured a cup of supper coffee for both of us. I took a chair and asked, "Is he like this all the time?"

"He's been who he is since the day I married him. His Ma said he was a colicky baby."

I surrendered and forked up a piece of flaky crust and juicy berries. She sat across from me, warming her hands around her coffee cup. She continued, "Nothing gets done around here until breakfast or lunch is eaten, a nap is taken, or the paper's read. Then, come hell or high water." She chuckled, as only a woman who'd lived with a man like Sam for so many years could. "Will Walton got so mad at him one day, I tell you. The cows were out eating Eva's posies. They do like her flowers. Sam had finished his lunch and was taking a nap on the couch. You know what happened?"

I picked up the last yummy piece of the pie. But, of course, I didn't know what happened, and she didn't wait to see if I did.

She said, "Will pulled the garden hose in here, inside my house, and he set it on Sam. He had it on full force." She laughed. I'd kill Will Walton if he'd done that to my house. "I about killed both Will Walton and Sam that day." Then, again, she laughed at the hi-jinks between the long-standing neighbors.

I was hungrier than I thought, or the pie was the best I'd ever eaten. It was both. Sarah Roe has a reputation for being one of the best cooks in Frytown. Plus, I hadn't eaten since the coin-operated lunch at the bus depot. I pushed back my plate after licking the fork clean.

"Want another piece?" Sarah asked.

Of course, I did, but I said no thanks. "I'd eat your whole pie if you'd let me."

"It's why I make them," she said, smiling. "I like having someone eat them."

I sipped coffee, feeling more relaxed and warmer. Sarah was one of those motherly women who made you feel immediately comfortable no matter the situation. "Good coffee."

She said, "I like a cup after dinner. For most people, it keeps them awake. But not me." She nodded. "You should get out of those clothes. You'll catch your death."

"I'm leaving as soon as the storm passes." I didn't mention the cows again, pretty firm in my expectation that as soon as the storm passed and the classifieds were read, I'd be on my way with a clear road ahead of me.

"Where've you been to on a night like this?" she asked.

"Coming back from Iowa City. KETV. You know, *Iowa's History and Its People* show?"

She nodded. "Bobby Bowen. I like that show."

"Well, it was on tonight."

"Oh, dear. I clean forgot." She said, "It was a special on the Carter fire, wasn't it? I wanted to watch it."

I told her what had happened, about how Chief Simms and Tim Johnson were on.

"Tim's a good boy," she said. She wanted to know why I was on the show, and I reminded her I was the one who called in the fire.

She reached out and patted my hand. "Right time, right place. We're put where we needed." Sam and Sarah were Lutheran.

I told her about how Carol and the boys showed up, too. Sarah was hanging onto each word.

Her face lit up. "Who?"

"Margaret Dillard."

She froze, her cup held halfway to her mouth. Then slowly, carefully, she set the cup down on its saucer. "Meg Dillard?"

I nodded. "The very one."

"Oh, dear." She half stood and yelled, "Sam, are you hearing any of this?"

Since Sam couldn't hear me when I'd been standing right in front of him, I was sure he hadn't special powers to enable him to listen to us talking in the kitchen.

But in he came, newspaper hanging down to his side. "Did she say, Meg Dillard?"

"That's what she said." Sarah stayed half standing.

Sam came over and took a chair. "I'll have me another piece of that pie, Sarah." While she was getting him a plate and a slice, he folded his newspaper carefully. His expression was both sad and curious. "Who was with her?"

"Man named Edgar Pike. Know him?"

He nodded. Not nodding like "Yes, I know him," but one nod, straight up and down. He didn't like Pike, either. "I told Amanda to send his tail flying when he came sneakin' around. Told Meg he was her half-brother. Man's got no proof." His lips pursed as if whatever was in his mouth tasted so bad he could spit.

"Meg gave Carol Carter a fifty-thousand-dollar check tonight on the Bobby Bowen show," I informed him.

Sarah came over and set Sam's piece of the pie in front of him. He dug right in. A drop of berry juice spilled onto his whiskers.

My mouth watered. I considered asking for another piece.

"Oh, dear," Sarah sighed. "Do you know about Meg?"

I shook my head. "I thought she was dead. But I do know Horace Dillard was murdered."

Sarah asked in a hoarse whisper, "Who told you that?" The same stunning response as Amanda Hayes's.

"Clarence Salzman."

She looked over to Sam. I turned to him, too. "Pike introduced himself on the show as Meg Dillard's brother."

Sam, finished with his pie, was methodically scraping the side of his fork against the plate, picking up the flaky left-over bits. Finally, he stopped and addressed himself to Sarah. "I told you, Sarah. When he came around, I said it was goin' to lead to trouble."

Sarah nodded.

I asked, "Pike, you mean?"

Sarah said, "Folks say Horace and Pike's mother were married. But if that's true, it's never been proven, as far as I'm aware. No legal papers or they'd have shown up years ago." He went on, "A woman by the name of Beatrice was the housekeeper. She was a young spit of a girl." He explained, "This was before Horace married Gertrude." He continued. "Horace was rich because he was a Dillard. He was a good catch, and this gal probably thought he'd keep her on permanent if she kept his house good enough." He glanced at me as if saying *If you get my meaning.*

"She wasn't the first girl to think like that," Sarah said. "Where were her parents is what I want to know. They should have stopped her from taking the job in the first place. A young, single girl in a house alone with a man like him. She was asking for trouble."

Sam added, "Yep. Her parents should have. But they were poor people. I doubt she asked for the trouble, Sarah. Girls young like that never think the trouble will find them. And they don't always have a whole lot of choices."

"I know they don't, but still, nothing to be ashamed of being poor."

I wasn't following their conversation very well. So I tried to catch up. "Are you saying this girl married Horace Dillard? That she was Meg Dillard's mother? And Pike's?"

"No. Not saying that," Sam said. "I'm trying to tell you that Horace had his way with this young girl, and then he ran her out of town once she got pregnant."

"It was different back then," Sarah added.

I thought a minute, "Did you say the woman's name was Beatrice?"

"Beatrice was a familiar name back in those days," Sarah said. "They called my mother's sister, Bee."

Things were beginning to make sense to me. "Why would Meg Dillard have taken him in as family without any proof?"

Sam abruptly got up from the table. "Best get those cows in before they trail over and start eatin' posies, and Will Walton calls the police."

Sarah began gathering the dirty plates and cups. Then, she said over her shoulder, "Sam will herd those cows back inside for you, and you'll be able to get by."

But I wasn't leaving. I walked over to the sink and took a dish towel, although I knew she wouldn't like having a guest help clean up. It gave me a reason to stand beside her and ask, "Why was Meg staying at the Hayes's house?"

Sarah's hands were in the dishwater, and she kept her eyes on what she was doing. "I don't think there was but one doctor in Frytown back then. The town was much smaller than it is now. Dr. Hayes, Amanda's father, took care of our family. My mother said he doctored just as many animals as people." She stopped as if thinking back, or maybe she was thinking about how much she wanted to tell. She started washing dishes again. "Horace was hard with his wife and daughters, especially Meg. That's why she was staying with the Hayes family. She stayed there a good deal of the time before the fire. She's…well, she's not right." Sarah's face squeezed for the right word before she shook her head. "I know they call it different today, but they called it retarded back then."

"Mentally challenged," I informed her.

"That's it. It makes it not sound so bad. And it ain't bad. Never was bad. People just didn't understand what was wrong. Today those people can go on living their lives. There's better schooling to help them learn. And I'll tell you that Meg is the nicest person you'll ever want to meet. She wouldn't hurt a hair on a rat's head. Ask anyone."

"Was she staying with the Hayes family the night of the fire? Is that why she survived, and her sisters didn't?"

Sarah rubbed the berry juice off the plates good and hard. Harder than what was needed. "They found Meg in the cornfield with a gun in her hand and gasoline on her nightie. They took her to Dr. Hayes, and he told everyone if she was to be sent off, she'd be drugged up and caged like an animal. They didn't treat people right then. They put them in a room and threw away the key."

"They thought Meg killed her father and set the house on fire?"

"The town was divided. Some said she did, and it wasn't right for her to get away with it, no matter her age."

"You may not think it was right to protect her. It was a crime. A horrible, horrible crime. Some still think she should have gone to a place for people like her or prison. But it seemed like the right thing at the time." I figured her parents must have been on the side of Dr. Hayes. She said, "She couldn't have known what she was doing. It had to have been an accident."

She paused, checked her emotions, and then continued. "The Hayes family took her in and took care of her. The Dillards were rich. There was plenty of money from Horace Sr. to provide for her. We all felt bad about Gertrude and the girls, but there was no bringing them back alive. And here was this young girl. Poor thing."

I heard Pike's voice threaten Dahlia. *You'll be the one who'll be sorry.* Was this his ship? Meg Dillard? If Meg was his half-sister, he might be using her to get back at her for killing his father. Or to get what he thought was his.

"Meg never got into more trouble?" I asked.

"Not a bit."

After the dishes had been finished and put away, I thanked Sarah for the pie and the Dillard story. I told her the pie was the best berry pie I'd ever eaten. Then, I started to leave but stopped. "Sarah?"

She was pouring herself another cup of after-dinner coffee. "Is Charles Kaefring married?" I asked.

She inclined her head, confused maybe by the change of topic. "Why yes. He married Rita Probst, Floyd, and Katherine Probst's daughter."

"Oh."

"Rita's been sick for a long time now. She lives in a home upstate, has for over, what, fifteen years? Poor girl. She became ill in her early twenties."

I wanted to ask what her illness was, but I was afraid of the conversation that might take place. Although Sarah would eventually hear I spent the night with Charles.

If he was married, but his wife was sick and couldn't live together, did that mean he might be looking for someone? If that was true, maybe it was also confirmed he didn't want to lay me off work because of our being together. Perhaps he laid me off because we worked together, but wouldn't he have talked to me first and waited for me to find another job? I would have looked for another job.

Sam had the cows off the road by the time I went outside. I went to the Mustang and got in, becoming wetter inside than I was sloshing through the puddles. I could complain about how my car had been ruined, but it'd been worse. I turned the key. The car coughed and wheezed like it'd come down with a good case of pneumonia.

"Hey-yep, car won't start?" Sam asked. A big brown cow with an innocent white face stood behind him as faithful as a pup. Sam looked inside. "Wires probably got wet. You need to give'r some fuel. Step down on that there gas pedal when you turn the key, and don't let up.

I saw the famous hole in the fence because more cows came back across the ditch and onto the road to join us.

I sure didn't want to be stuck out this far from town all night. I worried if I messed with the car too much, I'd never get it going again. Sam was a farmer, not a mechanic. I considered calling Clarence to see if he could come and get me. Tomorrow I could come back and see to the car. I also thought about calling the gas station at Highway 218 to see if Percy was working. Drunk or sober, he was a good mechanic. But neither of those sounded like a quick fix.

It was still hot and muggy. The sky was darker than the night, with the moon wholly forgotten. Another storm could follow this one.

Sam said, "Push down on the pedal and start her up."

I did as instructed. The car coughed and wheezed. I pumped the gas.

"Don't pump her. Just hold her down."

The car wheezed and wheezed and wheezed, whined, then started shuddering like I was strangling it.

Sam must have seen my lack of confidence. "Hold to'er, Lillian. Don't give up."

The Mustang began to sputter, then purred as good as new. Well, not new. I'm exaggerating that part.

He patted me on the shoulder. "Nothing wrong with it but being a little wet. It'll get you home." He looked at the sky. "Another storm's close." He sniffed. "It's moving south, though. It's done with us for tonight." He gave my shoulder another pat and turned around.

Seeing four of his cows back on the road, he let out a whoop. "Didn't I tell you to get in that there pasture?" He slapped the butt of the one next to him, and it began to retreat, hips moving up and down at a leisurely rate.

It was a few more minutes before all the cows headed back inside the fence. Then, afraid the Mustang might go dead on me again, I took off as soon as the road was clear.

I didn't go straight home. If Sam was wrong and the storm hadn't moved south, I could be straddled again with wet wires. And next time, it might not be easy to get started again. Oaks Manor was within walking distance of the condo. A long walk but doable. Besides, I needed to know what Dahlia knew and what Pike warned that she shouldn't tell anyone. Did she know that he wasn't Meg Dillard's half-brother? What was Pike up to?

Mary Niles greeted me from behind the desk. "Stormed up good, about rattled my teeth loose."

I stretched out my blouse and wrung out a few drops. "Not the best weather for driving a convertible."

"Convertible? You trying to kill yourself?"

"Not tonight." I started to go down to Dahlia's room. "I thought I'd stop by and check on Dahlia."

Mary shook her head. "She wasn't feeling well. So we put her to bed early. We've been run ragged by this flu, and she's probably coming down with a batch."

"I'll just peek in." Even the flu couldn't keep Dahlia down. She never missed a day at work, no matter how sick she was. So I was surprised to find her lying on her side, a blanket pulled over her shoulders.

Her eyes were shut hard, and her face creased. I wished I could say she looked like an angel lying there, but I couldn't. She looked tired. Strained. I decided to let her sleep.

I got home without further incident. Bacardi was starved, so I fed him. The answering machine was blinking red. I figured it must've been a message from Nelly or Marilyn notifying me Dahlia wasn't feeling well. Instead, a voice I didn't recognize came on.

"I hope this is Lillian Dove's number. It's the number she has on her resume. Miss Dove, this is Mrs. Tate, the woman who interviewed you at Hartfield. I was very impressed by our talk and your resume."

I hadn't called Marilyn and told her I'd put her down as a reference or explained how I was slightly exaggerating my experience.

"I would like to offer you the position."

Maybe I was the only one who'd applied. Mrs. Tate had said they were desperate to hire someone."

"It would start at thirty thousand a year, and health benefits begin after thirty days of employment. Hartfield also offers a 401K. So please give me a call by Monday and let me know if you would like to accept my offer. Or if you have any questions, please call. I will be back in the office Monday morning. I think you and I would work well together."

At the sound of thirty thousand, I didn't care why Mrs. Tate was offering me the job. I planned to call her back first thing in the morning.

As I was taking a shower, trying to ward off the chill from the storm, I mulled over the day.

I wanted a full-time job, a career, and was offered one.

I wanted a family. And, I saw something in Dahlia I'd never seen before, vulnerability. She'd threatened Pike to protect me.

And Charles? Was he ready to divorce his wife and start life over again with someone new?

None of what I wanted came to me how I would have ordered it if given a menu and asked, "How would you like that prepared?"

CHAPTER SIX
OVER THE PAST

I wasn't feeling well when I woke up. My forehead was sweaty, and my tongue thick. It was Saturday. With nowhere to be until afternoon, I pulled further down into the bed, worried I might have picked up that nasty ol' flu bug and brought it home.

The phone rang. It continued ringing while the thought squeezed its way in that Dahlia hadn't looked so good when I left her. I got up. By the time I reached the kitchen, the ringing had stopped. The answering light came on. Lieutenant Manville asked me to come down to the station to make a statement.

I made some coffee, and while it was perking, I moved to the couch. Bacardi was lying on it with his front paws stretched straight up, and his back legs elongated. I gave his belly a rub and was about to join him when the phone rang again.

"Hello, Lillian, it's Carol. I just wanted to let you know Burt was released this morning. They dropped the charges. And I want to thank you for helping us out."

"I didn't do anything."

"Oh? I thought you must have told them it wasn't Burt."

"No, but maybe they figured that out for themselves." I told her I was glad everything worked out and asked if the women's club was still holding a sale for them today, not adding that the club may have rethought the idea after the fifty-thousand dollars was presented.

She said excitedly, "Yes, of course. And we'll be there even though I'm busy. Burt wants to be in Des Moines by next week. He has a tip on a job."

"I thought you'd be rebuilding here."

"No. After the show, I tried to give Meg back the check she gave us, saying we couldn't take it. It was too much. We told her we would move once Burt found another job. Burt doesn't want to stay in Frytown. I think he feels let down after being arrested. It'll be hard for him to live around people who believe he could do something like that.

"And you know what Meg said? She said she wishes she'd left. She wants us to have the money. She called it a present. The trust made out the check. It's what the insurance will pay on the house. No one thinks Burt started the fire. It was caused by lightning." She paused and said, "Of course, Edgar wasn't happy. He called me and said the money could only be used to rebuild the house. He wasn't going to charge as much rent as the house would be worth after it was restored and updated." She sniffed. "Like he owned the place. Meg gave us the money as a gift. It's ours to do with as we see fit. Right?" She didn't wait for me to agree. She said, "And you know what else that man had the gall to say. He said he thinks Burt set the fire and should get what's coming to him."

"The fire department found gasoline at the fire," I reminded her. "Lightning could have started the fire."

"Then it was a wire or something. It was an old house. Burt did not set the fire. They wouldn't let him out of jail if they had any proof he did." She hurried to end the conversation and said someone was at the door. She thanked me again and asked me to wish her luck. I did, but I wasn't sure what kind of luck she was asking for.

I went over to the fridge and considered eating something to calm the rumbling in my stomach, but nothing looked appetizing. The thought of eating Strawberry-Kiwi Jell-O made me queasy. This wasn't a good time to be sick. I took out some bread, peanut butter and jam, and made myself a sandwich with the hope my stomach was giving me a bad time because I hadn't eaten much other than Sarah's pie. I downed the sandwich with a glass of milk and then returned to the telephone. I found the number I'd written for Mrs. Tate at the Hatfield.

The phone rang. Damn, how did I get so popular? This time, it was Clarence. "Lillian, I tried to get you earlier. Do you think you could take over the store for me today?"

I hadn't known Clarence ever to take a sick day. "You aren't pretending to be sick to give me more time on the clock, are you?"

He grunted. "Believe me, I wish I were. I've been sicker than a dog."

It didn't sound like he was kidding. I told him to feel better and hung up. I glanced at the time. It was going on noon. Clarence opened the store at ten, on the dot.

I felt better after having eaten. I quickly dressed and fed Bacardi the usual. I rushed out of the condo and almost bumped into Albert. "Hey Albert, I haven't thanked you for coming in and feeding Bacardi."

In his fifties, Albert was rumored to have over nine children. He wore a tool belt at his waist, with several screwdrivers and a hammer. "I should have left a note. I got thinking about the little guy and wasn't sure how soon you'd be home. I hope that wasn't what got you all nerved up the other night, calling the police?"

"No. I must have been shaken up still from the fire."

He nodded. "Something like that can stay with you awhile."

I thanked him again and headed out to the Mustang. It was still wet but started.

Percy Hastings was sitting on the steps at Discount when I drove up. He sat with his head in his hands. What he didn't need was another drink. "You okay, Percy?"

"Could be better." He uncurled his body. I saw the twenty clenched in his hand. "Got a gut ache." He followed me in.

"We don't sell Pepto."

"Hell, I don't need no Pepto. I need something stronger. My father swore two fingers of whiskey would kill whatever was ailing him. And I got somethin' ailing me bad." This answered many unasked questions. It explained Percy's propensity for drinking and that he might be coming down with the flu.

"Flu's going around," I told him, still not so stable on my own feet. I pushed a pint of whiskey across the counter. "Don't know if this can cure that kind of bug."

He took the pint in hand and looked at the label. He may have thought to ask for one a little better than I offered, but instead, he moved over to the refrigerated section and pulled out a couple of six-packs of beer.

Whiskey Sour If I were to think of Percy as a drink, he'd be a: Whiskey Sour. Shake bourbon, juice, and sugar well with cracked ice, then strain into a chilled cocktail glass. I enjoyed mine with a maraschino cherry.

I'd never taken the morning shift before, so I didn't know what to call busy or not busy. Finally, at one o'clock, my Saturday regulars began arriving. Some asked if I'd heard Burt Carter had been released. Most agreed with Carol that he should never have been arrested. One person offered his opinion that Detective Leveque should be fired. I replied, "I tend to agree."

By afternoon, those who'd come from lakeside said the sale was getting a good turnout. One or two mentioned what a good thing it was for Burt and Carol to get some money to get their lives back again. No one referred to the giver of the check as being Meg Dillard. I'm not sure if that was because every person in Frytown was keeping the secret or if most people had more things going on in their lives than remembering a twelve-year-old girl and a tragedy that happened over sixty years ago. Most just wanted to get what they'd come in for.

Customers dried up by late afternoon. By then, I could have used some Pepto myself but sucked on a couple of popsicles instead. Besides dispatch, I had Donna's home number on my cell phone and called to see what she knew about Burt being released. I also wanted to see what she'd tell me about Meg Dillard.

Her answering machine came on. "Busy, Busy, Busy. Leave a message." She was probably helping down at the sale.

I went into the back room, where Clarence kept deliveries. I carried cartons to the front and unpacked what he hadn't gotten to. That done, I cleaned my nails, swept the floor, and Windexed the windows on the inside. The glass was so hot from the outside that it didn't do much good. I counted how many fifths of rum would set on one shelf without the shelf tipping over. There wasn't much to do.

Messing with all the bottles made me thirsty. I pulled out a Pepsi and snapped open the can. I'd read somewhere Coke was initially sold at drug stores to cure hangovers. The original Coca-Cola was created from coca leaves. Yep, the same said leaves that produce cocaine. Drugs aren't something new. The drug stores sold the soda drink big time.

I sat down and took a big sip. My stomach churned—too much sugar. I needed food. Real food.

My thoughts returned to finding Percy on the store's steps. Maybe he'd worried Clarence wasn't going to show. A gut ache wasn't his only reason for needing a drink. You're not looking for the high when you start. You're trying to ease the pain. You're pissed-off life is nothing like what the Brady Bunch promised, and you start telling yourself everyone else got the Brady Bunch lottery, but you won the Addams Family. Your world shuts all the way down to only me.

My world stank. My father drank. My mother hated me. Or worse, she never saw me. My brothers clung to me like leeches in dirty water, wanting to be fed, hugged, put to bed, and offered sweet dreams. Hitching a ride to Davenport at eighteen seemed like my only chance for something better. I could understand why Beatrice had hoped to become a permanent fixture in Horace's life. I under-stood how she couldn't see herself having any other possibilities.

Choices aren't easy to see if you're feeling desperate, especially if you're blind drunk.

Davenport had promised a whole new world. Until after a week of living in Bill Cumingham's Nova, I returned from begging for "spare change," feeling good. I'd made enough for gas, a bottle of Ripple, and some pork sandwiches from Porky's—and found the car gone. I figured he couldn't have gone far. We were out of gas. It was the main reason he'd sent me for change, so we could get a couple dollars' worth of gas and move to Madison or Dubuque. He'd said Davenport was just too damn big, and we should move upriver.

It was one of my winters of discontent. There would be another fifteen.

Denial set in at first, not unlike early frosts before the first snowfall. I told myself Bill must have gone spare-changing, too, although it was a job he said I was better at doing. I tried to convince myself someone heard him playing and recognized his talent. He got a gig in one of the bars. I searched as many as possible, going from bar to bar, using all my spare change. He'd been trying to get a bar to hire him. We'd sit drinking my spare change while he checked out the right band to join. Bill loved his guitar. To him, it was like another woman. It went everywhere with us. Bill's stroking me lessened over time, but he could always sit and stroke that damn guitar for hours. Many of the bartenders already knew me, so my ID was never checked. And most of the bars I began calling "home" were so beyond the road less traveled that only we of the most faithful could find them.

Was I jealous of a guitar? Nah, I never really liked Bill. I mean, I wasn't in love or anything. He was just a way out.

Burt's guitar was the one thing Jim Johns had right. If Burt had been planning to burn down his house, he'd have placed his guitar where it'd be safe.

Five o'clock. Not a customer for over an hour. I still didn't feel right and didn't like going down memory lane. Not my memory lane. I closed the store. Plus, thinking about old times made me thirsty…I mean, hungry.

I'm not sure what I expected down at the lakeside—a few signs, maybe, and some familiar faces helping. Probably ninety percent of the population of Frytown had watched television Friday night, and with what was going on, I guessed a third of them had been glued to the Bobby Bowen show. After seeing the Carters' money, I'd expected most people to stay at home. They'd figure Burt and Carol wouldn't need their help anymore. So I didn't expect to see large yellow signs reading: Help Burt and Carol Get a Leg Back-Up; Show Your Cougar Spirit, Car Wash; and Honk If You Love Burt and Carol.

A group was washing cars, trucks, and SUVs, even though it was getting late in the day. Cheerleaders wearing short-shorts and wet T-shirts were soaping up the vehicles while hunky football players, shorts hanging low on their hips, chests muscled for the new season, managed the hoses.

Even the city brass was out. Wearing an enormous cowboy hat and boots, Councilman Richard Brenner took advantage of the gathered citizenry by moving from one person to another, shaking hands, and kissing babies. Mark, his son, was a twin to his father. Both were wearing some kind of campaign button. I couldn't help but notice the belt buckle on Mark, a large gold one still shiny. Was it the famous steer roping prize buckle?

Out from between two booths, Edgar Pike slithered into view and sidled up to Councilman Brenner. The councilman said something to his son, who moved on a little farther before stopping. Pike pointed in the opposite direction of the car wash, said something, and the councilman nodded. Councilman Brenner soon left and walked to where his son waited. The two matched gaits as they continued. When I looked again for Pike, he'd disappeared.

"Crazy, isn't it?" The voice was close to my ear. Leveque cozied up next to me. He smelled freshly showered. I stepped away, not enjoying his nearness or ability to invade my space without any alarms warning me.

He was dressed in jeans and a button-down shirt showing dark curls on his chest. I ignored him. But my ignoring him didn't stop him. He said, "There was this time in Central Park. It was a busy summer day, not much different than today. It gets hot in New York, too." He said it as if New York were a foreign country people in Iowa never experienced. Of course, I'd never been to New York, but he didn't know that. He continued. "People were out listening to music. Shopping. Then a gun was shot—just one shot, not two. Everyone panicked. People started shoving one another to get out of the line of fire, even though none of them knew where the shot was coming from or who was doing the shooting. A woman got knocked down and trampled to death. Several injured."

I turned to him. "What's your point?"

He smiled, his white orthodontist-straight teethed smile. Yes, he was good-looking. He may even be called handsome if you like the type. Men like Leveque are like eating a chocolate bar with a creamy smooth caramel center. Can't stop at one bite. Have to eat the whole damn bar. Next thing you know, you've got a cavity. And it hurts like hell.

"It means people react before they have the entire picture. They don't take the time to access what's there. I think folks around here might say, "Not everything is how it appears."

"Look, back off," I said. "You're not fooling anyone so that you can quit your little game. You may think you're better than the next person, but you're not. And I'm not interested."

He didn't appear impacted by my rage. His dimples popped. "Watch them." He pointed to the people walking by the booths across from us. "Everyone here appears like they're helping one another, being a good neighbor. But really, aren't they here so no one can say they weren't a good neighbor?"

He moved closer. "I saw you the other night on television. They say TV adds five pounds, but I'm here to tell you that those pounds went to all the right places."

I shuddered with disgust. I should have walked off but doing that meant he was affecting me, and I didn't want to give him the satisfaction.

His voice came so close his breath moved across my ear. "The Carters got fifty thousand dollars. Do you think any of these people have seen that much money in one lump sum? So, tell me, why are they here? Not to help the Carters."

He had a point. It was the same question I'd been asking myself.

"They want their fifteen minutes of fame, and they want to see if Burt will show up. Burt Carter set that house on fire. I'm going to prove it."

I whipped around. "Are you here to make your five minutes of fame? Why are you here, Leveque? Burt was released. You arrested the wrong person. Do you think he's guilty because there was an empty can of gas at their campsite? Because insurance money was given to his family? You have no motive. And you're not a local. If you stopped any of these folks, they'd tell you that you're wrong. They've known Burt Carter all their lives. He's not a criminal. You're mistaken."

The celebrity smile faded. His dimples filled. His fingers went to his mustache, dark, trimmed over swollen pink lips—eyes soft brown. "If you're right and I'm wrong, I'll come and put security on your place so you won't have to bother the police next time you get a little spooked. Did Burt Carter know Meg Dillard would give him the fifty big ones? There's a motive. And if I were given that kind of money and weren't guilty, I sure wouldn't be taking a hike out of town. When folks here learn he set the fire for the money and then took some of theirs with him, he'd better run, or he'll be tar and feathered. Good neighbors? People you know, friends, will turn on you faster than any stranger."

"Your point doesn't add up, Leveque. Carol was shocked to get the money, and Meg knows the Carters are leaving Frytown."

Nothing. No reaction. Not a tick or twitch or ease of stance.

He asked, "Where did you get your information? From Carol Carter?"

Ohhhhhhh…he is such a jerk.

"Sit back and learn, baby." He continued. "I watched the show, too. I grant you that Carol Carter looked pretty surprised. But then, your jaw dropped open when Meg Dillard came on the program. Maybe Burt didn't let Carol in on his plan." He paused, scratching his head. "I wonder, why is it your boyfriend never told you about Meg Dillard? No pillow talk?"

I broke away, moving quickly in and out and around the people on the sidewalk. I could hear him laughing. I'd show him. He'd better get his toolbox out.

But when I slowed down to a normal pace, my irritation simmered. I had to admit that he might be right. Burt was still the only person who had a good reason to burn down his house. He could have known about the insurance money, and he could have talked Meg into giving it to him. Carol called me this morning to thank me. But she had to have known I didn't tell the police anything to get Burt released. I publicly stated that I couldn't physically identify the person at the fire. Did she call me just to plant the idea Meg wasn't upset about them leaving? But why would she call me? Unless she thought what she told me would get back to Charles. And Charles didn't mention Meg Dillard surviving the fire. Neither did Clarence or Amanda. Why? Were they still trying to protect her? Was she not as frail as she seemed? After all, she was younger than Dahlia. Could she have set the fire?

I hated Leveque. I hated how he thought he was right.

Donna. I spotted her sitting at a table marked Bake Sale. She waved me over as soon as she noticed me. "Hi, hon. Can you believe this turnout?"

"Did you know Burt Carter's been released?"

She nodded enthusiastically. "I told you, didn't I? Burt couldn't have had a hand in burning down his own house. It's like Jim Johns said when I spoke to him, Burt would have taken his guitar."

I reminded her. "You did say Burt couldn't buy the kind of evidence Leveque had. Weren't you hinting that Burt might have had insurance on the house? Did you know Meg Dillard did and that she might give it to Burt?"

She looked confused. "Did I? No, darlin'. I was trying to tell you what Jim Johns said. His guitar was his insurance. You can't buy talent like Burt's. Have you ever heard him play?" She pushed a small sack of brownies towards me. "Double chocolate, only two dollars."

I didn't notice the two girls who had walked up to the table. One was saying, "He always has car trouble. Don't you get it?" They were wet, probably from washing cars.

I moved over so Donna could do her bake sale thing.

"Hungry, girls?" she said. "Annie Roth, you're drenched."

The girl was in cutoffs, threads hanging around her thighs, and a wet tank top displaying perky breasts. She was also wearing a button reading BRENNER'S WESTERN MUSEUM. She was Annie, Melvin Roth's daughter.

"I'll have those brownies," Annie said, pointing.

Donna gave her a scrutinizing look. "Aren't they bad for that waist of yours?"

It was a waist I was sure Donna hadn't seen in her lifetime but envied, thinking thin girls were happy girls, like the saying, *Blondes have more fun.* Go to any bar. You'll see a whole row of blondes living the good life.

"She's not buying them for herself," the girl next to Annie said. She was wearing workout pants, also wet, offering a camel toe. Both girls had been playing mischief with the boys. "She's getting them for Darrell."

"Darrell Carter?"

Annie shyly nodded.

"Darrell's a nice boy." Donna packaged the brownies, handling them carefully. "He's lucky to be getting these brownies. I tasted one. They're delicious. They're made with chocolate syrup."

I glanced over at the car wash, looking for Darrell Carter. My answer came from Annie. "He's working at Hy-Vee today. I thought I'd take him something."

"He's always working," the other girl stated. "Why do you have a boyfriend that never takes you out on a date? And that broken-down car of his, geez." She wrinkled her nose in distaste.

"He's the captain of the football team," Annie said.

"Was," the girl emphasized. "He quit, remember?"

"Well, he had to." Annie shot back. "He's got to work. That's why we don't go out as much. His parents are moving to Des Moines, but he will stay here. He and I are going to UI next year."

The camel-toe girl whipped her hair over her shoulder and hunted for split ends while talking. "I bet he's not going to get to stay. Would your mom and dad let you stay here while they lived elsewhere when you're not even out of high school? And if you think you're one of his goals, Annie, you're fooling yourself. I was at the Hy-Vee this morning, and I saw Cindi Whit bending over his checkout counter, giving him a good peek-a-boo at her big boobs. He didn't look like he was thinking about you or your goals. He's all famous since the fire."

"Shut up. You're just mad because Alex dumped you."

"He didn't dump me. I dumped him."

"Whatever." Annie handed Donna a couple of dollar bills. Donna gave her the bag of brownies as Annie said to Donna, "Darrell has his future all planned out. He's going to UI, will become a great writer, and we're going to live somewhere like New York or maybe California. Nothing's going to stop him. You wait and see. He'll do it. I'm going to help him."

After they had moved off, Donna said, "I wonder if Melvin knows she's prancing around looking like that?"

"Do you think Burt and Carol will let Darrell stay here on his own?"

Donna shook her head. "Carol's kept those boys close to home. Both good boys. And the family's close. They don't do much if they don't do it as a family. But you can't trust a teenager. If he turns eighteen and has his mindset, he will stay here. It's why I never wanted kids. Except for Sugar, of course." Sugar was her dog. "You always have to stay one step ahead of them."

I didn't know about ordinary families and typical kids. But all the decisions I made when I was a teen came from feelings of desperation, emancipation, alcohol depletion, and sexual stimulation. So my family stayed a safe distance from one another.

Suddenly I began to feel strangled. My chest was tight. *Think forward, not back,* Cressie would caution me whenever my head started replaying family life at the Dove house. The hidden pain began ballooning to where I felt I'd burst and disappear if I didn't do something immediately.

"You all right, Lillian?"

I took a breath. Swallowed. My throat was dry. Licked my lips. I needed to change the topic. "Councilman Brenner must be getting closer to having his museum?"

"The man's always cutting deals. He's like a snake in the grass. You don't hear his rattle, and it strikes before you see it." Her hands continued to fondle the baked goods, putting them in an orderly arrangement. "If I know Richard Brenner, and I do, he'll get what he wants. Some say that's what makes him a good councilman." She glanced around. "Those who are saying it, of course, are probably those whose pockets he's in."

What about the money the Carters got? Could Burt have known Meg Dillard would give it to him?"

She shrugged. "I don't think so. If he asked and she said she would, he was a fool to believe her. The decision isn't really Meg's." She selected a baggie and lifted it to get a good look. "That woman's sweet innocent. She'd hand it over to you if you asked her to give you the only meal left on earth. She loves those boys. They call her Aunt Meg. She spoiled them rotten when they were kids. She won't like seeing them leave." She opened the baggie and extracted two melting chocolate chip cookies. She handed one to me. I took it just to let the eating thing drop.

She took a bite of hers, and gooey chocolate dripped off her bottom lip. "Yummy," she cooed. "I'm off my diet today." She licked the chocolate off her lip. "Carol came by and told me she's busier than a squirrel. She resigned. She said Maurice Thompson, principal at the elementary school, wasn't happy getting the late notice. So she and Burt are leaving next Friday." Donna took another bite. My cookie was warming in my hand. "She said Burt's got a good tip on a job. This money we're making will help them get started again, along with Meg's money. That was nice of Meg. Well, actually, Amanda. She holds the signature on the trust."

"Meg Dillard seems to have been a big secret in town."

She chewed slowly. "Not such a big secret. I can't say I've been around her a lot, but I knew about her." She gave me a strange look. "All you had to do was ask."

She was right. I hadn't asked. "Okay, so what do you know about Edgar Pike?"

"I can't say I've had the pleasure of meeting him. Some people say he's her half-brother. Guess he's a good guy, or Amanda Keiff would have sent him down the road a long time ago."

I noted that comment, again wondering why Amanda hadn't mentioned Meg when telling me the Dillard story. I took a huge bite of my cookie, thinking about what next to ask.

"Lillian. Nice to see you." I whirled around and saw Charles standing beside the table with a woman I'd never seen before. She was tall like him and slender. He was in uniform, and he had his arm around the woman's shoulder.

I couldn't talk. I looked to Donna and made a silent plea, *Some help, here, please*.

Charles said to the woman, "Maxine, I'd like you to meet Lillian Dove. She's the one I told you about."

"You told her about me?"

"A little bit." He turned slightly red.

"Swell." Addressing the woman, I said, "Well, he didn't tell me anything about you. Not a word."

I took off with my dignity flaring, outrage in my step, and my reputation tarnished.

Leveque stepped into my path and grabbed my arm. "Hey, where are you going?"

I snapped my arm out of his hand and turned around. Charles was watching me. So was the woman beside him. I twisted back again. I put both hands alongside Leveque's face, pulled him to me, pasted my lips onto his, and gave it the best I had. I even coiled my leg around one of his.

He tasted of chocolate chip cookies and Juicy Fruit gum. Not a bad combination. When I went to pull away, his hand came to the small of my back, brought me further into him, and *he* kissed *me* this time. When he *finally* let me go, my head spun, and my toes tingled.

I glanced back toward the bake sale table. Charles and his wife were gone. Donna was staring at Leveque and me, biting and chewing cookies so fast that it was a surprise she didn't choke.

"Get off me." I pushed Leveque away. "Don't you ever, *ever* touch me again."

"Maxine." I got into the Mustang repeating her name. "Maxine? Maxi? Max?" And then it hit me. Clarence had said Charles's wife was Rita.

I twisted the key in the ignition so hard that the Mustang had no choice but to start. Rita, for God's sake, the name sounded nothing like Maxine. How could I have been so stupid? Who the hell was she? Another girlfriend? Someone else who had been out to the farm?

And what had I done?

I rubbed Leveque off my lips.

When will I ever stop being such an idiot?

I was angry enough at myself to take on Dahlia, so I headed to Oaks Manor. I checked the parking lot and curbs before going in—no old green cars in sight. Pike wasn't visiting. Too bad. I felt like taking him down, too. And he'd better not make another visit, or he'd have me to deal with.

I was hot, I tell you.

I threw open the door to Oaks Manor. I ignored Nelly at the counter, smiling at me and ready for a chat, and went straight to Dahlia's room. I would make her tell me why Pike had been threatening her and what she knew about Beatrice.

The room reeked of vomit.

"Dahlia, are you sick?"

She opened her eyes a slit, saw who it was, and shut them again. She said something, but I couldn't hear her. I leaned over.

In a flash, I saw her leaning over me. I was sick, so sick I wanted to die. I was fourteen. I'd been puking most of the night, and when Dahlia came into my room and asked what was wrong with me, I told her I had the flu. But, of course, it wasn't the flu. Instead, I'd drunk a bottle of cherry vodka all by myself. The bucket I'd put by the bed offered the evidence of pink vomit and the leftovers from a pepperoni pizza.

She didn't yell at me. She didn't say something like, "Don't lie to me. You ain't got the flu." Instead, she left and came back with a cold washcloth. She wiped my face and then placed it on my forehead. She said, "The key to life, Lillian, is admitting you can't always get your way." She took out the bucket and brought it back clean. She never said another word about the incident.

The key to life?

My anger softened. "Dahlia? Don't you feel well?" She mumbled again. She was wearing the small cross necklace I had given her one Christmas. I'd almost forgotten it existed. I bent so far over that my cheek almost touched her lips.

"Mind your own business."

What the hell? "Mind my own business?" I erupted. "Did you know Pike was Horace Dillard's son? Do you know something about the Carter house fire? Is that why he was threatening you?" I was pacing, my hands flying. "Mind my own business? Want to or not, you've become my business."

I must have been loud, for Nelly came running into the room. "Lillian, what's wrong?"

Dahlia began vomiting. Nelly shoved past me.

I ran. I ran down the corridor, across the lobby, and through the entrance doors. The heat outside after the cooler building made me that much angrier. I kicked the Mustang's tires. I grabbed hold of the car top and wrenched it loose and up. I would have kicked it open if duct-taping the plastic back window hadn't been such a bitch.

Damn car. Damn Dahlia. Damn Charles. Damn Leveque. Damn, damn, damn. I dared the air conditioning not to work. It took my dare, blowing out tepid air.

My cell phone rang. It was Oaks Manor. I wasn't willing to listen to Nelly's maternal wisdom. *God gave me her to work on patience.* And I didn't feel like someone asking if I was all right. No, I *wasn't* all right. Anyone could see that. I put the Mustang into gear and headed out.

I let the act of driving vent unspeakable fury. I began to howl, scream and bang on the steering wheel. I continued until I couldn't stand all of the pain anymore.

I pulled off the road and started blubbering like a little kid. Snot ran into my mouth, and tears dripped off my face. When I noticed the chocolate stain yet again on another blouse, right on the imprint of a very erect nipple, I laughed until my ribs ached and my stomach burned. I saw the keys for Discount in the cup holder in the console. I thought Clarence wouldn't notice a pint gone. He'd count it as an inventory error. It'd be so easy. Nobody would know.

You would know.

I pulled back on the road and headed out of town, unsure where I was going.

Absolut Stress: Equal shots of vodka, dark rum, peach schnapps, orange juice, and cranberry juice. Shake well and pour.

My cell phone rang. The caller ID read Oaks Manor. I ignored the call. I still didn't want to talk about Dahlia. I was done thinking and talking about Dahlia.

"Letting you go, Dahlia," I yelled at the phone.

Guilt stabbed my heart. I shut my mind off to it by telling myself she was okay. I never saw Dahlia take a sip of alcohol. She didn't allow my father to bring any inside the house. She had no weaknesses.

When you drive back roads, you can't have your mind on things other than driving. You must watch for oncoming traffic. Watch that a deer doesn't jump out to cross the road. You need to keep track of whether or not you've got your high beams on when a car passes.

Maybe I unconsciously knew I was driving to Charles's farm. Or perhaps I was very conscious of that fact because my foot eased coming to the driveway. The floodlight on the security pole lit the house and grounds. I shut off my headlights and let the car roll to where I could get a good, long look without being noticed. A strange car was parked over by a big tree. Two figures moved inside the screened porch. It was warm, not too humid, a good evening for rocking in the two large, antique rockers. Comfy.

Who was Maxine? What kind of name was that? Was she staying the night? Would he try to use the weather as an excuse? But there weren't any storms. Not tonight. Not a meteorological one anyway.

Or maybe Charles didn't need to come up with an explanation with her. He'd had his arm around Maxine's shoulder, easy-like. I'd thought, *He's done this before. I bet he'd brought lots of women to the farm.* Did his wife know about them? Seemingly the town did because he led Maxine around like arm candy.

Was I now one of Frytown's secrets? The thought unnerved me. Keeping secrets was a sick compulsion. One decadent act could open a whole bottle of other troubles until you are buried in denigration. Your cup runneth over in phony pleasure. My list could grow longer.

When I'd bumped into Charles at Louise's, Beulah, the restaurant's owner, asked Charles if he wanted his table. I didn't think of it as that big a deal at the time, but thinking back now, Beulah and Charles had always exchanged a knowing smile. *Your* table. I should have known.

I put the car in reverse and slipped back on the road. I drove a few hundred feet before putting on the headlights. I didn't go back to the condo. Instead, I replayed Sunday morning, turned between the cornfields, and drove down dried ruts to the Carters' burned house. No, not the Carters'. I now knew it was Meg Dillard's house.

I parked in front of an ash-riddled burned square where the house once stood. What remained was pushed into a heap of charred wood and blackened dirt.

I shut my eyes and envisioned the house, black smoke, flames tonguing from windows. I opened the car door, got out, and took a deep breath. A faint hint of ruin remained. Forcing my memory back, I again felt the heat. I saw the flying cinders. I smelled the acrid destruction of wood, furniture, and memories. I looked to where the window had been and saw the face. Quick, but I was sure now it was a man's face. Not the soft features of a woman.

It was not a ghost.

The wind picked up. I watched small whirlwinds of ash form and move like a spontaneous ballet. I didn't think of life as linear. I always thought of it as more circular. Like the Bible says, the sins of the father are inherited by his children. I was like my father, and I was living his life. But I didn't want to end up like him, dying of a pickled liver. I chose recovery instead. Watching the whirlwinds, I continued to think about life. What had the Dillard children inherited? Meg? She was the only one to survive unless Pike could also be counted. I remembered his mother, Beatrice, as being a nice woman. Pike seemed malicious. *Mean as Horace Dillard.* Pike met that legacy. The Carter children? Were they like their parents? Burt was a nice guy. Carol was a good teacher. The boys weren't known to be trouble.

Maybe life wasn't linear or circular but a mass of random events. Bill and I could have gone to Dubuque instead of Davenport. If we had, I would have never met Cressie. Or, if I'd still have met someone like her, maybe I would have gone with that person to a meeting. And if I hadn't met Cressie, maybe her sobriety would have held. Perhaps it didn't matter what we wanted or chose. In fact, I was beginning to think there was no choice. It's a roll of the dice, baby. And I kept winning crap.

The whirlwinds formed and fell, moved together to make one, and separated again. They picked up ash and left it in random spots.

I got to thinking that maybe life flows like these whirlwinds. The universe pulls you in, and you get tossed out if you understand your choices. But if you don't choose and only go along on whim or feeling, pleasure or fear, you stay in the whirlwind. Horace Sr. got his wealth from greed and death. Horace Jr. inherited his father's money, and he was mean. If Pike believed Horace was his biological father, then the whirlwind was gaining strength because Pike was both mean and greedy.

If Pike knew about the insurance money, he may have set the fire, thinking arson wouldn't be suspected, and he could talk Meg into giving the money to him. Or, if he heard Burt ask for cash from Meg, Pike may have set the house on fire to get rid of the Carters. Could he be that mean? Neither made sense to what happened. I knew I was grabbing for answers. Because if Pike knew about Meg's money, he had to know Meg couldn't make any decisions. Donna said the decision wasn't Meg's, and she'd mentioned how Pike must not be too bad because Amanda hadn't chased him down the road.

I wasn't sure all this thinking was helping me. I turned away from the whirlwinds, looked out over the corn, and saw lights twinkling beyond the cornfield. I hadn't noticed lights on Sunday. I hadn't seen another structure other than the tool sheds. Nor did I remember seeing any other car coming off the road. But now I remembered Charles telling Chief Simms the police had evacuated the other place. And I remembered Meg telling Bobby Bowen she lived close to her father's old house.

I got in the car and slowly retraced the route to Rohert Road. Finally, I found a slight separation in the cornfield, more like a tractor path but big enough for a car. I took it, and it ended in a clearing. Cornfields gated both sides of the road, fading away into the distance as if having no end. A small scraggly stand of woods curled where the road seemed to stop. And in the middle was a single-story house, old, sad, gray, possibly a worker's home from the old Dillard days.

Was this where Meg Dillard lived? No cars were parked out, but two rooms were dimly lit.

It was hard to imagine how a young, twelve-year-old girl shot her father and then set the house on fire. And why had her mother and sisters stayed in a room upstairs? Unless Gertrude Dillard had heard a shot and, being a protective mother, gone in to make sure her daughters were safe.

Pike lived in New Liberty then, nearly an hour away. He said he had dated Dahlia in high school. I knew my grandparents had been pretty strict. They wouldn't let Dahlia date until she was eighteen. She set sixteen as a rule for me. Of course, a young boy raised by a single mother would have been curious about his birth father. Had Beatrice told him about Horace Dillard?

Did Dahlia know Pike was related to the Dillard family? Beatrice might have told him. Did he have something to do with the first fire? The murder of Horace Dillard Jr.? It didn't take much to imagine he could be responsible for the second.

I thought about how Pike looked when he saw Meg Dillard hand Carol the fifty-thousand-dollar check. *Ship comin' in.* Nelly said every time the fire was mentioned, Dahlia became agitated. Nelly thought Dahlia was worried about me. But Dahlia had never worried about us kids unless we were doing something to cause her a pack of trouble. *Don't have time to run after you all the time.*

It could have been Pike I saw in the window. He would be about the right size and shape. The more I thought about it, the surer I became. I squeezed my memory, trying to match what I saw compared to the slouched way he had of standing.

I drove back down the dirt road, between the cornfields, out to Rohert. I was feeling pretty good. If I'd have found Sam Roe's cows out again, I don't think it would have bothered me. But instead, I felt good that I may have been successful at figuring out who'd started the Carter fire and why.

I spotted the green car as soon as I turned onto my street. Lights out. It was parked between two other vehicles. Someone was sitting in the driver's seat.

I parked my car in the lot off the side street. By the time I got back to the front, the car was gone.

The answering machine light was flashing red. Two messages. One was Clarence saying he was still sick and asking if I could handle the store again. "With the way I feel tonight, Lillian, you may have to take the whole week. I'm plum knocked off my feet." Again, I wasn't sure if he was sick or trying to help me out. The second message was from Nelly. I was just about to push the delete button when I heard the word, *hospital*.

"She's become dehydrated. The doctor said with her heart condition, we'd better bring her right in—nothing to worry about. No emergency. We've had several residents go to the hospital this last week. This pesky flu won't let up."

If Nelly wasn't worried, there probably was nothing to worry about. Nelly wasn't one of those who got dramatic to take the spotlight or hear her own voice. So, I didn't think I needed to go to the hospital to check. I'd call the hospital later. Besides, hadn't Dahlia told me to mind my own business?

I fed Bacardi, then double-checked to ensure the front door was locked and the sliding doors barricaded. Finally, I showered and got into bed. I was exhausted. What a day. It felt good that I may have figured out Burt hadn't set the fire, but I would need proof if Leveque still came after him. And still, something was bothering me. Something I couldn't put my finger on.

How did Pike know about the money? He could have seen the insurance policy if he'd been snooping in Meg's house. Would Amanda have let her keep documents? He could have heard Burt ask Meg for the money. But why did Pike think he deserved it? And why had he moved to Frytown in the first place? Did he have proof he was Horace Jr.'s son? Or had Meg, in her innocence, accepted him as her brother without evidence? Again, I could hear Donna say, *Guess he's a good guy, or Amanda Keiff would have sent him down the road long ago.*

If Donna could have seen Pike with Dahlia at Oaks Manor, she'd know he wasn't a good guy. But what did Dahlia know that threatened him? And why had he parked outside my condo? Did he think I'd been told something? Had he broken into my condo the night I thought someone was hiding in the bathroom? Had he come in to threaten me?

There were too many questions unanswered. I hadn't figured out anything.

I needed to visit Dahlia and talk to her, but it'd have to wait. My days would be pretty full since I'd be working at Discount full-time. But, sick or not, I was grateful to Clarence.

I thought back to the call from Hartfield Center for the Elderly offering me a job. I wasn't aware I was being interviewed when the woman at the desk asked me questions. Should I take the job? Should I move to Iowa City?

Bacardi jumped onto the bed and sat cleaning his face and paws. "What do you think, Bacardi? It'd mean a whole lot more Feline Delight." I grabbed for him, wanting a hug, feeling insecure. Instead, he jumped away and off the bed. He scurried out of the room.

My insecurity continued as my bedfellow and Charles came into my mind. *She's the one I told you about.* Why would he introduce me to someone else he was dating? Why would he have told her *anything* about me?

Out of respect for the community, Clarence never opened Discount until after church services. So I got to the store by noon, on the dot. Within minutes, the bell jingled a chorus of customers. Some were still in their Sunday best. I didn't usually work on Sundays. Clarence often covered the entire shift, so most people were curious why I was there and not Clarence. Once I mentioned he was down with the flu, they all wanted to tell me their flu stories.

When I got a break, I gave Donna a call. First, she wanted to know why I was at the store. It's not every day I get ahead of Donna. She then proceeded to fill me in on the commotion down at the lakeside.

Two guys and only one camping spot had created a fistfight. "Too many beers and too much sun don't always make for a whole lot of fun," she sang. Next, she told me about Carl Sand being arrested for battery. "Course he was drunk as a skunk. So was Paula. They both go at each other after a few beers. I don't know what keeps them living in the same house. And hon, did you hear Abbie Scribner reported a violation of her stay-the-heck-away-from-me –order? They caught Corte hiding in her bushes again."

Donna had told me that after Abbie Scribner's divorce, she had garnered the interest of Corte Braught, a seventy-year-old who'd been peep-in-tomming around Frytown for years. Abbie got a protective order. Her ex-husband was a lawyer. So Corte wasn't allowed within five hundred feet of her house. According to the law.

"I think the court order got him going that much more," I told Donna.

"I don't blame her. I wouldn't want a woody old man lookin' in my window, either. Only, I don't think Corte's got any wood left." She waited while I laughed, then said, "It's this damn weather. It's muggy, and not a cloud in the sky. You can feel another storm coming. Weather like this will set anyone on edge."

She mentioned how she would spend the afternoon helping Carol get ready to move. "We did well at the sale. We made over two thousand dollars."

But I heard the bell jingle. "Someone's come in." I asked her about Meg's financial situation and Amanda's legal responsibility to Meg. I wanted to know if Meg needed Amanda's permission to give the money to Carol Carter. If not, then Burt or Carol may have asked for it after Burt set the fire.

Still, that didn't prove he set it.

After hanging up the phone, I stayed for a moment longer, letting any and all scenarios play themselves. If Meg didn't need Amanda's permission, it didn't explain why Meg would have given him the money before the investigation into the fire was completed unless she genuinely thought of the money as a present. Was Meg Dillard a rich woman? Could Horace Sr.'s money have lasted this long?

There was also another way the fire could have been started and the Carter family given the money. They may have known Meg set the fire. She seemed frail, but she could get around with her walker. Did a twelve-year-old girl sneak out of the Hayes's house, walk the mile or two back home, start a fire in her family's house, and repeat the same act sixty-five years later? Could she have killed her father? Was Amanda paying Burt and Carol to keep Meg's crime secret again? Were there other secrets she was paying to keep quiet that Meg may have been responsible for?

That still didn't explain about Pike. He was involved in this somehow. I was sure of it.

When I walked into the store to help the newest customer, I found Edgar Pike at the counter. Percy stood beside him, and they were four sheets to the wind in full sail, wearing campaign buttons for BRENNER's WESTERN MUSEUM. The councilman must have been paying for rounds at one of the local bars.

I said, "Hey, Percy, how you feelin'? Did the whiskey help?"

Percy grinned big. "It'll kill anything, probably even me one day."

Pike had a hungry look on his face, like a dog that hadn't eaten for a very long time. His jaw was moving, tongue darting in and out across his lips. "Lillllllllllian. You look better every time I see you."

Again, I spoke to Percy. "Scraping the bottom of the friends' pile, aren't you, Percy?"

Pike's head snapped. "That mouth of yours needs a good soap scrubbing. It looks like Dahlia didn't teach you good manners."

I returned, "What about you, Pike? What did your mother teach you?"

Percy was looking between Pike and me as if watching a tennis match. I gambled, "Did she teach you to lie to an innocent woman about being her half-brother?" I let that sink in a second, then guessed big, "You looked pretty upset when Meg gave Carol that money last Friday night. You didn't know about it, did you? Did you think you'd get the money?"

Pike lowered his head, peeking up at me as if he was inside a protective shell. "What are you jawing about?"

"Burt had nothing to do with the fire. And while there's a story that says Meg once set her family home on fire, she couldn't have set this one. I'm an eyewitness, remember? It was a man, not a woman. I'm sure of it." *Or pretty sure.* "I don't know why you'd do it, but I'll let the police figure out how and why. I saw you in that window. You set the Carter house fire."

I'd been thinking out loud and guessing big. Something told me Pike wasn't innocent of anything that had been happening. What Dahlia knew had to be related to the fire. My guess paid off because Pike stared straight at me as if I'd hit the mark.

Percy spoke up, his body twitching. "What're you saying? Pike here wouldn't do anything like that? Burt was let out of jail, didn't you hear? The fire was an accident."

I focused on what was coming around in my mind. What could have been Pike's biggest mistake?

"You let your mouth run too much. You told Dahlia. Didn't you think she would tell me all about your ship coming in? Did you think she'd keep what you'd done a secret?" He flinched, and his eyes moved away from mine. I went on, still gambling. "Your boat's sunk. The Carters got the money, and once the police get back the forensics and I tell them it was you I saw, you'll need to brush up on your manners. I bet prison requires a lot of please and thank yous."

Gambling can become addictive. But I was throwing craps now like a pro.

A shadow fell across Pike's face as a black cloud falls across an already dying day. "You'd best be careful, girlie. I took care of Dahlia. I'd hate to have to take care of you, too." His hands formed into fists. His shoulders hunched.

I should have stopped, but I was high on adrenaline. Small jackpots were paying off, and the big prize was coming around. I could feel it. Hell, it was standing right in front of me—one more twenty. Come to mama. Baby needs diapers.

Percy didn't like the charged atmosphere. "Hey, Edgar's a good guy." He slapped Edgar on the back.

Edgar shook him away. "Get your hands off me."

Every gambler says they shouldn't before reaching for their last twenty. Like every drinker says, *This will be the last one before I hit the road*. I never stopped at the last one, and I couldn't stop now. I had Pike in front of me, and I didn't know whether I'd get the same chance again.

I wanted to be right so bad.

Pike was strong in his ability to feed off other people's weaknesses. He had been one of my dad's drinking buddies. Now he was Percy's. Somehow, he got Meg to believe he was related to her. And he was involved with Councilman Brenner. It all tied together if I kept stringing.

"Sharing a bottle is no different from sharing a cup with the devil, Percy." I reached around and picked up a pint of Jack Daniels. One of the best. I passed it to Percy. "If you need a drink that bad, I'll give it to you, free of charge."

Pike grinned. "Your daddy wasn't one to be choosy."

The comment stung. He was the thrower now. "Since you and your mama got to sharing, did she also tell you how she and I would run off together?" He turned to Percy. "I tell you, her mother was so into me, I couldn't get out." He laughed, cruel and dark. There was a heat coming off him now. Musky, sour.

"You shouldn't be talking about her mother like that, Edgar. It's not right." Percy's fingers quivered. They wanted to touch the bottle.

"Don't you be telling me how to talk." Pike glared at him before twisting back to me. "This girl knows a thing or two. She's been around. Hell, from the way I heard it, you could get your dick off by buying her a single glass of malt."

I tasted blood from biting down on the inside of my cheek. I slid the bottle a little closer. "Go on, Percy. My treat."

I didn't want Percy around Pike. The Percys of the world need saving from men like Pike. Unfortunately, they aren't strong enough to see the evil beyond the buddy slapping. They don't realize they're tapping glass salutes with someone who'll use them, then toss them off to more ruin and unhappiness.

"What the hell?" Percy asked Pike, not sure what to do. He licked his lips.

"Take it and get out," Pike growled.

I could tell Percy wanted to split, but he stood looking at the two of us. He needed me to give him the okay. I gave him a nod, and he said, "Thanks, Lillian. Just put it on my tab." Like Percy had a tab. He took the bottle and let the door jingle behind him.

I'd won if Percy was what Pike and I had been fighting over. But I think I'd lost sight of what was truly at stake.

Pike flattened his hands on the counter, looking like a rattlesnake wound uptight. I realized I'd rattled him too much and regretted cutting Percy out of the threesome. I wished I could take back telling Pike I'd seen him in the window at the Carter house. Unfortunately, my gambling may have hit on more of the truth than I could handle by myself.

I glanced out at the parking lot, hoping to see another car drive in. Unfortunately, I didn't see Percy.

I knew Clarence had a gun hidden beneath the cash register. He took me out of town after the store closed one summer evening and taught me how to use it. We shot at empty liquor bottles. "Just in case," he'd said. "A girl should know how to shoot." He'd mentioned how the world was changing. The crime was rising, even in towns like Frytown. I told him I would never feel comfortable shooting at a person.

But I shifted slowly over towards the cash register. Pike shadowed me. The energy between us was so charged that lightning could have struck at any minute.

"You've hurled your hash one too many times," he said, eyes narrowed to slits, bloated face blackened. "Stay out of my way, or I'll burn you down. You hear me, missy?" Then he made a motion that caused me to think he was coming at me.

I leaped back and pulled the gun from its hiding place. I lost my grip and fumbled it. The gun fell to the floor. Before I could get to it, Pike hit his fist on the counter. "Tend to your own, or you'll need tending yourself."

I stood still, not knowing whether I could get to the gun before Pike got to me.

He sneered. "A gun's not going to help you. If you're going to kill a man, you got to know how to *handle* a gun."

He whipped around and started towards the door, saying, "There are two ways to skin a cat. From the tail up or the head down. It's not the direction that matters. It's the fur. I've taken care of the head." He stopped. Hot air came in from outside, triggering the air conditioning. "The tail's even easier. No one's stopping me from getting what's mine. Not Dahlia. And especially not you."

When he left, the room seemed to lighten, as if the darkness he carried was heavier than the lights overhead and the sunlight coming in through the windows. I didn't realize I'd been holding my breath. When I did breathe, a shudder passed through me—*stopping me from getting what's mine.* Was he talking about the money Meg gave Burt and Carol? Or something more? Whatever it was, he sounded as if he would attack every ship until he found the one he'd waited a lifetime to board.

I thought about calling Charles and telling him what Pike had said. But would Charles believe me? I had no evidence. Pike hadn't confessed he'd burned down the Carter house. The security camera on Discount's wall would only show Pike and Percy coming into the store. Percy got a pint and left. Pike stayed. And while it'd looked like he was going to leap over the counter at me, when I thought back, I realized he'd barely moved. My reflexes had been as tight as rubber on a sling.

I picked the gun up from off the floor. The safety was off. Clarence said it was always best to keep a gun loaded, one bullet in the chamber, and the safety off because there may not be time to load and fire. I saw he didn't always do as he preached, thank God. I was damn lucky I didn't kill myself. I put the gun back. Weapons weren't my thing.

I locked the door, just in case Pike thought he made a mistake leaving like he did when I was all alone in the store. I turned the OPEN sign to CLOSE and then went in back. I called Donna. Did Meg have something else Pike wanted? I asked her to find out about Meg's will.

"How am I supposed to find that out?"

"Are you saying you can't?"

"Well, no. But it's going to take me some time."

"Call me when you have the answer." If forensics came back with any evidence on Pike, I wanted to have the motive figured out.

I gave Clarence a call and left a message on his machine. I told him I'd take care of the store until he got back on his feet. "I'll take Monday and Tuesday. Then, we'll see how you're feeling on Wednesday. After that, I'll take good care of the store, as good as if it were you. Don't push it, Clarence. From what I'm hearing, this flu is a bad one."

Before locking up and leaving, I called Oaks Manor to check on Dahlia. Mary Niles said Dahlia was still in the hospital. "I didn't call you to tell you because I thought you'd already gone there."

Frytown's General Hospital is small, only around fifty beds, and was more of a clinic for those who couldn't afford to go to Iowa City or didn't have insurance for a specialist. The emergency room was generally the busiest department with car and farm accidents, fights from the lakeside, or a scuffle at one of the local bars. Frytown was known for its nine churches and eight taverns. The two go hand in hand. Drunks pray either for their next drink or not to take the next one. And those who go to church pray not to become what they fear is hiding inside them. They're pretty much the same people.

I walked up to the reception desk at the hospital and asked for Dahlia's room. I told the volunteer responsible for patient inquiries that Dahlia had been brought over from Oaks Manor. The volunteer checked the computer, "Room 227."

I hate hospitals. They smell like sick people and death. I pushed open the door to Room 227, finding two beds. A woman was propped on pillows reading People magazine in the bed closest to the door. Jennifer Aniston's photo was plastered on the front cover again. The other bed held a lump of a body surrounded by IV tubes, beeping machines, and a doctor. He was standing at the end of the bed, making notes on a clipboard.

I walked over. "I'm Dahlia Dove's daughter. How is she?"

He continued jotting something down on the chart while saying, "She's doing a little better. We had a go of it last night."

"What do you mean, 'a go of it'? Oaks Manor left a message saying she was dehydrated so that they would take her to the hospital. Why didn't someone call me if it was more severe than that?"

"I don't know." He looked at the chart. "The chart states to contact Oaks Manor. When you came with your mother, didn't you ask to be notified of any change?"

"Oaks Manor placed her in the hospital."

"Your name?"

"Lillian Dove."

He made a couple more notations and then put the chart back at the foot of the bed. "I've noted for them to call you and Oaks Manor. Be sure to leave your number with the nurse at the desk. I'm standing in for Dr. Hampton, who is out of town. He's her regular physician." He held out his hand. "Dr. Spencer Martin."

It was a nice hand with a wedding ring on the ring finger. I had a new respect for a man who wore his wedding ring. Charles didn't.

Dr. Martin's attention went back to Dahlia. "She was dehydrated. Her blood pressure was low, and we put her on fluids. I saw from her history that she had prior heart trouble."

"Did she have another heart attack?" I moved over to the side of her bed. Her expression was no longer strained. She looked younger, wrinkles somehow minimized, eyelids having a bluish tint. Her breathing was faint.

My stomach clenched. My heart froze in fear. I was afraid she might die.

Dr. Martin interrupted my anguish. "I'm not sure what caused it. We've ruled out this flu that's going around. I've asked Oaks Manor to send over their medication list. I want to check if she's been put on any new medications and if what we see here is not a bad side effect. I've also taken blood samples. I'll know more when we get the lab results in the morning."

He came over to the bed and placed his hand on Dahlia's covered shoulder. "I've known many great women like your mother. She's strong-willed. She'll be fine." He went toward the door and stopped. "Make sure to stop at the desk and give them your number. They'll call you if there is any change in her condition."

After he had left, I pulled up a chair next to her bed. "Dahlia? Can you hear me?" Her body was warm to the touch. Her usual spit-n-fire was gone. "Dahlia?"

What if she died? What if every time I'd wished for her to die, leave me alone, someone, something had been keeping count? And now I was being granted my request? If she died, then she would be gone. Forever. I always thought that the event would rock my world, but Dahlia'd always been in my world. She'd acted as a place card for me. My thoughts were often preceded by, What would Dahlia say? How would she react to this?

I'd never know why she'd enabled my father for so many years. Why she had placed him ahead of us kids. I'd never understood the key that gave her strength. How she kept moving forward even though life kept knocking her back. Now, I'd never get it. I'd never be strong like her.

I'd have no....no...mother.

She lay right in front of me, but already I missed her. "Mom? Mommy, it's me, Lillian."

Tears fell from me onto her. She gave no sign she knew I was there with her.

"Please don't die. I love...

Pike's voice reverberated through me. *I've taken care of the head. Dahlia?*

Oaks Manor took good care of its residents, but the flu outbreak had bombarded it. And Mary Niles hadn't been aware Pike was there the night he trapped Dahlia in the corridor.

That night. What would have happened if I hadn't come along? Had he planned to do something then? Did he find another way to make sure whatever she knew wouldn't get out?

I wasn't able to help Dahlia in the hospital. But maybe I could stop Pike.

I needed to eat and calm myself down so I could think. So I drove to the lakeside. I walked into Louise's Italian Kitchen, noting that the table Charles and I usually sat at was empty. And Beulah didn't ask if I wanted *my* table.

The restaurant was packed but mostly with out-of-towners. Usually, you could catch a breeze coming off the lake this late at night. But not tonight.

CHAPTER SEVEN
OVER THE MOMENT

The sun must have been off doing a beautiful sunset somewhere else because the horizon north of Frytown appeared nothing less than ominous. Clouds had come in.

I headed back to Rohert Road. I wasn't sure what to do, but I knew where I was going.

I turned at the road between the cornfields and parked out of sight on the other side of the toolshed at what used to be the Carter house. Then, pocketing my keys, I walked down the small tractor road leading to Meg Dillard's.

I hadn't gotten halfway when I heard a buzz of a motor. Bright headlights glimmered on the cornstalks and then veered towards me.

I jumped between the corn. The car drove past. It was Pike. I kept my head down until he was well down the road and the dust settled.

I kept to the corn. Yellow cobs poked me and jarred my progress. It would have been much easier to move back out onto the road, where a ghost of light remained from the diminished sky. But I didn't want to gamble that Pike hadn't seen me. He might have been back-tracking on foot.

I saw his car parked by a small shed when I got to the clearing. Staying in the shadows, I moved slowly through bushes and trees until I came to it. The shed was an old chicken coop.

The two same lights were on in the house as the last time I'd come. I sprinted over to the smaller window, careful not to trip over something.

The window gave a view into the kitchen from over the sink. Pike was there. He was taking something out of a brown paper bag. A box. Yellow. It reminded me of the rat poison Dahlia used. He left the box on the counter and went over to a cupboard. He took out a bowl, moved over to the stove, and spooned in what was simmering in a pan. He carried the bowl over to the counter. Stopped.

He turned toward the window.

I jumped back. My heart thumped in my chest. Had he seen me? What would this man do if he caught me out here? What was he ca-pable of doing? Had he tried to kill Dahlia? His threat in the corridor at Oaks Manor may have upset her enough to cause her another heart attack.

Every nerve triggered every hair on my arms and head. I was afraid of being afraid. If I didn't find out what he was up to, Pike would get away with everything.

With every ounce of gumption I could summon, I forced my eyes to the edge of the window again and looked in. No, he hadn't seen me. Or if he had, he wasn't ready to let me know. He was sprinkling what was in the box into the bowl. I tried to see the print on the box, which was about the size of a package of cornstarch, yellow, with a lot of black type. But the front was facing the other direction.

He picked up the bowl and left the kitchen. I followed, skirting two old rose bushes, long thorns pricking. I remembered the rose bush outside my patio wall. I hoped to catch a view of Pike's arms. I bet I'd find scratches.

The next room was larger, a living space. Wearing a rose-colored sweater over what appeared to be a nightgown, Meg Dillard sat in a chair with a quilt stretched over her legs, and her head drooped on her neck. Pike called her name. Her head jerked up. She saw the bowl and shook her head. She pulled back, like how Dahlia reacted when seeing Nelly come after her with the syringe. Pike set the bowl on the stand behind the chair. She turned to shove it off and moved to get up, but he caught her and pinned an arm across her chest. Then he began force-feeding her. Was he poisoning her? Frailer than the last time I'd seen her, she was no match for him no matter how hard she struggled.

I needed to do something. I thought about going back to get my phone and taking a video. But could I get there and back fast enough? I had to try. I needed proof. What light the sky offered was gone by the time I got back to the car. Returning is usually a faster process than going, but not when you have to look back over your shoulder constantly. I found my phone and went back. But by then, Meg was alone in the room. She slumped in her chair. Was she breathing? I couldn't tell. I took a video. I knew I needed to get help. This was becoming more than I could handle on my own.

Where was Pike?

I couldn't take the time to look for him. He could have poisoned Dahlia, too.

Several times I thought I heard someone behind me. Finally, when I saw my car, I ran to it, but I forced myself to drive more slowly than my frightened state demanded. If Pike hadn't heard me, maybe I could do something to stop him. If he had and came outside, I didn't want him to hear the motor or notice headlights leaving the area. If he saw it was me, he'd do anything to stop me.

I drove to Charles's farm. This time, I left the lights on. The unknown car was still parked by the tree, and the house was dark. I went to the back door and knocked. No one answered. Nothing in the house stirred. Until one of the horses in the feedlot whinnied. Cooper came, barking his head off, then seeing it was me, began wet nosing my hand for a head rub.

"Wake them up, Cooper." Stopping whatever was happening in there was all right by me.

Still, no one came to the door. I went around to the front porch. Front porches weren't used regularly around Frytown. They were saved for people selling what you didn't need or the Jehovah's Witnesses who came now and again from Iowa City. The bell rang. I pushed the button over and over again until my finger hurt. Then it dawned on me they may not have been inside.

I went out to the shed where Charles kept his Ford Ranger. Cooper seemed to like the game we were playing. He ran ahead, letting off a bark or two. The doors were open. Sure enough, the shed was empty.

It was late for a drive. Dinnertime was long over. Where'd Charles gone?

Cooper loped ahead as I returned to the house, trying to figure out what I should do next. First, I needed to tell someone what I saw and show them the video. Second, I needed to tell someone why I thought Dahlia was sick. I wanted Pike caught, and if I acted quickly, he would be.

I got back in the car. I thought about picking up my phone and calling Charles, but he could have been with Maxine. I could have called dispatch, but I'd sound crazy over the phone. Neither of those choices seemed right, but I needed to show someone the video. Someone who had the authority to go out and arrest Pike.

Most everyone knew where everyone lived in Frytown. This time, I knew where I was going. I drove back to town to Leveque's small clapboard house.

Lights were on inside. Music was high. It was a jazzy type of music, with a bass and a distant saxophone. I knocked on the door and heard movement. A woman laughed. Then I heard the sound of two people scrambling.

Leveque came to the door wearing only his Levis 501s, unsnapped. Dark hair offered a pathway from his navel to the jean's opening. The same dark hair covered the muscles on his chest. The curls on his head were mussed, his eyes sleepy. I'm not sure who he'd thought would be at his door, but I figured he hadn't expected me by his double-take. Then he smiled, slow and easy.

A voice from inside called out, "Who is it, Jacque? Tell'em to go away. You're not done here."

He laughed and twisted around, shouting back, "Have another drink, baby. But, don't worry, I can get you revved up again if you cool off." He leaned casually against the doorjamb like he had all the time in the world. "What can I do for you?"

Keep your eyes on his, I warned myself. Not an easy thing to do at the moment. "I need to talk to you."

"Unfortunately, as you can tell, I'm taken for the night." He looked down at his jeans. A prominent bulge.

Don't look. Stay focused. "Burt didn't set the fire. Edgar Pike did. I think he's becoming desperate because he thinks I saw him upstairs in the Carter house."

"Why does he think you saw at the Carters?" He glanced back into the room behind him.

"I told him I did."

"I thought you told the Chief you couldn't identify the person?"

"But Pike wouldn't necessarily know that. He and Percy were in at Discount. That's when I told him I knew he set the Carter fire. I think he did it because he'd thought he'd got the insurance money. He never thought there would be an investigation. Only Meg Dillard gave the money instead to the Carter family. He's old and wants his due. I don't know what he's up to, but it can't be good. I think he's poisoning Meg Dillard. Right now. Right this minute. We have to stop him. He may have poisoned my mother, too."

He was waking up, becoming more interested. "Why your mother?"

"She knows something."

"What?"

"I don't know. But, Leveque, listen to me. Pike told me he'd taken care of my mother and threatened that he would take care of me if I didn't mind my own business."

He leaned back against the door frame. "How do you know he's poisoning Meg Dillard? Right this minute."

"Honey, come on," the voice whined from inside.

I had to convince him. "I was just at Meg Dillard's. I saw him making her soup, and he stirred something into it. I'm not sure what, but I know she didn't want it. She tried to fight him off, and she doesn't look good."

"Like she has the flu, maybe?" he snapped. "And you saw all of this when they invited you over for dinner?" He stood straighter, one hand on the door as if ready to shut it in my face.

I knew I sounded crazy, but he needed to believe me. "I was outside."

The declaration didn't surprise him. He stepped out to where I was standing, drawing the door closed behind him. I wasn't sure what he would do, so I stepped back.

"Now listen to me," he muttered. "You quit nosing around before getting yourself in a box with all the sides nailed down. You couldn't answer phones, and you're no policewoman. If it takes arresting you for being a public nuisance, I'll be the first one to take out the handcuffs."

All right, he had every right to disbelieve me. I was saying everything too quickly, and it wasn't making enough sense, even to myself. "Look." I held my cell phone, showing him the evidence I'd collected. "I'm telling you what I saw. Do this one thing. Go out there. See Meg Dillard. If I'm wrong about the poison, he's abusing her. And there are laws to prevent that."

"You've shown me a video of an old lady taking a nap in her chair. Go home."

"Jacccccccque…," came a call from inside.

He went back in and shut the door.

I don't know why I thought he'd open it again, but I stood there, waiting for him to do just that, thinking once he got inside, he might consider what I'd said, put whoever was waiting on hold, get dressed, and check out my story.

I got back in my car. The only other option I could think of was to call Lieutenant Manville, but I wasn't sure he liked me or would believe me any more than Leveque had. I had no other choice. I called Charles. The call went to voice mail. I told him exactly what I'd said, Leveque. It sounded even nuttier on the second telling.

CHAPTER EIGHT
OVER COMPULSIONS

I'd considered my choices. I could have called dispatch. I could have told them I thought someone was being poisoned and given them Meg's address. But if asked why I thought a crime was being committed, it'd have been too long of an explanation to give over the phone. I could have tried to stop Pike myself. He would have opened the door if he'd seen it was me. I could have pushed past him. Could I have overpowered him? And what if Leveque had been right and I'd been wrong? What if Meg wasn't being harmed? Could what I'd seen be called abuse? Pike hadn't hit her. He'd been feeding her soup against her will. I'd come to my conclusion based on what I'd seen in the corridor between him and Dahlia and what I'd witnessed while peep-n-tomming. I needed more evidence. Leveque had been right. I wasn't the police.

I planned to go straight to the hospital in the morning. If Dahlia's test results showed she'd been poisoned, and if Donna found out the answer to my question, I would have both evidence and motive.

Both would have gotten either Leveque or Charles to take me seriously.

I only hoped Meg would still be alive. Then I thought of calling Amanda. She might have listened to me. Or at least, she might have gone out to make sure Meg was all right.

I got back to my condo and found the front door ajar. I pushed it fully open. Listened.

I took a couple of steps in and turned on a lamp. A footstool had been knocked over. Papers were pushed off onto the floor. I pulled out my phone and dialed dispatch. "Helen, it's Lillian. I think I've had another break-in at my condo."

"Where are you?"

"Inside the front door."

"Turn around and go straight back out. You hear me this time, Lillian? Get out. I'm sending a car."

The siren told most of Frytown that something criminal was going on. When Officer Miner came, several residents were out of their condos, standing in the corridor. Most were in their bathrobes, including Earl.

Miner came into the hallway. "What's going on, Lillian? I heard you called in a ten-fifteen." His gun remained in his holster, but the strap was loosened.

"My door was open when I got here." I told him what I found when I came home.

At this point, Officer Richards checked in. "What's up, Miner?"

"Lillian thinks someone's broken into her place."

Richards unstrapped his pistol.

Miner turned to those standing out in the hallway. "Everyone back inside. I want this hall cleared." Then, he asked, "Is this the only entrance?"

I shook my head. "There's a back patio."

Earl said, "Come wait with me, Lillian."

I followed him back to his unit, leaving the door open a crack. Miner drew his gun and took the lead while Richards covered him as they entered my condo. I came out and followed them in, hearing "clear" repeatedly as they moved through the rooms. Then Miner spotted me. "I thought I ordered the hallway cleared." He waved me in. "Come on. No one's inside. But you're right. Things are knocked around. It looks like you've been burglarized. You want to look and let us know what's missing?"

Richards came in from the kitchen. "A real mess in there, too."

I found the litter box upturned in the kitchen, and kitty litter was strewn across the floor. Bacardi's kibble bowl set upside down. Water had spilled. Someone had scared Bacardi.

With Miner following me, I moved from room to room. The kitchen was the worst.

"Anything missing?"

Richards came over saying, "Your television and computers are still here. If this were a burglary, the laptop would have been lifted. It's an easy sell in the drug market."

It came to me then what was missing. "Where's Bacardi? Bacardi's missing."

"Who?"

"My cat." I got down on my hands and knees and looked under the couch. Dust bunnies but no Bacardi. "Bacardi, where are you?" I went into the bedroom, another hiding place, especially if there was a storm. I found the same dust bunnies under the bed. They were breeding like rabbits. "Bacardi?"

Richards said, "Your door didn't completely latch when you left. So he must have got out."

"I always lock my door. It was locked. Bacardi doesn't make a mess like this."

"Think back, Lillian. Do you remember locking the door? You could have forgotten. Everyone makes mistakes."

Why weren't they taking me seriously? Leveque. He'd played up in the office about the last time I called in, saying someone was in the condo. Plus, Richards had come to that call, too.

Richards said, "I know if I crack the door, my pup tries to get out."

Miner joined in. "You ever watch that dog whisperer show?"

"I locked the door." My voice moved up a pitch. "Someone has stolen my cat."

Miners and Richards exchanged glances.

I called, "Bacardi? Here kitty."

I looked under every piece of furniture. I opened every closet door. I opened the bottom drawers in the kitchen. Once, when he was a kitten, he crawled inside the pans drawer and got stuck inside. Only, today, no Bacardi.

Officer Templeton came into the condo. "What's going on?"

"Lillian thinks someone took her cat."

"Why would someone grab your cat?" he asked.

I pushed past them. People had returned to the hallway. "Has anyone seen Bacardi?"

No one had. A couple of residents who didn't know I had a cat were discussing whether pets were allowed.

I visited every section of the complex. I found each exit door closed. Tight.

When I returned to the condo, Earl's door was still ajar. He came out. "Don't worry, Lillian. He's somewhere around."

Did I lock the door? Why did I doubt myself? I always do. I will never forget it. "Bacardi? Here kitty, kitty, kitty."

I went outside to find patrol cars and officers standing, talking, and laughing. I thought the department was understaffed?

Miner saw me and came over. "I used to have a dog that got loose all the time. They're a lot like kids, you know? I finally figured out that he'd come back on his own if I didn't chase after him."

Really? "Cats aren't dogs."

"There's that, but there's not much difference between them when they're hungry. I bet tomorrow morning you'll find him meowing to get in."

"Don't you have a call to take?"

He stepped back, holding out his hands. "Just trying to help here."

I immediately felt terrible. "Sorry."

"What do you want me to do?" he asked. "I don't see any signs of force. Either someone had a key to get into your place, or you didn't get the door closed."

"If it wasn't for Leveque, I bet you'd believe me."

He glanced away.

My bottom lip quivered. What if something happened to Bacardi because of me?

Miner was looking toward the patrol cars. "Okay. Tell you what. The boys and I will do a three-block sweep looking for the little fellow. But if we get a call?"

"You would do that?"

"Sure." He squeezed my shoulder. "Happy to do it." He returned to his patrol car and stopped, "And Lillian?"

"Yes?"

"Sorry about the layoff. You got a raw deal. And don't let Leveque get to you. He gives everyone a hard time. He just jokes around, you know. He'd be the first to want to save your cat if he knew it was in danger."

The tears wanted to come, and the little girl in me wanted to stand crying, screaming at how cheated she felt. I rammed the palms of my hands up my face, shoving the possibility of tears away. Crying gave in to the possibility I'd never find Bacardi. But I had to believe he was okay. It was like Miner said, he'd be here in the morning. Hungry. He wouldn't venture very far.

Still, I got in my car and drove one block after another, up one street and then the next, calling his name out into the night. Miner was good on his word. I crossed the patrol cars doing a slow sweep of lights over neighborhood lawns and bushes.

"Bacardi?" I followed behind them, "Here, kitty, kitty."

When I did get back to the condo, I couldn't stay still. So I searched every cranny I could think of where he might have crawled. Then I went back outside.

I went without the Mustang this time. I walked and walked and walked the night away, calling, "Here, kitty."

Several cats answered my calls. They padded quietly up to me, purring as they rubbed against my legs. Others merely meowed back a hello. None were Bacardi. I know Bacardi's yowl. It wasn't until I came dragging back, exhausted, with a voice hoarse and feelings of failure, that I allowed myself to take in the idea, "What if he never comes back? What if something bad happened to him?"

Pike?

The following day, I called Clarence. If he felt better and could work the store, I could spend all day looking for Bacardi. He wasn't an outside cat. He didn't understand real-world concepts like traffic, dogs, and outdoor cats needing to defend their territories. With his puffed-out coat of hair, someone could think he was something besides a cat. Something rabid.

Clarence's phone rang and rang before the answering machine picked up. I hung up. I didn't want to bother him. I had said I would handle the store longer if necessary. He was counting on me.

Before leaving for Discount, I unplugged my computer and printer and took them. As soon as I opened the store for business, I planned to hook them up in the back room. Then, during breaks, I could print MISSING signs.

I poked my head out the window the entire way to Discount calling Bacardi's name. Comforting thoughts attempted to penetrate my terror. *Don't worry. He's just got himself locked inside someone's garage. He nosed his way into one of the condos and hasn't made his presence known to the owner.* I made a mental note to ask Albert if anyone had left on vacation or for a medical procedure, and if so, could he check their condos?

But after I ran a finger over the comforting possibilities, the terror returned. What if Bacardi traveled clear to the highway? What if he ran into a mean dog? What if…

Luckily, the store was pretty slow on business, so I was able to create a great flyer before the first customer. I had a lot of photos of Bacardi. It took me a few minutes to choose the right one. Then, I needed to decide how many phone numbers to include for the finder to call. I didn't think Clarence would mind me adding Discount.

Shortly before noon, a couple of boys biked in and tossed their bikes down in the parking lot. They had towels tied to their bike handles and were wearing swim trunks.

"Going to the lake?" I asked, demonstrating my great talents at deduction.

"Yep," one said, coming to the counter with two cans of Fiesta Orange pop and a large bag of hot Cheetos. I glanced at the other boy, who was choosing his chips carefully. He was more of the variety type, pulling smaller sacks of different flavors off the shelf.

I got an idea. "How would you like to keep your money?"

The boy buying the Fiesta took the bait. "What do you mean?"

The other boy turned his head. He looked familiar, but I couldn't place him at first. Then I recognized him as David Carter, the Carters' younger son.

"I need flyers around town." I went into the back room to get a handful. David had set his stuff down on the counter by the time I came back out. The boys were whispering.

I set the flyers down. David seemed interested, giving them a good look. "That your cat?"

I nodded. "He came up missing last night."

The other kid, whom I didn't recognize, said, "It's a pretty ugly cat."

"I know."

David seemed embarrassed by the comment. His face turned red. "Not so ugly." He said, "This is our last day to go to the lake."

"You're David Carter, aren't you?" He nodded. I said, "I'm Lillian Dove. I was the one who reported your house fire. I met you at the Bobby Bowen show."

He nodded his mutual recognition, then turned to his friend, maybe trying to figure out how that obligated them. They whispered to each other. Heads shook. I thought I might need to get a little friendlier before asking for favors. "I bet you and your brother hate leaving your school."

David shrugged. "School's school. My dad said I could play on a Little League team or something in Des Moines."

"But your brother's a senior, right? I heard he might not move and still in town."

David's voice took on a more mature tone, possibly copying his father's. "Darrell says he ain't going, but he's going, come hell or high water."

The possibility of drowning appeared worse than going to hell. The other kid said, "Come on, Dave. We could put a few of them up on our way down to the lake."

"That's all I need." I began putting their things into plastic bags, strong enough to be carried on their handlebars. I also put the flyers in one, along with some duct tape I found in the back.

David wasn't so convinced. "It's already pretty hot, and it'll take up most of our day." He was looking down at the counter. His friend gave him a *Where're you going with this?* kind of look. But I knew. He was negotiating. People had been giving his parents things, and he expected more from me than just pop and chips.

I started the bid. "So, do you guys need anything else? A bag of M & M's, maybe? I like it when the chocolate melts in the candy shell. Or there are some sandwiches in the cooler over there. I think we're out of popsicles, but an ice cream bar might keep you cooled off on the ride."

No hesitation. David went about gathering all of it. He picked out two bags of candy and grabbed four sandwiches. The boys un-wrapped the ice cream bars while I put everything into the sacks, counting how much I would owe Clarence. Thirty dollars? I was being robbed, but what else could I do? The boys would have the flyers out before I closed the store.

I watched as they excitedly hung the sacks on their bike handles and peddled off, ice cream dripping, licking, and laughing. When they reached the corner to turn into town, I saw a heavy plastic bag thrown toward the ditch. I was pretty sure it wasn't the M &M's.

Damn kids.

There was nothing else to do but go out and salvage what I could. When I got to the bag, I saw something on the ground not far from where the sack landed. A small dog? Dogs were sometimes dumped out in this area. Its belly was bloated, flies buzzing. I pictured Bacardi, his fuzzy little body swollen larger than his head, with a fuzzy, long tail protruding from a mound of fluff. Would anyone recognize him from the flyers? Would someone who saw fresh roadkill stop to check and think, "I should let Lillian Dove know"?

When we were kids and stuck together in the backseat of the car for a long ride, Frank, Patrick, and I would play a game, "What is it?" When we spotted roadkill or Dahlia warned something was coming up on the road, the goal was to be the first to state what it'd been when it'd been alive. If it weren't readily recognizable, we'd beg Dahlia to slow down or stop to determine which of us was right. She never did.

I went back to the store. I brought the stool from the back and sat with my sack of flyers on my lap while waiting for customers. A heavy dread circled me, weighing me down. The hands on the clock seemed to move so slowly that I got up twice to check the time with my cell phone. I called the hospital and talked to April McDonald, who told me Dahlia was still stable and there had been no change.

I put my idea of poisoning into April's head. "Maybe Dahlia ate something that poisoned her. The doctor told me he didn't think she had the flu."

"A side effect of a prescription acts like poisoning in the body. But I don't think that panned out. I haven't seen her file, but I believe the test results were negative. So don't worry, Lillian. Dr. Martin is an excellent doctor. Are you coming by later?"

"Tonight."

"Good. Let's hope she's better by then. I'll personally call you if there is any change."

I hung up, hearing Pike's words: "You can skin a cat two ways, from the head down or tail up."

Dahlia was the head. The tail?

No matter what I'd promised Clarence, I couldn't stay selling pop and beers, chips, and ice cream while Pike could've been getting away with murder.

I called Charles.

"Hello, Lillian. I got your message."

Relief. "Are you going to Meg's?"

"I went by last night."

"Then you saw how sick she is."

Sounding a little impatient, he said, "With the flu, Lillian. She's not being poisoned."

"Are you sure? That's what Pike would want you to think."

"It's what she told me. And her doctor confirmed it."

"You talked to her?"

"I did. She said she's been sick, and Pike took her to see her doctor."

It sure hadn't looked like she wanted what Pike had been feeding her. "She wouldn't know she was being poisoned. Not if he was doing it slowly. Did you look in the kitchen for the box I described?"

"Dried noodles. Yellow box, right? It was still on the counter."

"Dried noodles?"

"I paid a visit to the hospital this morning. I spoke with Dr. Martin."

I prayed for a customer to enter the store so I would be forced to hang up. If Charles told me I was mistaken about Dahlia being poisoned, I was wrong about everything, which means Leveque could be right. Maybe Burt did set the fire. Maybe he heard about the insurance money somehow and figured it was his best solution. Or, if Meg had set the fire and Burt had seen her, Burt could have asked for the insurance money.

But Burt wasn't the type to blackmail or set a house fire. And where did all of that put Pike? I was sure he'd done something that Dahlia knew about, so bad he'd tried to kill her. Hadn't she said, "Someday you'll show up, and I'll be dead."

"Your mother has had a bad side effect from sleeping medication," Charles said.

"I talked to April McDonald a couple of minutes ago. She said those results came back negative."

He audibly sighed. "You need to let us do our job. Leveque and I are handling this."

"He's wrong, Charles."

"Lillian?"

He wasn't listening. "Did the Kaefring's side with the Hayes's? Is everyone still trying to keep what Meg did a secret?"

"One incident has nothing to do with the other."

Dead air.

"Charles?" Had he hung up on me? "Charles, are you still there?"

He said, "I heard about Clarence. Sorry, Lillian. It's nice of you to take care of the store."

I wasn't in the mood for chit-chat. And if he thought he could change the subject and that I would just let what I believed go, well, he was wrong. "I've got to go."

"Miner told me about your cat. You've been given a lot to handle in the last couple of days. But, look, if your cat's not found, I'll give you another one. One of the cats out in the barn had a new litter. And I'm fighting the city to get you back, part-time, but…"

Like Bacardi could be replaced?

"Lillian, are you still there?"

"I'm not coming back to work at the station."

"Look, we need to talk. I think you got the wrong idea about Maxine."

"You don't need to explain anything to me."

"I wanted you to meet her. She's my..."

I hung up. "No, I'm not still here."

I turned the sign in the window back to CLOSED and went outside. It wasn't just hot enough to fry an egg but hot enough to barbecue a whole damn chicken.

CHAPTER NINE
OVER CHOICES

I hurried past the reception counter and went straight to Dahlia's room. An intravenous line connected her to a couple of intravenous bags filled with clear fluids. The machines were still buzzing and beeping. I took a glance at the heart monitor. I had no idea how to read the numbers but figured the beeps and burps meant she would live.

"She's doing better." The woman in the next bed sat up and dangled her legs over the bed.

"Is the doctor around?"

"He was just here. You may still be able to catch him. I think he's doing his rounds."

I turned to leave, and then I remembered my manners. "How are you doing?"

She perked up. "Oh, I'm much better. I've been released. I'm waiting for the nurse to come in so I can get dressed. Melvin is going to come down and get me. He said the shop wasn't busy, as hot as it is outside."

It must be Melvin Roth's mother, I thought.

She continued. "I don't like hospitals, but I hate the thought of going home. It's at least cooler in here." She smiled.

"But I bet you'll be happy to be home in your bed." I moved to leave. "Stay well."

She said, "Your mother said she's never been so sick. She thought she was going to die."

"She's awake?" But, then, I'd been wrong. She was getting better, fast.

"She was, but I think they've given her something." The woman laughed. "You're mother's quite the character. She said the devil would have to work harder next time."

I stared over at my mother's sleeping form, saying aloud. "She must have had the flu or a side effect from a prescription."

"That's what I heard the doctor say," the woman said. "But your mom told me she started feeling sick right after they gave her the second shot."

Second shot? "Did she tell that to the doctor?"

"Why, I don't know."

I went to Dahlia and shook her. "Dahlia?"

The woman continued to talk. "Everyone says she'll be fine in a couple of days." Then, "Where is that nurse. Melvin's going to be here any minute." Then, "He takes good care of me."

"Dahlia?" I shook her again. "Mom?"

Her response was a strangled snore from having her sound sleep interrupted.

I left, heading off to find Dr. Martin. But instead, I found Laura Dell. "I need to talk to the doctor about Dahlia."

"Oh?" She said, "Don't worry, your mother will be fine. I don't think he's left yet. I spoke with him earlier. You'll to happy to hear that the tests showed it wasn't a side effect from the medication.

Well, not exactly. She was mistakenly given too much medication. We're lucky it didn't cause an overdose."

"Overdose? How could that have happened?" But I knew. I was already answering my own question.

"We've notified Oaks Manor," Laura continued. "Marilyn's checking the files and questioning everyone over there."

Edgar Pike wouldn't be hanging around Oaks Manor. If he'd gotten wind of the overdose prognosis, he might be thinking of leaving town. Fingerprints, DNA, something would show he tried to kill my mother.

"Oh, and Lillian?"

I stopped.

"Sorry to hear about Clarence."

"Yeah, this flu. Go figure."

When I got outside, I stood, trying to think. My phone rang. It was Donna. "I got your answer, hon, and let me tell you, it wasn't easy. I had to pull some favors."

"What'd you find out?"

"You were right. Meg tried to change her will."

"Did Amanda tell you this?"

"I know Doreen over at the law office. She said someone else brought Meg."

"A man?"

"Yes. How did you know?"

Pike. I asked, "Does the Chief or Leveque know this?"

I could see her shrug. "Leveque doesn't discuss his cases with me, and I haven't seen the chief. He's been in and out. Do you think I should call and tell him? Is this important?"

It was important. Very important. Pike had lost some of Meg's money, but he was going for the rest of it. I hadn't been entirely wrong. Not about Dahlia. And not about Meg Dillard, either. If I had two right, then I was right on the third. Burt was innocent.

But before I clicked off the call, Donna added, "Your name's come up around here this morning."

"Yeah? By who?"

"Leveque. He and Lieutenant Manville went into the chief's office.

I got into the Mustang and headed back to Rohert Road and Meg Dillard's. The Mustang knew the way like a well-trained animal. I didn't ease the speed until I turned down the middle of the corn-fields. Nor did I slow more than necessary when I raced down the narrow tractor road. Dust flew up behind me, creating smoke sig-nals. If Pike could read them, then he'd know something was coming at him and fast.

I didn't care. He tried to kill Dahlia. He probably killed Bacardi.

The house appeared quiet—no green car. I got out of the Mustang quietly, cautious. Was Pike gone? Or was his car in one of the sheds?

I kept my eyes on the windows and the front door. I wasn't afraid. Not yet.

The front door wasn't completely closed. I pushed it open and walked inside. "Meg? Anyone here?" I saw the blood.

Red droplets spotted the floor. "Meg? Are you all right?" *Stop and call dispatch*. It was the most sensible choice to make. I moved towards the kitchen. The door was closed. Was Pike hiding behind it? I pushed open it open and saw a puddle of blood on the floor. So much blood, if it was Meg's, as fail as she looked, there was no way she'd have survived.

A shiver ran through me. My stomach flip-flopped. "Meg?" From the kitchen, I went from one room to the next. With each turn, I expected to find Meg's dead body. In each room, I forced myself to look carefully for any signs of violence.

Finding none, I went back to the kitchen. I followed a blood trail to the back door. It opened easily, not latched tight. The trail ended here, inside. There was no blood outside the door, but there were footprints from a puddle of water where someone had used the hose. And beyond, a yellowed dry lawn and cornfield.

The field of corn appeared to be an endless green sea bordered by a dark threatening horizon. Clouds were moving in. The air was turning sticky-wet. Then I saw them. Three flew low above the corn-field as if the wait wouldn't be too long, circling lower and lower. Buzzards.

Had Pike killed Meg and taken her out into the field? It would be an excellent place to hide a body, and he'd have no reason to believe anyone was coming to look for her. Charles had come out and found she was all right.

Did Pike find a way to get Meg to sign papers leaving the estate to him?

His ship was coming in. But if he'd heard about the overdose being discovered, he may have wanted to hurry his ship along.

The corn was green. Pike could be long gone before they found her. A farmer harvesting may not notice the machine's wheels burying frail Meg beneath the stalks.

The corn welcomed me, parting before my hands, allowing me to pause to stop and look and calculate the direction of the vultures' flight. It wasn't long before the rows seemed to narrow and grow tall above my head. The dense stocks shut off the flow of air. It became hard to breathe in anything but hot, stale air and dust. Then the rows changed as if suddenly the field reasserted itself. Stalks began pushing back, making it harder for me to go through. Their green leaves ripped at my face and hands. Thinner, sticky leaves reached out for my hair. Hard cobs like hard fists jabbed me. The further I went in, the more the stalks stirred and rustled, becoming a chorus of murmuring voices. *Watch out. Look. She's here.*

The air became a furnace. I was lost. I had no sense of direction. I couldn't see above the stalks. I couldn't find the buzzards. Were they still flying overhead, or had they landed and were feasting on a corpse?

My lungs hurt. My head hurt. The same feeling of death I'd experienced in the house came back to haunt me.

I panicked. I ran.

The stalks resisted, tortured me, and jeered at me. Finally, I ran down a row, stopped, turned, in the wrong direction, and raced down another, only to turn again. Where?

I pushed out onto the tractor road. I'd circled a half-horseshoe around to the front of the house, where I now saw a car. Pike's. He was looking out the window.

I glanced over to the Mustang. Could I get to it in time?

Bang!

I ducked back into the corn without checking if the sound was a car backfiring. The air immediately turned dead, the stalks hanging curtains. I ran, losing direction. The stalks moved in closer, higher. I was somewhere in an endless row, stalks like a labyrinth of flames offering too many possible paths and yet no direction at all. Each row imperfect, no solid wall to follow. I became itchy. Disoriented.

I heard something. Someone else was in the field with me. Stalks rustled. Heavy footfalls. He'd come into the field after me.

He couldn't see me above the stalks, but neither was I able to see him. I ran until I realized his only sense of direction would be the noise I was making. I slowed down and concentrated on each step I took, careful to knock stalks aside.

And yet, no matter which way I moved, no matter how careful I was, the sounds of movement behind me never seemed far off. He wouldn't stop until he'd taken the cat by the tail.

I came out on Rohert Road and, by a miracle, thank God for miracles, saw a cloud of dust and then a green car moving in my direction. Pike. It roared past me. But this time, I hadn't leaped back and hidden farther than a couple of stalks. Not even the threat of a gun could get me to move back into that cornfield.

As soon as I was sure he was well on down the road and hadn't turned around, I returned to the house and ran directly to the Mustang. I found my keys in the ignition. My purse set on the seat. Why hadn't he taken them? I didn't want to take the time to reason Pike out. Instead, I grabbed my cell phone, skipped dispatch, and tapped in Charles's number. He answered, and I didn't wait for him to say hello.

"He's killed Meg. Blood's all over the house."

I locked the car doors and kept my eyes on the road in case Pike came back. Charles must have been at the farm. He was the first to arrive and pulled his car up to mine. He jumped out. "Lillian? What the hell is going on?"

"In the house," I yelled. "Pike tried to shoot me and chased me into the cornfield, but he's gone now." I told him what Pike's car looked like, old and green. Not much of a description. Then I remembered a dent on the back, right side.

"How do you know he hurt Meg?"

"There's blood, Charles. Lots of blood. In the kitchen. You'll see."

Charles said, "Get in your car and lock the doors."

"He's gone."

He gave me a push toward the car. "Don't you move until I come back."

He waited while I got inside and closed the door. I opened it again slightly when he went back to his Ford Ranger. I heard him call dispatch and give Donna the description of Pike's car as I'd given it. Then, he unholstered his gun and started towards the house. He turned briefly and yelled, "Not an inch, Lillian. Stay where you are."

I nodded, but there was no reason for me to stay in the car when I could show him where the blood was and show it trailed to the back door.

He must have heard the click of the car door. "Stay there."

"He's not here. I told you, he's left." I entered the house just steps behind him. "In the kitchen."

He went into the kitchen and came immediately back. I trailed slightly behind as he moved from one room to the next, finding each room empty as I told him. He holstered his gun. I heard sirens as I followed him back toward the kitchen. He stopped and angrily said. "Go outside. You've contaminated a crime scene."

"I was careful," I returned. But, at least, he believed me now that it was a crime scene. But then, how could he not believe me?

His brows furrowed. "I thought you said Pike came after you."

"He wasn't here when I first arrived. But, I told you, I came in looking for Meg, saw the blood, and then saw the buzzards circling in the cornfield. So that's where he must have taken Meg after killing her."

We both moved outside and looked out toward the cornfield. Not one buzzard was flying.

"They were there just a few minutes ago. When I couldn't find her, I came back to call you. That's when Pike saw me. He'd returned to the house, and he must have seen my car. He was waiting for me."

"You should have called me as soon as you found the blood. No, hold it. You shouldn't have been anywhere near here. You could have been killed."

"Oh, and what? I should have let Pike get away with almost killing my mother and killing Meg? I tried to tell you, Charles. I tried to tell Leveque. But neither of you would believe me. And now he's getting away."

Patrol cars were parked in front of the house, several situated along the tractor road. Lights whirling, a cloud of dust settling. Voices shouting. It looked like the entire force. Officer Miner and Officer Richards hurried toward us, Miner shouting, "What's going on?'

Charles shouted back, "House is clear. Richards, get some men to tape off the entire area, including the cornfield, and tell everyone not to trample the place. No one's to go into the house until we get a forensics team here."

"There're footprints outside the back door," I said. "I think he used the hose to clean himself off."

We walked around the house to the back. Charles squatted down and studied the prints. He put a finger in the puddle of water, checking its temperature, then wiped it dry on his pants. Finally, he said to Miner, following us, "I want officers out in that field. Take it one row at a time and follow it all the way to the end. If Meg Dillard's out there, I want her found." When they left, he turned to me. "Go to your car and wait there."

This time I did, although I felt useless watching officers come and go. Finally, Sergeant Wheeler arrived and went over to confer with Charles. The second shift was being called in to help. The forensics team arrived, and Charles followed them into the house. When one of the team came back outside, he had an evidence bag in his hands and a large, bloody knife inside. Only, I hadn't seen a knife. Where did they find it?

Lieutenant Manville arrived. Then Leveque. He glanced over at me in the car and frowned. Both went inside the house.

It was a long time before some officers started coming back from the field. I figured it was safe, so I headed over to the house, wanting to hear what they'd seen. When I walked up, Miner told Charles, "Nothing out there except for some dead animal. That's probably what the buzzards were after. Or what there was left of one."

"What do you mean, what was left?" Could it have been…?

I didn't notice Leveque when they came up to where the rest of us were standing. "We found Pike."

"Where?" Charles asked.

Leveque said, speaking to me, "Stevens called in and reported Pike's car parked in front of the hospital. He found Pike in Emergency having his arm stitched."

I shook my head. "That can't be right. It doesn't make sense."

Leveque said to Charles. "According to Pike, Lillian had been stalking him. He said she was out here last night, and he caught her gawking in the window. He said she came back out this morning, and she was waiting for him behind the kitchen door. He claims she stabbed him."

"*I* stabbed him?" I sucked in my astonishment.

Leveque said as if I wasn't standing right there beside him. "She came to my place last night talking about how Pike was trying to kill her mother or something like that. I told Lieutenant Manville she was going to be trouble. It looks like she took matters into her own hands."

I turned to Charles. "Why would I have called you about Meg then, Charles? And why would I have called to tell you I found blood here if I attacked him?"

"To pull suspicion off yourself," Leveque said.

"You're crazy, Leveque."

"And you're trouble."

"Pike is lying, Charles. Check the knife, it doesn't have my finger-prints on it. When I went into the kitchen, I didn't even see a knife. He must have cut himself with it when he couldn't find me in the cornfield. It may be the weapon he used on Meg. He's trying to blame me." I steel-eyed Leveque. "Where's Meg? Can you explain where she is?"

Leveque pointed to my clothes. I looked, seeing blood on my shirt. I must have bumped against something.

"It's not Pike's. It's Meg's blood."

Leveque grabbed my arm. "Chief?"

"Okay." Charles nodded. "Take her in. If nothing else, it'll keep her out and away until I figure out what the hell happened here." He stomped away with Sergeant Wheeler.

Leveque grabbed me. "You're under arrest."

"Don't you touch me, Leveque. What are you doing, Charles?" I jerked away from Leveque. "Leave me alone." Leveque grabbed hold again, and there was no possibility of throwing him off this time. I continued to yell, gathering interest from some of the other officers, and struggled, making it difficult for Leveque to put on handcuffs. "You have no evidence to arrest me. You have nothing but what Pike said. He's lying. You're a fool, Leveque. Pike's the one you should be arresting."

Leveque's teeth gritted together as he tried to keep a hold of me. "You are under arrest on a public nuisance charge."

"A public nuisance? I'll sue the department."

He pulled my hands behind my back. Hard. "Will you quit? Stand still." He cuffed me. "This time, you'll do like you're told."

I had to get him to listen to me. I stopped yelling and tried to reason. "If I'd stabbed Pike, and I'm telling you, while I wouldn't have minded stabbing that son of a bitch, I didn't touch a hair on his head. But if I had, it still doesn't explain where Meg's is. Did I kill her, too?"

"Are you confessing?"

There was a smirk on his face. He couldn't be serious. I glanced over my shoulder for Charles. I saw Lieutenant Manville and he huddled together. Sargent Wheeler was walking toward them with something in his hand. It looked like the rose-colored sweater Meg was wearing when I caught Pike forcing her to eat. I shouted over, "Meg, Charles. It's her sweater. I saw her in it. She has to be in the corn."

I tried to wiggle free of Leveque by kicking him in the leg.

"Settle down," he yelled, almost losing his hold on me.

Then the lieutenant came up, stopping Leveque from continuing to lead me over to his car. "Uncuff her, Leveque."

Leveque's face drained like a child who was just told he had to give up his toy. "You've got to be fucking kidding me."

"The chief said to take off the handcuffs." Lieutenant Manville said, "If you go into the office without any trouble, we'll take you in without the cuffs." I nodded in agreement. He said to Leveque. "We're doing another check of the field before we lose daylight. I called Steven's. He's bringing Pike in for questioning. I want you to go to the hospital and speak to the doctor who saw him."

"Then Charles believes me? I was right. It is Meg's sweater."

Lieutenant Manville nodded. "We've notified Amanda Hayes. She hasn't heard from Meg and didn't know she was ill."

Lieutenant Manville turned and went back to the investigation. I jerked my arms, still held firmly in Leveque's hands. "You heard him, Leveque. Take the cuffs off."

But he didn't. Not right away. He dragged and pushed me to his car, enjoying my predicament. When he did take the cuffs off, he pushed me into the backseat of his car.

The back seat smelled of male sweat and Fritos. A barrier separated the front and back seats, which kept me from beating Leveque
over the head. Which is what I really, *really* wanted to do.

I was worried. Officer Stevens was a reserved officer. Pike would
trick him and get away. I kept my voice calm. I needed to present
what I knew to Leveque. If he heard me out, he'd understand why I
was so sure Pike had killed Meg.

"Detective Leveque, please, hear me out. "Pike set the Carter fire.
I think he told my mother something that could implicate him. I
called Donna and had her find out some information for me. Pike
took Meg down to her lawyer's and tried to get her will changed."

No response. I kicked the back of Leveque's seat and demanded,
"Stop this car.

"You're going to be sorry, Leveque."

"If Pike's statement sticks, you could be charged with attempted
murder. The evidence will tell us who's lying and who's telling the
truth. DNA doesn't lie. If you're innocent, as you say, then you have
nothing to worry about. If Pike is guilty and gets away, you're helping
him. You're only getting this VIP treatment because you're sleeping
with the chief. Be a good girl so I can get on with my job."

I moved forward, so close to the glass my lips fogged the barrier.
"I am nobody's girl."

Donna's voice came over the radio. "Give me your position, over."

Leveque pulled up the mic. "I'm five minutes out from the station. What's going on, over."

"Officer Stevens has called for backup. Edgar Pike has disappeared."

"See, I told you," I shouted in Leveque's ear. "He's getting away."

"Lillian, is that you?"

Leveque slowed the car down as if trying to decide what to do next.

"He tried to kill my mother. He's killed Meg Dillard. He's not going to stick around." Leveque glared at me in the rear-view mirror. "We need to go after him."

I was probably telling him to do precisely what he wanted to do. Only, I knew he hated that it was me telling him. He spoke into the mic. "Has the chief been notified of the situation?'

"He's on his way back in town."

Leveque made an illegal U-turn. "Ten-four. I'm headed to the hospital now."

Officer Steven's car was still in emergency room parking. Leveque jumped out of the car and hurried in. I checked for Pike's car. It was missing. I began looking for a way out of the car.

Then I saw David Carter on his bike on the other side of the street. "Hey, David. Over here."

His head turned as if hearing someone, but he wasn't looking across to where I was waving in the back seat of a police car. I screamed at the top of my lungs, "David. Over here."

He stared over at the police car. I calmed down and gave him a, *Hey, how are you doin?* kind of wave. He looked around, possibly to see if anyone else was hearing me, then he got off his bike and came across the street to the car.

"Hi, David."

He bent to look through into the backseat, moved forward to check upfront, then came back to me. I sat, calm and relaxed. "Hey, David, I need you to open the door for me."

"What'd you do? Did you get arrested?"

"Of course not. I'm with Detective Leveque. We're following up on who I saw at the fire at your place. I told the police it wasn't your dad." *See, I'm on your side.*

He wasn't so convinced. "If you weren't arrested, why are you in the back seat?"

I raised both my hands. "Do you see handcuffs? Detective Leveque went in to see about your Aunt Meg." I gave him a laugh, *it's the funniest thing,* "I forgot all about there not being handles back here. I'm stuck, and I need to tell him something. A call came in for him."

He shook his head. "I don't want to get into trouble." He started to lower his bike. "I'll go get him for you."

"No!"

He jumped. I'd frightened him. He glanced at the hospital doors and then looked back to the street. "I've got to get home." He started to get back on his bike.

I thought quickly. "Do you have a cell phone?" He nodded and took it out for me to see. "Terrific. If you let me out, I'll take a picture of you sitting in the back seat."

He thought that over. "With handcuffs on?"

"Sure. I'll just need to go inside and get Detective Leveque's hand-cuffs. Then I'll cuff you up, and you can sit in the back like we've arrested you."

He thought a moment. "I'd rather sit up front like I was driving." David Carter, a professional negotiator.

"No problem. Detective Leveque might even let you turn on the siren."

The thought of the siren did it. He opened the door. I ran.

The sky darkened. Thunder blasted and rolled.

Where would Pike go? Would he go back to New Liberty? Or would he just head towards Canada? I saw a police car, lights flashing, Leveque. I jumped into a doorway. He sped past me. He was pissed. Which is why I turned at the next corner and ran between buildings. Thunder tumbled above me.

Then I saw Pike's car. It was badly parked at the back of a building as if left in a hurry. The car was empty.

The lights were off when I opened the door to the building. Shelves of hinges, switch plates, and other hardware faced me. It was Melvin Roth's hardware store. I heard voices, Annie's voice.

Thunder rumbled again so hard, the sound took me back to the Carter house when explosions roared downstairs, and the roof threatened to cave in.

"You can't do this," Annie shouted. "Let us go."

Pike.

I grabbed a hammer off a wall peg.

Then I heard another voice. "Don't cry, Annie."

I followed the voices, moving toward the front, disbelieving what I thought I'd just heard, and keeping my eyes open for Pike. The front door was closed. The window filled with a quick, brilliant light, and then a crack resounded as if the very sky was being torn apart.

"Stop it. I can't think."

"Why are you doing this?"

"For us."

The voices were coming from a small, side room. Cartons were stacked everywhere. There was a small desk and a couple of chairs. Meg Dillard sat in one of them. She was wearing her nightgown. Her feet were bare. She was alive. Annie Roth was seated close to her. And I saw Darrell Carter. He was holding a gun.

I gasped. His head whipped around and saw me. "He heard you. He ran out, out the front." He held up the gun, showing me. "He dropped this. He was going to kill us."

"Call the police." I ran back up front, unlocked the front door, and ran outside. Rain sheeted down. The wind howled. The street was empty.

I went back inside and out through the back door, thinking he'd circled, and went back for his car. It was still parked. I checked and found the keys in the ignition. I took them out. I went back into the office." Did you call the police?"

"They're on their way," Darrell said, staring hard at Annie. They all had to be scared.

"I'm cold," Meg said.

I quickly calculated if we would be safer staying until the police arrived or leave. Thunder made my decision. "We need to get out of here in case Pike returns."

"No," Annie broke, her head falling into her hands, sobbing.

"Shut up, Annie," Darrell said, his voice coarse. "She's right."

Meg whined, "I'm cold."

"I went over to her." Come on, Meg. We'll get you someplace warm."

Darrell went to Annie, who shouted, "You don't understand."

"Hurry," I told them.

I half-carried Meg through the store and out back into the storm. I opened the passenger door of Pike's car, helping Meg inside. I shouted to Darrell and Annie, "Get in the back. Hurry."

Rain turned into hail. Annie refused to get into the car. Darrell said something. She got in, and Darrell slammed the door and headed for the driver's door.

"I'll drive. Get in the back." He grabbed my arm as I passed him. "Darrell, get it back. We need to get out of here."

I jumped in and started up the car. I drove into the storm, my ears listening for sirens, expecting to see Leveque's car any moment. He couldn't have been far away when Darrell called the police.

Pike's car was a touch better than my Mustang. Only my windshield wipers worked. Unfortunately, the rain flooded the window, and this car's wipers barely scrapped well enough for me to see three feet in front of the car.

Meg was talking, "loved my daddy," but it's all I heard. Although the temperature hadn't dropped much, she was cold from shock, but I had nothing to cover her up with. Then I felt something cold and hard against my head.

"Pull over."

I looked into the rearview mirror. Darrell. The gun.

"Darrell, don't," Annie yelled.

"Pull over, or you're dead," Darrell said as if playing a role in a B movie. He pushed the gun harder with his intention.

I did as I was told and pulled over.

"Now get out."

"I'm getting out, too, Darrell," Annie screamed. "You'll have to shoot me, too."

"You're staying with me." He yanked her back before she could get the door open. "We're getting out of here."

What was happening? I heard a groan and looked over at Meg. Her head drooped to her chest, and she might have fallen over if Darrell hadn't buckled her in.

My eyes caught Darrell's in the mirror. I tried to hold his attention, my mind racing. The front door. I'd had to unlock it. Pike hadn't gone out front. Darrell hadn't called the police. "What did Pike make you do?"

He laughed, short, sharp barks. His eyes moved from mine, glancing out the side windows, to Annie, back to me.

Thunder rolled. Lightning cracked.

I heard a groan and glanced over at Meg.

"Darrell, we need to get Meg to a hospital."

But mentioning Meg caused him to get angrier. "It doesn't matter."

"Darrell," Annie cried, "What if something happens to her? Put down the gun. Stop this."

He sneered, "Then she got what she deserved." He hit the gun against my head again. "Get out, and take her with you."

The rain beat against the roof, waterfalling over all the windows. If someone had noticed a car seemingly stalled, its headlights on, they wouldn't have been able to see what was happening inside the car.

"You're a shit, Darrell Carter. I hate you." Annie went again for the door.

Darrell grabbed her, threw her back, and hit her, with a hard, open-handed slap. She cowered back into the seat. He immediately crumbled. "I'm sorry, Annie. Oh, God, I'm so sorry. I didn't want to hurt you. I didn't mean to hurt anybody. Are you okay? Are you hurt?"

His voice saying those words pulled me into the room... smoke, there was so much smoke. I could hardly breathe. *Are you okay?* It wasn't Pike I saw in the window of the Carter house. I said to Darrell,

"You came over to me. You were worried I'd gotten hurt. You asked if I was okay."

He was half-turned toward Annie and to me. I couldn't see the gun. I didn't know if he was still holding it.

"How did you get out of the house?" I remembered commending Darrell's accomplishments at the Hy-Vee, one as a junior firefighter. "You were wearing a fire mask. You must have had oxygen." I kept my voice low. "Why?"

"I had no other choice. My folks were going to leave, and they would make me leave with them. I told them I could stay with Aunt Meg. I knew Pike wouldn't like it. He'd been kissing up to Aunt Meg, trying to get her to sign some papers. I saw him do it. He told her he had his lawyer draw them up and that once she'd signed her name, he'd be in charge, not Amanda. He said Amanda and the rest of us were only after her money. That's why we'd been caring of her all these years." He said to Annie, "I had to, Annie, don't you see? I'd heard Mom and Dad talk about how Aunt Meg burned down her parents' house and killed them. I thought people would just think she'd done it again. If Aunt Meg gave my parents the insurance money, they wouldn't leave. I'd finish school. Go to UI."

"How'd you know the house was insured?" I asked him.

I saw him glance over to Meg. I couldn't tell if she was breathing. "I heard Ms. Kieff talking to someone when I was at the library. I figured she was talking about Aunt Meg. She said fifty-thousand would be enough to cover the house in case of fire."

He looked back at Annie. "I thought they'd stay here. Not leave."

I cautioned him. "You haven't hurt anyone yet, Darrell." I nodded to Meg. "If she dies, you'll be charged with murder."

"Oh, my God, Darrell," Annie shouted.

Then I saw the gun, still in his hand.

"We'll work something out with your parents. Just give me the gun, Darrell."

I saw a car pull up behind us. Headlights spill into the backseat.

"Give me the gun, Darrell."

Tears rolled down his cheeks. His resolve was weakening. "Will they arrest me?" he asked in a little boy's voice.

"Yes." He'd have known I was lying if I'd said differently. "You'll get in trouble for what you've done, but you're only eighteen. You've had a lifetime to make different, better choices."

Then suddenly, Annie pushed Darrell, and he lurched over the front seat, slamming me into the steering wheel. The gun went off, and the front passenger side window blew out.

My door flew open.

"Drop the gun. Put your hands up where I can see them. All of you."

Leveque stood, legs apart, gun leveled. I raised my hands. "Do as he says, Darrell."

Darrell raised his hands.

"I'm getting out," Annie shouted.

"Stay where you are," Leveque warned.

But she threw open the back door and leaped out.

Sirens cried.

Thunder rolled in the distance.

Leveque yelled, "Where's the gun?"

Darrell mumbled. I said, "He says he dropped it."

Police cars pulled up and around us. Leveque yelled, "We've got a shooter."

I yelled, "We don't have a shooter." I said to Leveque, "Tell them to hold fire. We're getting out. No one is going to shoot." I said to Darrell, "Come on. Keep your hands where Detective Leveque can see you aren't holding anything. Follow me, and I'll make sure you're not hurt."

"Stay where you are, Lillian."

"We're coming out." I said to Darrell, "Aren't we?"

Leveque wasn't happy with my taking over, and he kept cover as I got slowly out of the car, Darrell sliding out behind me. As soon as Darrell cleared the car, Leveque grabbed him and threw him to the ground. I moved to get out of the way of the other officers moving in. I saw Miner and told him, "We need an ambulance." I hurried over to the passenger side. Margaret Dillard, the only surviving daughter of Horace and Gertrude Dillard was dead.

I stood with Annie on the sidewalk, both of us dripping wet. Leveque handcuffed Darrell and handed him over to Miner, who put him into the back of his patrol car. The ambulance arrived, and Ben Weaver took Meg's frail, limp body out of the car. It was then that I noticed the car. Same make and the same color, but this car had no dent.

It wasn't Pike's car.

It may never have been Pike's car.

CHAPTER TEN
WHEN LIFE BECOMES UNMANAGEABLE

D etective Leveque brought Darrell Carter out from one of the interrogation rooms and led him back to the holding cells. Darrell kept his eyes to the ground, his face expressionless. What had happened to him in the last few days must have felt like a nightmare. He was dream walking, waiting to wake up and go back to finishing his senior year and attending UI. Maybe make love to Annie. Plan his fantastic future.

I couldn't help but think of my choices at his age and how lucky I'd been to wake up before harming myself or others.

Carol and Burt came down the hall next, with someone I didn't recognize. From the briefcase, I assumed it was a lawyer. Carol briefly glanced over at me. Her eyes burned red from crying. No sympathy could alleviate her and Burt's pain. The son they knew was dead. The life they thought was theirs, gone.

Amanda and the Reverend Keiff, and Lieutenant Manville came next. They left the station together. Charles followed them, but he came over to where Officer Miner, Richards, and I sat along with other officers not out working the crime scenes.

Charles said, "The fingerprints on the knife found at the scene match Darrell's. He's been charged with first-degree arson and attempted murder."

"What about kidnapping?" Miner asked.

Charles shook his head. "The DA made a deal to drop the kidnapping charge for a guilty plea. Even still, he'll be doing prison time."

I tried to put together what I knew now with what I thought I knew when I went back out to Meg's attempting to prove Pike guilty. "So, Pike had nothing to do with this?"

"According to Amanda, Pike had a power of attorney drawn up and was trying to get Meg to sign it. When he took it down to Meg's attorney, the attorney told him Meg's trust was irrevocable. Dr. Hayes couldn't be sure Amanda would outlive Meg, and with Meg's innocence, he worried someone might take advantage of her, just like this. Meg's will states any money left is to be divided equally between Darrell and David Carter. She loved those boys."

The irony didn't escape me.

Miner and I talked for a little while, and then I went out to get some air. I stood outside the station, looking at the sky, clear, stars out. Something was still bothering me, a piece was left out of the puzzle, but I couldn't bring what it was to the front of my mind.

"You were right."

I turned to see Leveque standing next to me. He looked up, noticing all the stars, too. "A storm always clears things out."

I admitted, "If I hadn't been so set to prove Pike was involved, maybe none of this would have happened."

He placed his hand on my shoulder. I moved into the warmth of it. The storm still lingered unseen. Always there, beneath the calm.

I said, "If I'd stayed out of your way, you would have figured it out."

"Yeah, I would have." His hand moved down to the center of my back, rubbing, soothing. "That's why people need to let the police do their job and mind their own business. Innocent people can get hurt."

Mind your own business.

I stepped away.

"Come on, I'll take you home."

"No thanks. Miner said he'd take me to get my car."

And as if on cue, Miner came out. "Ready, Lillian?"

"Ready."

It was well after three in the morning when I got home. I fell into bed exhausted and immediately found myself on the island.

Dahlia was somewhere near me, I sensed her, but I couldn't see her. In her place, Cressie came out of the bushes and appeared before me. "Go to her." Her long blonde hair was down for a change, flowing to her waist. I could smell a scent about her, like powder on a baby, smelling fresh and new. "Help her."

"Who?"

"She's the key."

Something rustled in the bushes behind her. She wasn't alone. She began to fade. The undergrowth parted, and I saw someone else. Someone was waiting for her. He waved. I waved back.

I woke up. *Help her. She's the key.*

Dahlia.

THIRTY

I found his car parked a block away from the hospital. He would only know if he was in the clear if he knew Darrell had been arrested and the police were no longer looking for him. If he thought I'd lost interest, then he was very, very wrong.

The hospital was quiet. Nursing staff are held to a minimum during these hours. Doctors are still sound asleep. Patient visitations weren't for another four hours. I hurried through the lobby, past the reception, to the elevators, keeping my eye out for Pike. When the doors opened to the second floor, I stepped out and stayed hidden, waiting while two nurses finished a conversation before returning to their work. Once they did, I moved down the hall toward Dahlia's room.

Melvin Roth's mother was gone, her bed empty. So was Dahlia's bed. Had they released her? If she had gone back to Oaks Manor, April or Laura would have called and informed me. And if she was at Oaks Manor, why would Pike be at the hospital? Then I saw something on the floor. The cross necklace I'd given Dahlia. Had she dropped it, or did she leave it as a sign she'd been taken?

I found one of the two nurses I'd seen talking. "I'm looking for Dahlia Dove."

"I'm sorry. You can't be on the floor. Visiting hours aren't until…"

"Was she released? She's not in her room."

"She's not in her room? I just checked her blood pressure a …."

I said clearly, "She's not in her room."

The nurse's expression still didn't match the panic I felt, but she appeared concerned. "She gets up. The doctor was planning to release her tomorrow. Did you look in the bathroom?"

I held out the necklace. "Was she wearing this?"

The nurse nodded. "She asked me to get it for her. She said she felt safer with it on."

I took off down the hall, opening and searching each room. Some patients woke and wanted to know if something was wrong. A feeling of panic began to spread with my confusion.

The nurse caught up with me. "The wheelchair in her room is gone."

I tried to think. Dahlia wasn't going to make it easy for Pike to take off with her. She may have had the chance to take the necklace off when she first saw him come into the room. She could have dropped it without his noticing. Dahlia was not an easy woman to scare. She'd fight him each step. She'd shout for help. He would have had to gag her. Or maybe he injected her with something. He had to have been the one to give her the overdose, so he knew how to give an injection, and he'd gotten his hands on a sedative.

Think.

I knew Pike wouldn't chance being seen. He could have monitored the few nurses on the floor and waited until a break came when the nurses were in patient rooms and the corridor was free. He couldn't have pulled the wheelchair with Dahlia sitting in it up a flight of stairs. He couldn't have carried her. He also wouldn't have chanced taking her out into the open. His car was too far away. The opportunity for someone to see him or for Dahlia to wake and cause a fuss too great a risk for him to take her to his car.

Where would he go? I searched and saw an EXIT. "Where does that lead?"

"It's a stairway to the third floor."

"I thought there were only two floors."

The nurse shook her head. "It looks like only two from the front, but there are four floors. A basement and a floor about this one with offices."

"Is there any other access other than the stairs?"

"The elevator. But the button is F for facilities, not three. The offices are for staff only."

"What about the roof?"

"There's access at the end of the corridor on that floor."

"Call the police. Tell them Edgar Pike is trying to kill Dahlia Dove. Have them contact Chief Kaefring immediately. I'm going to the roof." Then I took off without further explanation. There wasn't time to explain. Pike could have already killed her and gotten away.

I ran to the elevator, pushed the F button, and held my breath, hoping and praying I was right. Because if Pike had risked taking her to his car, he'd be gone by the time I got back outside or the police arrived.

The elevator doors opened into a corridor.

Everyone on this floor worked a regular workday. It was dead quiet. It didn't make sense he would kill and leave her in one of the offices where she would be found as soon as people came to work. He'd want more time. If I were going to kill Dahlia, I'd do it where someone wouldn't find her until there was no chance of bringing her back alive. Pike was at least as smart as me.

I checked the offices. Two doors were unlocked and opened to equipment rooms, looking like electrical operations. The roof was the only other option. I ran to the EXIT. I eased the door open.

Pike had Dahlia down on the ground. He stood above her head, pulling her toward the roof's edge by her arms. He was going to push her over. Dahlia was fighting him every inch.

"Get away from her!" I ran at him, catching him off guard, and threw myself on him. He fell back and stumbled.

I squatted down by Dahlia. "Are you all right?"

Pike charged me, grabbing my arm and hauling me up. He walloped me across the face, grabbed my neck, and squeezed.

"Let her go, Edgar," Dahlia screamed.

I grabbed at his hands to loosen his grip on me. I reached for his face, trying to gouge his eyes. I scratched his face. He stood as if planted to the spot. His eyes were wide and wild. And then we were pushed. Together we stumbled. His grip loosened. I fell to the ground, choking. Looked up. I saw Pike slip to the edge of the roof. He stopped, and his body worked to keep balance, his arms raised as if he were getting ready to fly. I ran to him to grab hold and pull him back. He fell off the roof, landing on a concrete patio below. He landed on his back, staring back, his eyes still wide and wild. Dark red blood seeped around his head.

I turned. Dahlia stood gasping. I thought she was having a heart attack. I ran to her.

"Dahlia? Mom? Are you all right?"

She said, "Of course I am. Don't I look like I'm all right?" She went over and got in her chair and waited for me to come and take her back to her room.

Banging on the front door woke me.

I pulled on a robe and stumbled sleepily out of the bedroom into the living room. I opened the door and found Albert standing outside with something I thought I'd never see again.

"Bacardi!"

Albert said, "I found him in the Porters' place. Mr. Porter's daughter called, saying there were a few cartons she needed extra packaging for. Fragile stuff. She asked if I'd do it. Of course, I didn't mind. This little fellow must have followed me in, and I didn't notice him."

I squealed, reaching out to take Bacardi from him.

But Albert seemed to need to finish his story and continued to hold Bacardi, talking to him as well as me. "I went back to hand over the keys to Brian Drake of Drake Real Estate. He's got the listing. And this fellow here, he went running out between my legs. Nearly scared the shit out of me. Pardon, my language. I guess he wasn't going to take any chances of being stuck in there any longer." He gave Bacardi's head a couple of pats, then handed him to me.

I took him in my arms, crying, "I thought I'd lost you."

He yowled and jumped out of my arms before I could put him on the floor. Then, he ran straight into the kitchen.

Albert seemed embarrassed by Bacardi's behavior. "He's probably hungry. There wasn't anything to eat at the Porters'. Only water there to drink was in the toilet."

I wasn't embarrassed at all. I grabbed Albert and gave him not one kiss on the cheek but dozens. He was my hero. "Thank you, thank you, thank you."

He acted as if he were brushing the kisses off his cheek, reddening. "It was nothing. I didn't do anything but open up the place. I should have been watching more carefully. The little fellow could have starved to death."

Could have, but it didn't happen. Albert did more than he could know.

After I thanked him another five or six times, I went to the kitchen and stood there. The frizzed-out hair. The pugged face. He was perfect. Bacardi yowled. "I know. I know. You're hungry." I took not one, not two, but three cans of Feline Delight out of the cupboard. "I take it that you're happy to see me, too." I put all the cans into the best, only-for-company bowl I could find. We were celebrating.

I watched him eat, thinking I'd never get tired of watching him. I went over and pulled a Pepsi from the fridge and headed to the television. I stopped, seeing the answering machine. There were two messages. The first one was from Hartfield.

"I'm not sure if you got my message, but since I didn't hear from you, I had to give the job to someone else. However, I will keep your application on file, and should there be another job opening, I would be interested in interviewing you again."

I wasn't too disappointed. I wasn't crazy about the commute and wasn't sure I could work with people like Dahlia. I just didn't have Nelly's penchant for patience. The second message was a woman's voice. "Ms. Dove. This is Mr. Paul Chatman's office of Scribner and Chapman, Attorneys of Law. Would you please call Mr. Chapman at your earliest convenience? Our number here is…"

I returned the call, and the secretary put me right into Chapman.

"Ms. Dove? Let me first say I'm so sorry for your loss."

"My loss? Are you sure you have the right person.?"

"I believe I do. You are the Lillian Dove who worked for Clarence Salzman?"

I heard the past tense. "Yes, but I still work for Clarence."

"You aren't aware that Mr. Salzman passed away last Sunday night?"

I heard, *Sorry to hear about Clarence, Lillian.*

Chapman said, "He died at Frytown General of heart failure. A complication from the flu."

"But there was nothing wrong with him."

"He suffered from heart trouble, and his lungs were weak. He had been a heavy smoker when he was younger." He waited a moment so I could take this information in. "Again, I am sorry." He paused. Was he waiting for me to say something? I was wordless. Clarence? It was unbelievable. He continued. "I have some paperwork at our office for you to sign. Mr. Salzman named you as his beneficiary. He's left you his house at 722 Church Street, his store at 37309 Lakeside Road, and all his assets, goods, and properties. Of course, you will be required to wait for all debt to be settled, but Clarence Salzman wasn't a man to accumulate debt."

If he said anything else, I didn't hear him. I dropped the phone.

My heart was broken.

CHAPTER ELEVEN
ADMIT TO MAYHEM

C harles called and said that he'd spoken to Dahlia. She'd told him when she was dating Pike back in high school and how he had come back from Frytown smelling of smoke and gasoline. He'd told Dahlia he went to meet his father. She said his mother had told him all his life how his father was a wealthy man and how he would be rich, too, someday. Charles said, "When your mother heard about the fire, she figured he had something to do with it."

"Was he really Horace's son?"

"I don't think we'll know. Pike thought he was."

Charles asked me to meet him for dinner at Louise's. "I won't lie to you, Lillian. I never meant to lie. I thought you already knew. I'm married. My wife lives in a care facility. She's been there for a long time." He paused. "Damn, it'd be better to tell you all of this in person, but I want you to understand what I'm asking of you if you decide to have dinner with me."

He went on. "I meant the vows I said to my wife on our wedding day, in sickness and health. I still love her." He corrected himself. "I loved the woman I knew, but she isn't her anymore. She has told me to divorce her, but I won't. My faith forbids it. So, if you do decide to have dinner with me, you should know I like you. Maybe more than like you. You're the first woman I've wanted to have a relationship with for a very long time. But I can't offer much in the way of a future."

I told him I'd need time to think. Too much had happened to answer him right away. He agreed to give me time.

I pulled the bottle of Absolut from the fridge and took it into the living room. I snuggled with Bacardi on the couch. I was taking a day off from life. Just for today. I had decisions to make, but they could wait twenty-four hours. I mean, what could happen in twenty-four hours, right? Okay, a lot of things could happen in a moment that could trigger other moments.

I'd had that bottle of Absolut in the freezer for a long time. I contemplated throwing it away.

I'll admit it's easier to piece together someone else's life, and mistakes, and see how they're damaging their lives, but putting your head around your own isn't easy. My father had a problem with alcohol. Probably his father before him had issues. Or maybe it was his mother. It's not gender-sensitive. So why hadn't I seen that problem storming my way? Okay, I'd been twelve. But, still, didn't I know? Was I always thinking, *Not me*?

I blamed my life problems on everything but me: Life gave me a raw deal. I'd been born Lillian Dove instead of someone else. I had Dahlia as a mother.

But my choices weren't because of Dahlia. Not directly. She'd been determined to get through her life somehow. She resolved to lie in the bed she'd made for herself and keep it as clean and tidy as possible. I couldn't see it before, but I'll admit, Dahlia may have done the best job she could.

I'll admit, too, I'd fucked up. Me, all by myself. I may have been powerless over the decisions I'd made in the past, but maybe the power I had was deciding what I'd do next.

I was an alcoholic. I was a Pepsi addict. I was a chocolate fiend. I liked men. I wanted to love someone. I wanted someone to love me. I was independent but didn't feel comfortable in my skin.

I wanted the key.

I thought Dahlia was the key.

Maybe, just maybe, I found a bit of myself by jumping.

I scratched Bacardi behind the ears, enjoying his purr. Then, I got up, took the Absolut bottle, and put it back in the freezer.

THE END

PREVIEW - BOOK TWO, SUPPOSE

Lillian's back, again!

In this enticing second installment of D. J. Adamson's Lillian Dove Mystery series, big city problems wind up in a small town in the Midwest, threatening not only the safety and integrity of the community, but bringing imminent danger to the life of one woman who is just trying to move beyond her rocky past and navigate toward a more
positive future.

Trying to get your life back on track may be a little tricky when you're a recovering alcoholic five years sober, and you've just inherited a house and the local AAA Discount Liquor Store. Here in Frytown, Iowa, Lillian Dove is clearly aware that "life has its ironies," but she's determined to make the best of recent circumstances. With her cat Bacardi, she's been residing at her mother Dahlia's condo in Lake's Edge Senior Residential Complex, while the feisty woman is in a nearby convalescent home hell-bent on getting out.

Lillian's also been involved with the local Frytown Police Chief, a man she felt offered love and security, though unfortunately he also happens to be married. While sobriety and the unexpected new business acquisition have boosted her spirits, Lillian is haunted by the suicide of her best friend Cressie, a former addict who forced Lillian to face her own issues.

Suddenly, Cressie's onetime ne'er do well boyfriend is threatening to blackmail Lillian, claiming to have video proof that she was responsible for Cressie's death. Lillian knows his demands are bogus, but when his dead body is discovered at the condo, she's determined to uncover the truth and clear her own name.

Within this well-crafted storyline, the murder investigation is linked to a border-crossing drug operation that stems from a multi-million-dollar Chicago firm, and a CEO
involved in illegal money laundering. As Federal Agents and the local Police Department unite to catch the criminals, Lillian finds herself in harm's way when she's unwittingly dragged into the high-risk probe. From murder and a suspicious flash drive to vandalism, kidnapping, and surprise revelations, Lillian embarks on a winding, roller-coaster ride.

"For those unfamiliar with Adamson's evolving mystery series, a passing mention of Lillian's having been a prior witness to an arson case that resulted in near dire consequences for both Lillian and her mother, helps bring readers up to speed and also confirms Lillian's seemingly magnetic draw to trouble.

While chapter/segment titles indicate this story plays out over a short span of a few days, Adamson broadens the platform with a full range of characters and action. From the local mayor being accused of bigamy and a dispatch operator who equates to "Town Gossipedia", to the ghost of Lillian's benefactor assuring her that "everything will be fine" and the pirate-costumed nurse just trying to keep the ornery senior patients in line, all add engaging humor and lightness to the narrative in contrast with the greater tension and drama.

Like all good mysteries, Adamson creates a tale riddled with questions. Intertwined with bantering dialogue and heated conversations, Lillian's self-imposed ponderings about recent events help draw us into the heart and mind of the central character. As a soul-searching individual coming to grips with the past, Lillian's dream states offer a glimpse of her lost childhood and her fractured life. Adamson clearly has an eye for detail. Whether exposed in the sharp visuals of a crime
scene, or revealed in the aromatic constants of a nursing home environment perfumed by the fragrance of "urine, unwashed bodies, and the Wednesday night meatloaf special," the writing paints a colorful, and vivid picture.

Through the character of Lillian Dove, readers are introduced to a flawed, but tenacious female heroine who is genuinely likable. *Suppose* is a mystery filled with small-town heart, yet big city edge, unexpected excitement, and a touch of humor. Together they prove a smart, and winning combination.

5 Stars!
★ ★ ★ ★ ★
BEST BOOK
Chanticleer
Book Reviews

"A smart and winning mystery with small town heart and big city edge filled with unexpected excitement and a touch of humor.

Lillian Dove is a likable, smart-as-a-whip heroine!"

– Chanticleer Reviews

GET YOUR COPY TODAY!

THANKS TO MY READERS

Most importantly, I want to thank you for reading the first of the Lillian Dove Series, *Admit to Mayhem*. I hope you enjoyed meeting Lillian Dove and how she ends up finding herself in difficult situations.

While I am not a person recovering from alcoholism, I have worked the twelve steps in quitting smoking, my chocolate addiction, and my addiction to reading every book I hear that has a good story. Well, maybe I still need to work on the latter. My husband has refused to build any more shelves for me! But, I firmly believe that we all
need to look at our lives now and again and decide if "this is the real me or how I wish to live."

I would be greatly appreciative if you would leave a review. Reviews are the greatest value a writer can receive.

The Lillian Mystery Series goes on with Lillian becoming involved with a drug lord and the FBI in *Suppose*Book 2. Then, she stops to help an injured man and discovers his family murdered in Book 3, *Let Her Go*. If you are interested in exploring Lillian's continued journey, I have kept them on Amazon Unlimited for those readers who, like me, read without an overflowing pocketbook....or more room on the shelf.

And, if you like suspense thrillers, I think you will also enjoy:

At The Edge of No Return, Psychological/Paranormal Thriller

Approaching Storm, Young Adult/Paranormal Thriller

Into the Storm, Crime/Paranormal Thriller

Also, feel free to contact me at: http://www.djadamson.com/contact.html
I personally reply to all emails.

Happy tales to all of you.
My sincere best,
Dj

ACKNOWLEDGMENTS

Writing is a process, and my work has developed in many ways and genres for many years. For that, I am grateful to my creative muse.

Many writers wait until the end of a book to acknowledge those who assisted in its creation. I would not have braved putting my work out there without the support of many. These friends and family deserve a significant placement in this publication. First, love and gratitude go to "adopted" son Mario Alcalde for his enthusiasm, encouragement, and support. To T. J. Martin, who continually shows me life is made for living. Thanks to my professional creative muses: Moni Richie, Steven Shibuya, and Laurie Stevens, who read more drafts than they wanted to. To Melanie Wilken, who helped me create a lifetime of stories. Cheers to Samuel Joseph, a great cheerleader. I also thank the following for reading drafts and offering comments: Aaron Hudson, Liz Chai-Chang, Luanne Fose, Patricia Martin, and Sally Dykes. Special thanks go to Iowa content editor Kathy Shields, Law Enforcement street team: Community Officer Rachelle LaPan, and Reserved Officer Cody Shields.

To: Tabra Martin, Judy Henderson, Delaine Ploessel, Ruby Martin, Reneé Leeper, and Patty Doward. You will always have my loving gatitude for the service you provided. You are amazing women.

FRYTOWN

F rytown is a real unincorporated community in Johnson County, Iowa, about 10 miles southwest of Iowa City. The town has been town as Frytown since the 19th Century. Lillian's Frytown is a mixture of several cities and towns in Iowa, as are many other locations in this novel. It is fictional. All characters in this work are fictitious. Any similarities to living persons are coincidental.

ABOUT THE AUTHOR

International selling author D. J. Adamson has received awards for her Lillian Dove Mystery Series and suspense thrillers. She is the editor of Le Coeur de l'Artiste
which reviews books by national and international authors.

DJ's family homesteaded in the Iowa area in the late 1800s. The Lillian Dove books are based on Johnson County where her family settled and many still live, by creating an imaginative city Frytown using a mixture Oxford and Frytown, Iowa.